VANDEMONIAN SPIRIT

VANDEMONIAN SPIRIT

MISSY BIRCH

'It is not in the stars to hold our destiny but in ourselves.'
William Shakespeare

Dedicated to the memory of Louisa Wright whose story is at the heart of this work and to my other courageous pioneering ancestors, who also suffered and survived the brutal convict system of early Tasmania.

Contents

1

ST PAUL'S WALDEN

'Valley of the Britons'
Anglo-Saxon place name.

I was just another thief in a city of thieves. Throughout my trial, I watched the stony-faced judge who held my life in his hands. Slumped sideways in his chair, he never once looked at me, the proceedings seemed to bore him. When he retired to deliberate, I vowed he would never see my true feelings. Having treated me with contempt throughout, the judge's demeanour was very different when it came to passing sentence. He sat upright and alert and, in a booming voice, commanded me to rise.

'Hannah Fearn, you have been found guilty and will be transported across the seas for a period of seven years. God save the King. Remove the prisoner.'

That only hardened and unrepentant criminals stood emotionless in the dock was untrue, for upon hearing my sentence I stood similarly, powerless to move, even my tears refused to flow. Two prison officers took hold of my arms and all but carried me from the dock. I was numb, aware only of the sobbing of my grief-stricken sister. Borne along the underground passage linking the court and Newgate prison,

I was delivered to a cell, my convict number '513' chalked upon the board.

Over the next three months, I existed but did not live. Confined with several other women, the morning routine was the same every day. I dreaded the rattle of heavy metal keys which signalled the warders' approach. Every morning, the same careworn faces of my fellow inmates. Their lifeless eyes and their shuffling feet. Some were insane whilst others were trapped in misery and despair. They had nothing left to live for. I sat in silence, hour after hour, day after day, picking oakum. My hands bled and my mind wandered. I was surrounded by death and disease, the overwhelming stench of Newgate and the screams of its inmates disrupting my fitful slumber.

****

They finally permitted my aunt's visit three days after my trial. Aunt Elizabeth had offered me sanctuary in this abhorrent city called London. Only allowed to speak through the iron bars, she clasped my hands tightly in her own, and wept with me when at first words were too hard. This darling aunt of mine was as dear to me as my sweet mother.

'How has it all come to this?' I sobbed.

'You did what you thought you must,' my aunt consoled.

It was true. I stole the wretched watch to save my ailing sister. Bittersweet were the words that followed.

'Be assured, Martha is safe. Your grandmother arrived with medicine the day after your arrest.'

My heart was joyous at Martha's salvation, though its timing, a few hours after my capture, was a cruel blow. Oh, why couldn't Granny Ravens have arrived one day earlier? If only I'd known help was on its way! I apologized profusely for all the trouble I had caused and pleaded with her not to tell her children of my crime. Though I knew I would never see them again, I wanted their memories of me to be happy ones. My aunt promised me my cousins would never know of my crime, being told instead that I had gone away unexpectedly to gain work.

Now came the question I dreaded. Yet, peace of mind would elude me until it was answered.

'Is Granny ashamed of me?'

'Not at all!' came the quick reply. 'She, like me, is proud you showed such love for your sister and placed her welfare before your own.'

Be that as it may, shame consumed me. My parents would have expected so much more.

During my time in Newgate and over the following years, I would often think back to those amazing days of my youth. They were joyful, uncomplicated days spent in what seemed to be endless warmth and sunshine. Complete happiness can create such an illusion. In truth, the weather did not favour us all the time, but Hertfordshire was always green. We had blossoms in the spring and snow in the winter. Winter was my favourite season. Wrapped up tightly against the bitter chill, I wandered along the narrow lanes and across the open fields. I loved seeing the red berries covered with snow and the robins in search of an elusive worm. I would watch a fox or two at play, the burnished red of their fur bringing brightness and life to the frozen world around me.

'I will never forget the beauty and freedom of St. Paul's Walden,' I sighed. 'No matter where I end up, it will always be home in my heart.'

My aunt nodded sympathetically.

'My brother was fortunate in the life he led there after leaving London,' she declared.

The brother of whom she spoke was my father, Stephen. Dada was a quiet and serious man. A native of Stone Cutters Alley, he had become overly familiar with the dark, filthy streets of London from a young age. He was only five, when he joined his four older brothers working for their father, who was the Master Chimney Sweep of St. Giles. Their father did not resort to the cruel methods of his fellow masters. His sweeps were never prodded with pins, nor were fires lit beneath them to make them climb faster. But they faced danger and death every day.

'Your poor father's eye irritations, respiratory troubles, and twisted spine all began to develop within months,' my aunt said, and I remembered Dada's suffering.

Life was never easy for Dada and he plodded through life's struggles as though he expected yet another blow at any moment. He did, however, greatly honour and love my mother and expected all of his children to revere her similarly. With her bright, vivacious personality and amazing love of life, I never found any difficulty in loving her. Born in Codicote, she was the daughter of Thomas and Annis Ravens, both of who were from long-established local families. Her family was prosperous and she experienced an idyllic childhood, surrounded by beauty, encouraged in her musical and artistic pursuits, and never lacking the animated company of like-minded friends.

'I will never forget when Stephen brought Margaret home for the first time,' my aunt mused. 'She was visiting London for the celebrations surrounding King George's Coronation. Stephen went to sweep the chimneys where she was staying, and despite his blackened hands and face, and the vast class difference, it was love at first sight. There was heavy opposition from both families, but your parents' love conquered all and they were married at St. Clement Danes Westminster in December the same year.'

'And Martha was born five months later,' I said.

Aunt Elizabeth smiled.

'That's when your mother decided London was not the place to bring up her growing family. Your father offered no opposition, for whilst he had never left the bustling metropolis, he was as eager as his young wife to escape its perils. Visiting St. Paul's Walden for the first time, he fell in love with it, and whilst he knew nothing about farming, he purchased *Sweep's Farm* as soon as it became available.'

'Dada was so very proud of it,' I reflected, as my mind transported me back to the farm where my eight siblings and I grew up. 'He slaved to make it a success. I used to love the smell of the wool from the newly shorn sheep, feeding the chickens, and eating the freshly picked fruit.'

I remembered how we were always comfortable and cosy. Mam decorated our home with great artistry, and she loved placing vases of flowers throughout the house. *Sweep's Farm* allowed us a carefree upbringing, and though we had very few material possessions, we knew no different, and we made our own fun. As we gathered together around the hearth each evening, we were content in the knowledge that the love and affection of our parents would never cease.

'There was always your dear Granny Ravens too, don't forget.'

'I could never forget sweet Granny,' I said as the tears that had been slowly welling in my eyes, finally escaped down my cheeks.

As I took a moment to recover myself, Granny's darling face came to mind. Sitting there fireside, knitting another scarf or pair of gloves to keep us warm. Living four miles away in the town of Codicote, her medieval thatched cottage in a winding hedge-lined lane was a magical place for me. Mam took us to there whenever she could, the cottage always filled with sumptuous aromas from the newly baked goodies she prepared in our honour. There were delicious cakes and juice we would never dream of getting at home. Our mother was always too busy and we were too poor to afford anything other than the simple fare we ate each day. Granny Ravens' treats, therefore, remained planted fondly in our memories from one visit until the next. On the rare occasion I was allowed to stay one or two nights in this cherished abode, I truly felt as though I were in Heaven, especially when I had my adored Granny all to myself.

Becoming impatient at my aunt's extended stay, the gaoler jingled his keys, and cleared his throat forcefully.

'I will come again,' my aunt promised as the gaoler edged closer.

Kissing me through the bars, she urged me to stay strong. Watching as she was escorted from the dismal cells, my one small comfort was knowing that she was returning to my broken-hearted family and they would be consoled in the arms of this beautiful aunt.

Curled up in the corner of the cell, with sleep eluding me, I continued to ponder the wonderous days of my youth. Being the two eldest in the family, my sister Martha and I were afforded the privilege of having a room to ourselves. At that time, we used to willingly lie awake, talking about our dreams, hoping beyond hope they would come true. One of my most cherished dreams, was that I would one day own a new dress and bonnet, nothing overly fancy, just something with a little colour, adorned with some ribbon or lace. It would be made just for me, and not something passed down from Martha or donated by a neighbour. Young men also consumed our thoughts.

'I saw Frederick Banner again today,' Martha would say, hoping that I'd encourage her to tell me more. I always obliged her. 'He saw me walking past the bakery, and having just brought some mince tarts out of the oven, he chased after me to slip one into my hand.'

Martha saw it as a great romantic gesture which only spurred on her dreams of one day marrying him. With her pretty blonde curls and sparkling blue eyes, there was no doubt she would win his heart. Whilst my own hair was darker, my figure not so elegant, and my eyes lacking the crystal allure of Martha's, I was not totally unfortunate looks wise, and dared to dream of winning my own sweetheart, Michael Ansell.

'He's a cheeky young pup,' I heard countless people say, and I little doubted it was true, but I loved him nonetheless.

The Ansells were originally from Pirton, their father moving his family to Codicote in order to find work as a carrier. They were a family of five wild boys who always seemed to be in trouble. Like my own family, they clearly understood poverty and struggle.

The first time I laid eyes on Michael, I was thirteen. My family was attending the Codicote fair which was always held on the Monday following Whit Sunday. It was a bright sunny day and my family enjoyed a rare opportunity to be together, far away from the everyday grind. There was Morris dancing and many competitions on offer. Roving musicians entertained us and our bellies were kept full by special treats baked by Mam. Having won some hair ribbons in a foot race, I was dividing them between my sisters when we noticed a great uproar down the street.

'I wander what's going on,' I said.

As the general crowd was moving towards the scene, my sisters and I hurried to follow.

At the village green, we were just in time to see a young man being roughly herded down Bury Lane, an occasional clip across the ear being given by the local constable. A man I knew to be the local squire followed. Hurling abuse at the prisoner, he kicked out at the springer spaniel who followed the procession barking madly. As the parade reached the front of the *George and Dragon Inn*, the front door flew open and another young man raced into the street. The new arrival grasped hold of the young miscreant and tried to pull him from the constable.

'You won't be putting no brother of mine in the cage!' he bellowed, attempting to block the path to the single-cell lock-up.

A minor scuffle ensued, before the constable finally managed to brush the enraged brother roughly aside, and succeed in locking the young man away.

The crowd began to disperse and I looked towards the cage where the young man was now held. His spaniel sat beside it whining and I could hear its owner whispering words of comfort from the darkened cell. Having been left alone by my siblings, I headed down the laneway and patted the poor creature. Hearing me consoling his pet, the captive asked my name.

'Hannah Fearn,' I replied. 'What's yours?'

'Michael Ansell.'

Volunteering to mind his dog until he was released, Michael agreed and Chester the spaniel was entrusted to my care. How I doted on that sweet little creature! I even took him to bed with me, much to my parents' chagrin. I was terribly sorry when Michael came to collect Chester the following day, though very pleased to get my first proper look at his young owner. At seventeen, he was four years older than me, though most would probably have thought him much older. No one could say he was handsome, indeed, he was of average height with dark brown hair, hazel eyes, and the hint of pockmarks around his jaw. Mam enquired about what led to his incarceration.

'The old squire caught me hunting ducks on his property,' Michael informed her. 'Things became heated when the villain kicked this dear little fellow, and I gave him something to think about. That's when he summoned that miserable excuse for a constable.'

It was exactly this rebellious spirit and Michael's mischievous grin that instantly won my heart. When he caught me watching him that afternoon, he winked and blew me a kiss. I was powerless to contain the smile that burst forth from my lips at such brashness. Every fibre of my being told me to have nothing to do with him, for he was a wicked, wicked young man. Yet, impressionable as I was at that tender age, Michael was the most precious man on Earth to me. That afternoon when he left, he took my young heart with him. Although there was no reason for us to ever meet again, my heart would break if we did not.

Sadly, a tragic event, the death of Thomas, his sixteen-year-old brother, brought us together again later that year. Thomas was killed on the Welwyn Road. He fell off the wagon he was driving and was run over by one of its wheels. Greeting us, Michael offered his thanks for our support.

'You're the little girl who minded my dog, aren't you?' he said.

I didn't like being 'the little girl,' but was thankful he remembered me. I greatly admired Michael that day for his strength and courage. He was the one who remained by his mother's side, welcoming visitors and keeping the family functioning. He, too, completed the tedious and heart-wrenching business of organizing his brother's funeral.

Barely recovered from the loss of Thomas, the Ansell family was shattered by their mother's death at the young age of fifty-seven. Fleeing from the house of grief, Michael escaped to Hitchin, where he soon found himself in trouble.

'Those Ansell boys are in strife again,' Dada announced once evening. 'Young Michael stole a coat at the Hitchin Market. They have given him the lash, and now he'll spend three weeks in solitary confinement. That will earn him a criminal record for sure. And the eldest boy, Francis, he's been arrested and charged with murder after felling a man in a drunken brawl.'

Mama shook her head.

'It's his poor wife that I feel sorry for. Francis has only been married for a few months.'

Whilst Francis was later acquitted, his new wife, a local girl by the name of Annabelle Primett, fled back to her father's home, the settling influence that she had provided, going with her.

During those days, the Welwyn Market was a place for people to gather and sell their wares. It enabled my family to gain a little extra income through selling our seasonal jams and preserves, fruit and vegetables, and Mam's exquisitely fashioned items made from straw plaiting. My job was to assist in preparing the wares for market, ensuring we had enough stock to warrant the trip to Welwyn. If the quotas were not met, the trip would be cancelled, and the whole family would suffer. Mam usually operated the stall but as she was due to give birth to her seventh child, I was nominated to fill her place.

Market day turned out to be cold and miserable, the persistent drizzle severely testing my patience. Having sold enough to return home with ample funds to please my parents, I begun packing up my stall. It was then that I was joined by the dearest of all animals. Sweet little Chester stood beside me, his tail wagging animatedly. Clasping him affectionately in my arms, I quickly glanced up in search of his master. Michael wandered casually past, barely glancing at my wares. Stopping not far from my stall, he turned, slouched against a wall, and perused the scene in front of him. His eyes eventually met my own and my heart beat faster. Not moving from where he stood, he beckoned to me. Perhaps far too eagerly, I hurried to his side. He said nothing by way of greeting but reached out to remove a stray piece of wet hair from my forehead.

'You're frozen through,' he said. 'Come. Follow me.'

Ushered into the *White Hart Inn,* Michael found us a table by the fire, and I sat observing my new surroundings. The inn was not the dark, smelly place full of vice my parents always described. In fact, the *White Hart* had been part of Welwyn's society since the 1600s and was one of the main coaching inns on the road north from London. It was a popular choice for travellers and maintained high standards, doubling as the village's courthouse. A coach from London soon arrived and an influx of travellers started settling themselves as close to the fireplace as the remaining tables allowed. I loved the vibrancy of the place, the sights and sounds were so exciting to one like me, so used to a solitary life on the farm. A tray containing a pot of tea, two cups, and some cinnamon buns arrived and I was immensely pleased to cradle a warming cup of tea in my frozen hands and made short work of the cinnamon bun. Breaking the other bun in two, Michael fed half to my furry companion before consuming the rest himself.

Revived by the refreshments, I began to enjoy Michael's company more and more and feared my parents' disapproval less and less. My initial inhibitions gradually gave way to animated chatter. We both possessed an adventurous spirit and longed to see the world beyond Hertfordshire. During a lull in our conversation, I lowered my eyes to gaze upon the fire, knowing that Michael observed my every move like a hawk.

'You're certainly a pretty one,' he declared, and my heart was stirred.

Dada would surely have called his declaration brazen; I was secretly thrilled to discover his admiration. I do not know if I had ever been as happy as I was that afternoon with Michael. Thankfully, he was far more aware of time than I and eventually suggested that we should be leaving before Dada appeared. Escorting me back to the stall, he took my hand and kissed it.

'Until next time,' he whispered.

With a mischievous grin, he winked at me, whistled for Chester to follow, and quickly vanished from sight. Dada was by my side less than two minutes later. I was possessed of the all-consuming power of young love. Over the next few days, Michael's name rolled involuntarily off my tongue several times. When my amour was discovered, my parents warned me against becoming involved.

'You're far too young,' Mam declared.

'I'm almost sixteen,' I proclaimed.

'And Michael is nearly twenty,' she responded. 'That's a big difference at your age. Boys and men have different needs and desires to women, and it's always the women who are left to take the consequences. Surely, you haven't forgotten why Doritie Peerce was forced into the workhouse.'

'I have no intention of ending up like Doritie,' I declared, my pride wounded.

'Often the girl has little say.'

'Michael would *never* treat me like that,' I replied, quickly jumping to his defence.

Mam remained silent. Michael was wild, had spent time in gaol, and was incapable of holding down a steady job. My parents believed the life of a daughter married to Michael would be one of toil and sorrow. It was not the life they wanted for me. Michael was a young rogue and all my instincts told me that I should heed my parents' advice and distance myself from him. Yet, he was endearing and the more he winked at me, whistled, and blew cheeky kisses, the more I loved him. As a young girl believing herself in love, it was impossible to take in and accept my parents' objections. Choosing instead to disregard them, I eagerly awaited the next market day and a few more stolen moments with Michael. A tender word or two across a busy market stall would suffice, just so long as I was able to see him.

The late 1830s were harsh times for those like my father who battled to make a living on the land. Agriculture had seen massive changes. Hundreds of years of time-honoured practices were taken over by an industry operated by machines. With the increased pace and productivity promised, many farmers were purchasing the new machinery to ensure their properties remained viable. Dada could not afford to do so and, without such advantages, the farm ceased to be competitive. With a new son adding to his ever-growing family, Dada was forced to fall back upon his old trade, and began offering his services as a chimney sweep once more. My nine-year-old brother Henry became Dada's apprentice. I knew that my mother's heart was breaking each morning as she watched them depart for such dangerous and dreaded work.

With production on the farm having slowed dramatically, the Fearn family would not be attending that month's market. Mam entrusted our few goods to a kindly neighbour to sell on our behalf. On market day life on *Sweep's Farm* continued as normal. To say that I was devastated would be an understatement. Despite the clear blue skies, a black cloud hung over my head all morning. Michael would be at the market yet I could not be there.

Totally despondent, I desperately needed to escape and when my chores were complete, I raced straight to the barn. The better of our two horses was always off-limits, but I was allowed to ride the second one. Rapidly bridling it, I climbed the rungs of the fence, mounted without a saddle, and rode. At first, I rode out of anger and frustration, but then as my mind became clearer, I headed for the place I loved most – the river. Flowing close by *Sweep's Farm*, the Mimram's tranquil waters always soothed my soul. Believing myself to be alone, I removed my boots and stockings and plunged my feet into the ice-cold, crystal waters. Sending a shiver through my whole body, they instantly washed away my woes. In my reverie, I failed to notice the approach of a newcomer until a tan and white spaniel bounded into the water beside me. It was Chester, his master leaning upon a nearby tree in his customary fashion.

'I was waiting for you at the market,' he declared.

My sad story about our farm no longer producing enough goods to sell ushered forth a sympathetic sigh from him.

'Your family's doing it tough?'

I nodded.

'Well, you were missed,' he assured me. 'It wasn't the same without you.'

Sitting together upon the bank, Michael took my hand in his own and gently stroked it.

'You're a bonny lass, Hannah.'

I raised my eyes to his and smiled.

'Will you be my girl?' he said. 'My special girl?'

Placing his arms around me, he held me close and kissed me. It was my first kiss. What a moment! With burning cheeks and a pounding heart, I jumped to my feet, flabbergasted by the sudden granting of such a longed-for moment.

'I must go,' I declared. 'I'm needed at home.'

Michael grinned.

'I'll be here again tomorrow,' he said.

'It might be hard to get away,' I replied.

Michael was not fazed.

'Well, I'll still be here.'

Grabbing my boots, I hurriedly gathered my horse's reins and attempted to flee, but a whistle made me turn back. Michael stood twirling my stockings in the air.

'Forget something?'

Hurrying back, I snatched the stockings from his hand. He laughed loudly. What a wicked tease he was!

From the way Martha was watching for me when I arrived home, I knew I was in for a scolding. She swung the window open as I dismounted.

'Must you insist upon riding without a saddle? You're so very wild, Hannah.'

Granny Ravens, who was making a surprise visit, continued the chiding inside.

'Barefoot again!' she exclaimed, aghast at my appearance. 'Whatever will become of you?'

I made no apologies, for it was not the first time, and certainly would not be the last, that I would be reproached for my misdeeds. On the days Michael and I arranged to meet, I would scurry off following my morning's work, ready to slip my hand into his and we would laugh and frolic as we made our way to the river. Its lush, green banks became a place of sanctuary and delight for both of us, lost as we were in each other's company. I loved him for his roguish grin and his insubordination. The way he laughed at the world and mocked the heavy load it laid upon him made me proud to know a man of such strength. I vowed to strive harder when it came to accepting my own lot. Michael possessed an in-depth knowledge of local plants and wildlife, and I cherished the lessons he gave me about lichens and fungi, berries, and other unique shrubs. Together we would marvel at the beauty of the kingfisher and smile as the pipit sang its sweet song. He taught me to appreciate even the most common animals, the frogs and dragonflies, and showed me varieties of butterflies I never knew existed.

When I turned sixteen the following February, I naively celebrated being one year closer to independence and the freedom I so desired to explore the world. Dada blamed Michael.

'It's that Ansell boy,' he grumbled. 'He's making you discontent. You've got a very good life here, Hannah.'

At that moment, I failed to recognize the truth of my father's words. Michael taught me to think beyond the bounds of St. Paul's

Walden. One day I would escape and possess a bigger and brighter future than I could ever have imagined. Sadly, my dreams often blinded me to the blessings I already possessed, and the veil would not be lifted until it was too late.

St. Valentine's Day, the grand celebration of love and bonhomie, followed close on the heels of my birthday each year. Soon after sunrise, I spied my sister Harriet's friend, Evelyn Wright, creeping silently towards me. Having been charged with the secret commission of presenting me with an exquisitely pretty tussie-mussie, she handed it to me.

'It's from Michael Ansell,' she whispered, and I knew that it symbolized my sweetheart's great devotion.

Martha thought it very forward of Michael to present me with such a gift whilst Harriet and Louisa found it terribly romantic. Mam smiled at me tenderly and she fetched her *Language of Flowers* to look up the meaning of each precious bloom: Lily of the Valley (purity and happiness), Asters (love and patience), ferns (fascination), deep pink daisies (love), and ivy (eternity). As we examined my lovely gift, a small card suddenly fell from amongst the foliage. Harriet wasted no time in snatching it up, and try as I may, I could not extract it from her grasp. Its words were for my eyes only, and though I could not read them, I wanted to hold them close to my heart until Michael could read them to me at our next meeting. Mam was sensible to the hurt I felt and managed to retrieve the card from my sister's eager hands.

'Go to him,' she whispered, giving me a reassuring smile.

Hurrying to the river, I found Michael waiting. Taking my hand in his own, he read the gifted words of devotion.

So fair art thou, my bonnie lass,
So deep in luve am I,
And I will luve thee still, my dear,
Till a' the seas gang dry.
Robert Burns

Such beauty and love in so few words. I was smitten! My quest to have my parents accept my amour for Michael, however, received a setback two months later when his brother Francis was transported to Van Diemen's Land. Failing to be deterred by his earlier murder charge, Francis's list of offences now included breaking and entering, poaching, theft, and counterfeiting. When he was again caught poaching following a daring escape from Welwyn Gaol, the judge's patience finally ran out. Francis was sentenced to transportation for life and banished far across the sea. He was not mourned, and we quickly forgot him, consumed as we were in preparations for May Day.

Being descended from a long line of chimney sweeps, May Day always held an extra special significance for my family. Dada told us how sweeps eagerly awaited this day for, as warmer weather approached, Londoners would cease using their fireplaces. Amazing images filled my mind as Dada described the sweeps dancing through the streets, their clothes decorated with flowers and coloured paper, and feathers in their caps. Musicians would sometimes accompany their dance whilst at other times they used soot brushes and other tools of the trade to create their own rhythms. That year I would dance more joyously than any sweep, for Michael would be by my side and my heart was so full of youthful love.

May Day always began before dawn. Coaxed from the warmth of my bed, I would join Mam and my sisters wandering through the woodlands to partake of the ancient beauty ritual of washing our faces in the morning dew. Though none of us believed in the superstitions of times past, we still liked the notion that our faces would be made beautiful for the coming year. Sauntering back home, we laughed and talked whilst the younger ones practiced the Mayers' Song, an all-important part of the celebrations later in the day. Mam would have her basket and we gathered flowers to decorate our home, the woodland spirits granting good fortune to families who honoured them in such a way.

In a household of five girls, the crowning of the May Queen was always a significant event; Mam, Granny Ravens, and Granny's mother before her, having all been crowned. When Martha was declared Queen, Granny bought an exquisite white dress in London, hoping that it would be worn by all her granddaughters. Harriet, Louisa, and I all subsequently reigned, and this year it would be Adelaide, the golden-haired beauty of the family, who would take her rightful place as Queen. Festivities continued throughout the day including maypole dancing, an archery competition, and the Jack o' the Green procession. The day was blessed with sweet, fragrant breezes, and the night was heralded in by the most magnificent sunset.

Squire Hammond threw open the doors of his barn and, whilst the younger ones made their weary way home, the older revellers continued with an evening full of joviality, food, and dancing. The barn was decorated with garlands of May Day blooms and three fiddlers welcomed us to the celebration. Michael, in his Sunday best, was by my side, and we supped on delicacies we could indulge in but once a year: fowl, smoked goose and haddock, ham with veal and pigeon pies, brawns, custards, puddings, fruit tarts, and jellies, all washed down with Squire Hammond's home-brewed cider. Michael and I danced and sang, and when we were done, we lay in a haystack staring up at the bright stars above.

'That's Orion,' Michael said, pointing towards several very bright stars. 'He's known as the hunter in the sky.'

Raising himself on an elbow, Michael smiled as he gently caressed my cheek, and kissed me.

'We'll think of them as our stars. Let's promise that no matter where we are or what we are doing when we see those stars, we will think of each other.'

I promised solemnly to do so.

As we wandered home, I rested my head upon his shoulder. It was the most wonderful night of my life. My heart was so light and full of joy. Looking back now, it was the last truly happy evening for many long years. Perhaps I wasn't meant to be that happy. As my world came crashing in around me over the coming months, it was as if I was being punished for those fleeting moments of pleasure.

Unbeknownst to us, Dada had been suffering for the past few months from something he called a soot wart. Not wishing to further burden Mam, he initially kept the growth a secret from her, a decision we would all come to rue. When Mam was eventually told, she convinced him to see a doctor, and the wart was removed. He was given poultices to apply and mercury was prescribed, yet a second wart soon appeared. A new doctor gave the disease its correct name and Dada was diagnosed as having Chimney Sweeps' Cancer. So named because of its prevalence in sweeps, it was caused by their ongoing exposure to soot. We were all numbed by the news. My parents were still coming to terms with Dada's illness, when at the end of May, although barely recovered from the birth of Ethelbert, Mam discovered she was expecting another child. I had rarely seen Mam cry, but she cried for days after she was told the news. When she wasn't crying, she would sit staring into space, hardly speaking and could do nothing. I helped where I could with the cooking and the little ones, Granny Ravens visited daily, and Michael came to lend a hand on the farm. I struggled to understand why my family, so humble and inoffensive, who cared for their fellow men and never harmed another living creature, should be sent so many trials. Granny Ravens tried to console us using her faith and teachings from the Bible.

'Blessed is the man who remains steadfast under trial,
for when he has stood the test he will receive the crown of life,
which God has promised to those who love him.' James 1:12.

I am not religious and never was, so Granny's verses did nothing to relieve either my pain or that of my parents. I fought to adjust to life following these cruel blows and desperately tried to realise that, no matter how I mourned, nothing could be changed.

There is a commonly held belief that bad things come in threes and within days I was forced to acknowledge such a truth. It had been the warmest and sweetest of May days, and taking a brief moment from my work, I sat musing about nothing in particular, simply content to watch the sun reflect off the crystal-clear waters of the pretty Mimram. The pounding of horses' hooves woke me from my reverie and I turned to see Michael and his brother Richard approaching. Quickly alighting from his mount, Michael's countenance instantly told me something terrible had happened. Jumping to my feet, I hurried to him.

'Thank God you're here,' he said seizing me in his arms. 'I just had to see you. I must go away, my love. Such punishment awaits me if I am caught.'

His knuckles were cut and bled freely. I drew out my handkerchief and wrapped it around them. He smiled his thanks.

'What has happened?' I asked breathlessly.

'I couldn't help myself, Hannah,' he declared. 'This morning there was a man, a new tenant, moving into my grandparents' house, the house where I was born. My father has leased it out for years, fully furnished with quality pieces inherited with the house by my dear mother. I discovered this man casting out mother's cherished possessions in favour of his own. Her lovely furniture was being hurled into the muddy courtyard. Infuriated, I rushed forward and dragged him away from the furniture. We came to blows and the man fell. I raced to the barn and snatched up an axe, before setting to work to destroy his furniture. The constable was summoned, but I felled him too and threatened him with my hunting gun.'

I cried out at the horror of it all.

'I'm so sorry, sweetheart,' Michael whispered, still holding me tightly.

Our brief moment together was interrupted by Richard who urged his brother to hurry. I watched as Michael re-mounted and the pair rode off towards Welwyn. Such liberty, however, was short-lived. Having sought medical attention for his injured hand, Michael was arrested and put in the cage overnight. This time he would feel the full force of the law. Appearing at the St. Alban's Sessions, he was sentenced to six months' hard labour for criminal damage and assault. A further order was made that upon release he would be required to pay twenty pounds and keep the peace for twelve months. From whence he would obtain twenty pounds, I knew not. It was a huge sum of money. If he didn't pay, he would be returned to gaol, and my heart would be forced to bleed for him all over again.

As Michael rode to me that day, his gorgeous spaniel raced joyously alongside him, little knowing why his master galloped with such haste. With Michael's departure, however, the dog somehow sensed that it was not the time to follow and he remained dutifully by my side. Taking dear little Chester home, his loving nature and desire for comfort and attention, gave me something other than Michael's absence to dwell upon. Chester always held a special place in my heart. Now, standing in his master's place, he became dearer to me than ever.

Summer was short that year, or perhaps it just seemed that way, for much of it was spent inside. There were no evening walks, the Mimram having lost much of its sparkle without Michael. It was like a part of me was missing. Dada's health was also declining quickly and he grew weaker almost daily. As Mam's confinement drew ever closer, she struggled to divide her time between nursing Dada, nurturing my younger siblings, and having enough rest to ensure she and her unborn child remained healthy. Moving to *Sweep's Farm* on a permanent basis, Granny Ravens worked alongside Martha to run the household, my fastidious sister assuring me in no uncertain terms, that the best help I could render was to stay out of the way. Perfectly at ease with my banishment, I happily remained outside, contentedly milking cows and collecting eggs, whilst dodging all dreaded household chores.

Michael returned to me on a day almost as perfect as the one on which he left. Soft blue skies greeted me that morning, the sun casting its brilliant rays generously upon all God's creatures. For mid-October, it was a rare gem. Such were the glories of the afternoon; I was inspired to take a short walk by the river. With Chester bounding alongside me, I walked briskly, for my heart was light. Upon approach to the river, I spied a man sitting under one of the willow trees, idly shredding a blade of grass. Raising his eyes, he smiled. Six months imprisonment had changed him; he was pale and thin; his lovely hair shaven to the scalp. His eyes no longer held an impish sparkle and his face was careworn, but it was still him, still my Michael. With riotous barking, Chester leapt into his arms whilst I melted to my knees by his side. When Chester was finally lured away to frolic in the river's cooling waters, I resumed my rightful place in Michael's arms and was kissed like never before.

'Now that's what I've been waiting for,' he declared with a grin. 'I've celebrated every passing hour, every minute, for by their passing, they brought me ever closer to being with you again.'

Reaching into his pocket, Michael drew out a small silver disc and handed it to me.

'I made this for you,' he said, almost bashfully. Pointing to words engraved upon it, he read, 'I do love nothing in the world so well as you.'

I smiled at the sentiment, which Michael assured me was borrowed from Shakespeare. On the reverse side, Michael had etched the five main stars of Orion.

'They're our special stars,' he reminded me.

'It's beautiful,' I sighed contentedly.

Michael gently fastened the disc around my neck, before encasing me in his arms once more.

'I've done so much thinking over the past few months,' he declared. 'When I'm with you the world is a different place, and I need you by my side more than ever. But I have nothing to offer you. I'm a poor man and have spent a reckless youth, but this morning I took a job with the carter my father once worked for. I will learn the trade, gradually work my way up and, in time, start my own business. The great cities of Liverpool and Manchester offer amazing opportunities. I wish to have a home and children of my own, a family to love and protect for the rest of my days. And you, my love, are the girl I want to share it all with. I promise I will work hard and make you proud. My wild days are over.'

His words filled me with a warm, happy glow. He was planning a future, and that future included me. That evening, I re-examined my cherished necklace. I tried hard to remember the words Michael read, but could only remember their sentiment. The following day, I begged him to teach me. Word by word I learnt them, practicing each one repeatedly, the earth my parchment when pens and paper were lacking. In time, I knew the precious words by heart. My supreme efforts to learn the words of Michael's declaration signalled the beginning of my ability to read and write. My liberation from ignorance had finally begun.

It was a cold and blustery November day when Mam's new bairn arrived. Winter, it seemed, was coming early that year and we huddled by the fire waiting for the cries of our new brother or sister. All of Mam's children were born at home, delivered by Granny Ravens. Things, however, were different this time, and Mam was having difficulty delivering her bairn. Leaving the others, I went to sit beside her, holding her hand as I wiped her brow. Hours dragged on and Mam's condition worsened. The seriousness of her predicament was signalled by the summoning of a doctor, something usually only done in dire circumstances. It seemed an eternity before his arrival, and I could do nothing in the meantime to ease Mam's suffering. When the doctor eventually made his appearance, robed entirely in black, such was the impression on me that I nearly fainted. He pointed at me.

'Get that girl out of here,' he commanded, and I was hastily ushered from the room.

Staying by Mam's door, each of her screams pierced deep into my heart. Eventually, the cries of a child were heard within and I breathed again. Martha was quickly by my side and we waited eagerly to meet the new arrival. It was not long before Mam's door opened and Granny appeared, our new brother in her arms. I could see Mam lying on the bed and I began walking towards her. Granny, however, barred my way, thrusting the new arrival into my arms.

'Here, take him and wait outside,' she said, herding me back into the hallway.

My entreaties to be allowed admittance fell on deaf ears, and Granny closed the door upon my pleas. Eventually, the door opened again and Dada, who unbeknownst to me had been in the room the whole time, appeared. His face was ashen and tears streamed down his cheeks. Upon seeing Martha and me, he stopped and stared as though he didn't recognize us.

'She's gone,' he murmured before staggering off along the darkened passage.

With a wail of despair, Martha hastened to our mother's side. Following at a distance, I crept forward, my eyes fixated on Mam lying there so pale and silent. Granny Ravens looked at us. She was always such a tower of strength, but now she was crying tears for a daughter who only that morning had been cooking bread alongside her, happy and healthy. Her precious daughter had died in her arms well before her time.

As the reality of my mother's death slowly sank in, my resolve to be strong for Dada and the rest of my family, failed. The thought that our home would now be bereft of her laughter, her sweet song, her warmth, and her courage was unthinkable. Mam was the only person who fully understood me, the only one who never chided me for my wild heart or foolish childhood whims. Whilst mourning alongside my siblings brought a certain amount of solace, expressing what was deep in my heart could only be done alone. Forced to flee from the sanctuary of my bedroom by the arrival of Martha, I escaped to the meadows adjoining the church. The tranquillity of these meadows used to bring Mam much needed succor from life's struggles, and my peaceful surrounds had a similar soothing effect on me. I imagined Mam playing here as a child, dancing in the sunlight with a light-heartedness snuffed out since her marriage. She danced again now, free from her burdens and sorrows. The hearts of those she left behind may well have been broken and empty, but we had to find it within ourselves to celebrate her life and know that she was in a far better place.

Aunt Elinor arrived that evening and stayed with us until after Mam's funeral. Whilst loving us in her own special way, life with our aunt was certainly not easy. A stickler for routine, the homeliness of *Sweep's Farm* was soon brushed aside in favour of regimented order. With Dada in no fit state to care for our new baby brother, the task fell to Martha and me. According to Mam's wishes, we christened him John and took his crib into our room, my sister and I taking turns to feed and minister to him during the night. Despite his traumatic entrance into the world, John was thankfully a strong and healthy bairn who quickly won my heart, though I was sorrowful he would never know our mother's love.

Dada could not afford to bury his wife and it was left to my grandmother and aunt to see her peacefully laid to rest. Breaking with tradition, they chose to walk behind the coffin, escorting Mam to her final resting place in St. Giles' Churchyard. By now, Dada's health had deteriorated to such an extent that he was no longer the man we knew and loved. Despite treatment, his cancer spread rapidly and he spent his days in a great deal of pain. Laudanum offered relief, but clarity of thought was the price paid. With Mam's death, Dada lost the will to go on.

In a household reeling from the loss of our mother and whose father was suffering so cruelly through illness, there was little cause to celebrate my birthday that year. In times past, I found great delight in the sweetness of the early spring blooms, but today everything seemed inconsequential. I was turning seventeen, and as dear Dada took me by the hand, he wished me joy, assuring me it was a comfort to possess such a daughter. Embracing him tightly, I struggled to mask my tears and was quick to draw his curtains so that he might rest. Upon leaving him, my one birthday wish which was to see his pain vanish. With every expectation of seeing Michael, I headed out mid-morning and waited for him by the river. He did not come. More than once my mind tricked me into thinking that I could hear his footsteps, but in the end, I was left to wander home alone and disappointed. I never saw my Michael again.

Granny Ravens had arrived by the time I came home and we gathered around the kitchen table for a birthday celebration. Having baked a sumptuous pound cake, she allowed my sisters to decorate it with flowers from the garden. There was bread and cheese, Granny's homemade jam, and a delicious jug of lemonade. Seated comfortably in his armchair, Dada gently called me to his side and bestowed the gift of new shoes, a present we always received on our birthday, and something for which we were continually grateful. I knew that Dada would have been too ill to purchase them himself, and was thankful to Granny for ensuring that I still received a gift. Granny did so much for our family during this time, including giving Martha money to keep the household running.

Towards evening, Mr. Ansell brought me the devastating news that Michael was arrested in the early hours of that morning. He was caught in Poolemore Lane in possession of twenty dozen pigeons. His brother Richard and cousin Thomas were arrested alongside him. I was stunned. Michael had been so settled of late. He was doing well as a carter and making exciting plans for the future – our future. Mr. Ansell held out a bunch of violets.

'Michael wanted me to give you these for your birthday.'

As I took the violets, I wiped the tears from my cheeks.

'May I see him?' I asked.

'They won't let anyone see him.'

My beloved Michael was taken to Hitchin and placed before the Magistrate to answer questions. The Magistrate remanded him to be further examined at a later date. After thirty-four days of waiting, Mr. Ansell finally arrived with news.

'Michael and Richard will be tried tomorrow in the Hertford Shire Hall. The Marquis of Salisbury and Lord Dacre will be presiding,' he explained mournfully.

Mr. Ansell travelled to Hertford for the trial of his sons. I could only wait full of expectation and hope that Michael would soon be returned to me. The day after sentence was passed, Mr. Ansell arrived home and came to see me, looking more drawn than ever before.

'They are sending my boys away,' he said, in a broken, barely audible voice.

My heart stopped and my knees buckled.

'Richard and his cousin Thomas both got seven years, but Michael got life.'

Unable to hold back the tears any longer, I threw myself prostrate upon the ground and sobbed, knowing my heart would break for certain.

'My dear girl,' Mr. Ansell said, raising me into his arms. 'I wish it could have been different. Michael's last words were for you. He said that he would love you forever.'

Michael and Richard were hastily removed from the district. I heard from Mr. Ansell that they left for Van Diemen's Land six weeks later. They spent the intervening weeks on a rat-infested hulk anchored in the Thames. My heart bled for my poor, beloved Michael. He had been my great love, a man with whom I could always forget my cares, who brightened my days, and someone who made me feel special. Now he was gone. As he was borne thousands of miles away from me, part of my heart was going with him. Mr. Ansell revealed that the stolen pigeons would have brought in five pounds, a great deal of money for a man in Michael's position. The more I thought about it, the more I was sure he did it for me. Having spoken about a life together, Michael wanted to ensure our future security. Maybe the lure of some quick money was just too difficult to resist. Whatever the reason, at only twenty-one years of age, he would pay a ghastly price. My

Michael would be spending the remainder of his life in the place they called 'Cruel Van Diemen's Land.'

With three sons convicted and transported, poor Mr. Ansell was left with only one son to comfort him in his old age. Edward and his wife lived in Manchester, a city where both were employed in one of the ever-growing numbers of cotton mills. Upon hearing of his brothers' misfortune, Edward sent for his father, who, despite several misgivings, eventually packed his few belongings and headed north. I watched him leave with tears in my eyes. He cut a sad and lonely figure, as he walked slowly out of town, his small cart loaded with possessions. Michael's faithful little dog followed him. I offered to adopt the dog as my own but Mr. Ansell wanted to keep Chester as a way of remembering his son. It broke my heart to say goodbye and to see the dear little thing leave. What made it even harder was knowing Chester would never see his beloved master again or play in the green fields he loved so much. He was going to a big, dark, dirty city and his life would be changed forever. I will never forget his sweet face nor the joy it gave me.

Mr. Ansell was the last of his family to leave Hertfordshire, the family having resided there since the 1500s. I lingered beside the river that afternoon, musing upon my lost love and the happy times we spent together. I would rue my decision to dawdle, however, when I arrived home to find Martha waiting impatiently at the door.

'Hannah! Where have you been? Dada has been asking for you.'

Together we hurried to our father's side, but he knew not that we were there. His laudanum usage had increased with his pain, and he sat fireside oblivious to the world surrounding him. The following morning, he was lucid enough to admit himself to the Hitchin workhouse where he died a little over two weeks later. They told me that Dada made the best possible use of the workhouse, receiving care in his final days, something that would have been out of our reach if he remained at home.

Following Dada's funeral, Granny Ravens took Martha and me aside to discuss our family's future. In days gone by, women like us were able to run successful enterprises from their own hearthside. Now, however, machines were taking the work of thousands and girls like us were being forced into the factories to survive. In having a skill to fall back upon, Martha and I were luckier than most. Being tutored in the finer skills of needlework by our mother, grandmother, and aunt, Martha and I developed into rather fine seamstresses. At first, these skills were taught to me to improve my focus and tame my wild heart. Now they were able to secure me a position with one of our aunt's London acquaintances. I knew I should be thankful for this small mercy. Martha also gained employment with this woman. I was grateful that, in leaving home for the first time, my sister would be by my side.

The dreaded day of parting from our family and friends, from everything familiar and cherished, came on Monday 8th of June, 1840. The two of us rose early to prepare for the long journey to London, the inhospitable city where we would earn our keep. It was Martha's idea to plant a small rose bush on our parents' grave before we left. It would be a long time before either of us would visit again. Leaving the graveyard, I looked back as a ray of sunlight fell upon the pink blooms of the rosebush. It was the briefest moment of joy on this dismal day, for these blooms would be a lasting testament to our love.

With no funds to pay for a coach trip to London, a local farmer volunteered to take us as far as St. Albans on his dray. From there, Granny organized for a carrier to take us to London as part of his regular trip. As the dray pulled into sight that morning, my heart was heavy. Turning to embrace Granny, Martha and I settled ourselves amongst a cargo of barrels and we were soon making our last journey down the High Street. Watching the hedgerows go by, my heart was near to bursting as I bid St. Paul's Walden a sad farewell. With all her courage spent, Martha couldn't bring herself to take a last look. Laying back upon the straw, she stared mutely into the wide, blue expanse above.

2

LONDON

“The truth is, that in London it is always a sickly season. Nobody is healthy in London, nobody can be.”

Jane Austen, Emma, 1816.

The carrier deposited us at the Queen's Hotel in St. Martin's Le Grand later that evening, and we were greatly relieved to have finally arrived. Martha pointed to a garish plaque upon the hotel wall portraying a huge mouth ready to consume a bull in its entirety. She read the accompanying inscription.

'Milo the Cretonian an ox slew with his fist and ate it up at one meal. Ye gods what a glorious twist.'

As I stared at this remnant of the old *Bull and Mouth Inn* which once stood on the spot, I thought it an ominous welcome to London. Were we to be likewise swallowed up by this enormous city?

London was very different from what I had always dreamed and it did not take long for the initial novelty and thrill to fade. In this 'great' city, all was haste. With its chimneys belching thick, black smoke, it stood by way of stark contrast to my native Hertfordshire whose air was always so clear and refreshing. My lungs now struggled to cope with such dense, polluted air. Dirt and filth were a way of life here. Congested with every means of transport from hackney cabs, carts, and even live cattle drives, the roads we traversed daily were squalid, often ankle-deep with waste, and the smells emanating from them could produce instant malady. The buildings we frequented were covered by a thick grime that we would go to extraordinary lengths to avoid brushing against for fear of soiling our clothing indelibly.

We were to be in the employ of Madame Lucie Le Blanc. Aunt Elinor had known her as plain Lucy White, but since opening her up-market London boutique, she had assumed a more fanciful, French name, and transformed herself from a young, naïve girl into a severe, astute businesswoman. Her gentleman friend, Mr. Biggerstaff, kept watch over the business, ensuring that we seamstresses worked hard and obeyed the rules. Warned by those more experienced in the ways of Madame's establishment, we knew to be wary of this gentleman and tried our best to avoid contact with him altogether.

Being a seamstress in an establishment the calibre of Madame's was not such a bad thing. At the time of our arrival, London was flooded with workers from all over Britain and Ireland, so many, like ourselves, having fled their rural abodes in search of work. We were shocked by the number of unemployed and homeless people, as well as the widespread prejudice against the Irish. With so many living in dire circumstances, Martha and I were lucky to be employed by Madame. Ours was an industry that was acceptable enough for upper-class women who had fallen on hard times. As someone with no formal education, I felt fortunate to be employed in it. Provided with smart new attire so that we might elegantly represent the boutique, I felt more a part of modern London than I did in my faded, country check. Nothing, however, could stop me from missing the barefooted freedom of St. Paul's Walden, my stockinged feet now trapped inside tight boots each day.

Living as I did in the heart of fashionable London, I was exposed to everything my heart could desire: endless entertainment, street upon street of high-end shops, and a life of ease and merriment. Sadly, all the beautiful things I coveted remained well beyond my reach, my lack of funds dampening my enthusiasm for the city. Feeling miserable and unfulfilled at work simply added to my malady. As the elder and favoured sibling, Martha instantly took her place at the seamstresses' table which literally left me on my hands and knees crawling around the cold, hard floor picking up pins, scraps of material, and cotton. I was barred from going near any creation underway. I arrived in this city with the understanding that, if I worked hard and put my mind to it, I too could one day become a prominent London seamstress. How I would relish such an opportunity! The inherent tedium of my current role, however, severely tested my faith and commitment, and all I could think about was going home. Then, one morning, Madame entered the workroom.

'Hannah Fearn,' she commanded, and I gazed up from the floor.

There was never any distinction between the way she treated her workers, using equal disdain when dealing with all of us. The girls in the workroom were practised at keeping their eyes on their work but I knew that they would be secretly watching with interest as I, the newcomer, went slowly forward. I felt so alone as I approached Madame.

'I was told by your aunt that you have far more talent than your sister. Is this true?'

I remained silent.

'Come on, girl, there's no room for loyalty or modesty here. Are you or are you not more skilled than your sister?'

'I have always been told so,' I whispered.

Madame was satisfied. Producing a garment from behind her back, she thrust it into my arms.

'This work is well below the quality expected from my establishment and has been returned to us. Unpick it and bring it up to standard and you may have a permanent place at the table.'

Madame summoned the young seamstress who produced the work and I watched as she brought the poor girl to tears. Mr. Biggerstaff stepped forward to console the sobbing girl with a sort of grotesque, overpowering 'tenderness' that he seemed to revel in and which always left the receiver dreading further advances. Fleeing from Madame's office, the poor young girl's employment was at an end.

Work upon the returned dress was soon completed and the client was soothed. Madame was pleased with my efforts and, as promised, I was promoted to the seamstresses' table. I had finally joined the ranks of the needlework girls of London and my faith and drive were restored. My promotion brought new responsibilities. Working six days a week, sometimes up to seventeen hours a day, I was handling fine satins and laces, and could not afford to have rough hands or sharp nails. I therefore commenced the nightly ritual of the other seamstresses, rubbing my hands with cream before covering them with the cotton gloves that became a necessary addition to my sleeping attire. Keeping my hands as soft as a newborn bairn was now my obligation. The slightest pull or rub on my work would mean ruination of the garment. The subsequent chiding from Madame would be considerably worse.

Further progression along the seamstresses' table came around a month later: another's misfortune again benefitting me. Due to an unprecedented commotion in the workroom that morning, Madame appeared amongst us and demanded to know the cause of such disruption to our work. Learning that one of her seamstresses had not returned from an outing the previous evening brought a furrow to her brow and she declared the missing girl would steal no more of her valuable time. Commanded to resume our seats, Madame ordered us to begin our day's toil. During the morning, whispers circulated concerning the whereabouts of the absent Ella. London had been abuzz during recent days over the upcoming execution of a twenty-three-year-old Swiss immigrant named Courvoisier who murdered his employer, Lord William Russell. Public executions were becoming infrequent in London, but the public's interest was still sparked by gruesome deeds and forty thousand onlookers turned up at eight o'clock that morning to see Courvoisier hang. Ella was amongst them.

Around nine-thirty, we observed Mr. Biggerstaff escorting her into Madame's office. It was an all too familiar scene that played out and ended as expected with Ella's dismissal from the workroom. Shivers shot down my spine as Madame approached me. Swallowing slowly, I breathed deeply and rose to stand upon trembling legs.

'Ella's departure has left me without my best seamstress. Though you have been here such a short time, your skill has been noted. You possess far greater talent than any of the others. You will take Ella's place. Henceforth, you will sit at the front of the workroom. The completion of Lady Braye's gown awaits you.'

To hinder Madame's quest to be the best boutique in London was done at one's own peril. Following an examination of Lady Braye's gown, I suggested several ways the design could be enhanced. I fully understood that Madame's approval of the alterations was also her way of throwing down the gauntlet, challenging me to prove once and for all that I was worthy of the trust she had placed in me. Success would secure my future in the boutique, and in time would elevate me to be one of London's top seamstresses. Relying upon my intuition and creative flair, I set about broadening the gown's neckline, transforming the large gigot sleeves into smaller demi-gigots, and adorning the top of the bodice and cuffs with generous flounces of Honiton lace. Once completed, I am proud to say that the gown's beauty would have matched any in England. Lady Braye was delighted and Madame was impressed by my artistry.

When Lady Braye subsequently returned to commission a day dress, I suggested adding a second bodice for evening wear that matched the same skirt. Madame applauded my initiative, and my reward was the opportunity to design a dress for display in her boutique. It was a great honour. Allowed access to materials, threads, and trims from the workroom, I worked on it every spare moment. Knowing that elegance was achieved through the delicacy of design and stitching, I shied away from the temptation to produce an overly elaborate display of my talent. Choosing a cream challis whose subtle pattern incorporated wild strawberries, pink and yellow anemones, and bamboo shoots, I used it liberally throughout the design, adding a double ruched collar, three layers of sleeves cut on the bias, and a voluptuous dome-shaped skirt.

Labouring away as I was, Martha may well have felt abandoned had not an equally important mission consumed her own leisure hours. Having befriended two fellow seamstresses, she was introduced to a relatively new movement aimed at gaining political rights and representation for the working classes. Each Monday evening, Martha and her friends would attend a meeting for female Chartists held at the Abbey Street Trade's Hall. Whilst happy to work in the background sewing banners and distributing pamphlets, she was nonetheless stirred by the injustice that it was always men who were educated, given the vote, and held all the power. My shy and retiring sister suddenly had a new purpose in life and she began to fight against such inequality. Frequenting the Chapter Coffee House on Paternoster Row, Martha and her friends placed themselves alongside educated men; publishers, booksellers, and writers.

Having taken in the readings and discussed the affairs of the day, Martha would return to our tiny attic and impress upon me the necessity of my becoming more informed about the world around me. She understood that education was the key to this knowledge and, feeling blessed by the tuition she received during her time living with Granny Ravens, she was determined to teach me everything she knew. This process began with learning to write my name, a task at which I worked diligently until it was mastered. Each week Martha would also read me the next instalment of *Mister Humphrey's Clock* written by an author named Boz, whose literary talents we had been enjoying since the previous April.

Despite the busyness of our days, Martha and I still found time to spend together for pure enjoyment. Drawn to the exotic gardens at Kew when they opened to the public for the first time that year, we also watched as the finishing touches were put on the new square being built on the former King's Mews. Within this square, the building of a column to commemorate the victories of Admiral Horatio Nelson during the Napoleonic Wars had just commenced. We stood in awe as it crept ever skyward. With an abundance of gas lighting, the streets of London were always so bright as we passed through them of an evening, something that continued to delight and astonish us. At home, we could never have dreamed of such picturesque window displays nor such radiantly lit interiors.

As Christmas approached, we felt the bonds of kinship tighten, and were blessed to have each other during this first Christmas without our parents. Being far from our beloved siblings and Granny Ravens, we were indeed touched when one of our new friends invited us home for her family Christmas party. Abigail's family was different from all the rest, being from the professional classes. They lived in Knightsbridge, their Sloane Street residence rather isolated, separated as it was from the rest of the city by marshland. Our gratitude knew no bounds for what turned out to be a truly magical night. This family's kindness and generosity slightly eased the sting of our lost ones and we spent Christmas in relatively good cheer. Our yearning to be at home remained, however, and its distance from London never seemed so great as it did when trouble struck just a few months later.

It was one evening the following May, when Martha came stumbling into our attic, the pain and terror on her face unmistakable despite the dim flickering of our candle. Pale and shaken, she collapsed upon our bed in a torrent of tears, and I took her into my arms begging to know what evil had transpired.

'Mr. Biggerstaff,' she said in whispered sobs. 'He … cornered me …'
She could say no more.

'The monster!' I exclaimed, flying to my feet. 'I'll tell Madame.'

'No, Hannah,' Martha replied, quickly grabbing my wrist to impede progress. 'We must tell no one. We cannot afford to lose our positions here.'

She signalled the thin curtain which separated us from the other girls who shared our attic and held a finger to her lips. We were always mindful of what we said and did around our work colleagues, for we knew that any hint of scandal or gossip would see us immediately dismissed. In a city where so many needed work, young seamstresses were an easily replaceable commodity. In the few months we had been in London, Martha and I had seen the very worst this city could offer and knew exactly what life on the streets would mean. Nothing though could scare us like the thought that one day we might end up in the workhouse. That very thought now gave us strength, and we agreed not to report Mr. Biggerstaff's actions, whilst vowing that neither of us would ever be alone with him again. That night we did not sleep head to toe as normal but side by side, two heads on the one pillow, holding each other tightly.

Despite our resolve to continue as though nothing had happened, the following morning the decision was taken out of our hands when Martha was summoned to Madame's office. Though uninvited, I followed my sister into that beastly room and, standing beside her, clasped her hand. Madame stood menacingly before us, looking far from her usual immaculate self. Drawn and desolate, her hair was quite dishevelled. When the lecherous Mr. Biggerstaff entered, she turned her face from him, refusing to acknowledge his presence. Yet, despite her clear loathing, when Mr. Biggerstaff accused my sister of attacking him like a wild cat, he was believed. Aghast, Martha pleaded her case, but it fell on deaf ears. She was ordered to pack her belongings and leave before the others arrived for the day. Our parents raised us to never cower before bullies, and shy, gentle Martha did credit to herself by refusing to flinch in the light of these malicious accusations, standing instead with her head held high and proud. In contrast to my sister's dignified silence, I was blessed with a robust voice and, in times of peril, I always spoke out against injustice.

'That's cruel and heartless indeed,' I declared. 'Martha has told you the truth. She acted in self-defence. A woman should not be punished for proving herself pure and honest. If that man's behaviour towards the women employed here was ever exposed, your establishment would come crashing down around you.'

The look that Madame cast towards me was one of pure hate.

'You may join your sister,' she declared, a great deal of spite in her voice.

I informed her that nothing would give me greater pleasure. Still tightly clutching Martha's hand, I walked with her to the doorway, my sister pausing upon the threshold.

'I told you the truth, but your affection for Mr. Biggerstaff has willingly blinded you to what sort of man he really is. I accept my dismissal, and can clearly see you intend to punish me further by also dispensing with the services of my innocent sister. Our aunt always spoke kindly of you and held you in high esteem. It appears she was grossly deceived.'

Madame seemed shaken by Martha's words and turned her face sharply from us. Passing through the workroom for the last time, I spirited away the display gown into which I had poured so much time and effort. Upon reaching the safety of the attic, I pulled every stitch and embellishment from it, preferring to see it in pieces upon the attic floor than in Madame's clutches. Within the half-hour, our few meagre belongings were packed and we left Madame's establishment forever.

'Shall we go home?' I queried.

Martha shook her head.

'We don't have a home to go to any longer.'

'But what about Granny?'

'We cannot impose upon Granny. She's already got enough to contend with looking after the little ones.'

'We could take jobs as straw plaiters at the Luton hat factory,' I suggested.

'Don't be silly, Hannah,' Martha scolded. 'Some of those girls have been there since they were four years old. We couldn't match their skills.'

'Then what shall we do?' I asked anxiously.

'We shall stay with our aunt and uncle,' my sister declared decidedly. 'From there, I will think of a plan.'

3

ST. GILES

'Nothing but idleness, poverty, misery and ruin are to be seen; distress even to madness and death, and not a house in tolerable condition ...'

William Hogarth, 1785

We were so pious and proud upon arrival in London, vowing that we would never enter this unwholesome part of town; an area of ill repute in one of the worst slum areas of the city. Now we wandered through mud-filled, narrow streets, row upon row of laundry hung overhead in the desperate but futile hope of sunlight or warmth in this ever-darkened world. The London air was, at the best of times, heavily polluted, yet here in St. Giles, the smell from nearby tanneries, made it almost impossible to breathe. There was squalor everywhere one looked. Filthy were the streets, filthy were the shopfronts and houses, and filthy were the people who huddled together for some kind of comfort and warmth in this grim place. Dada once told me that the Great Plague of London started in St Giles. I little wondered why. Despite this, it had always been a place of refuge for people fleeing persecution and hardship. Now we went there begging for asylum like so many other unfortunates before us. Stay here or sleep on the streets.

Eventually, we found Stone Cutter's Alley and the narrow, three-story tenement that housed my aunt, uncle, and their six surviving children. Its dark and damp exterior with blackened windows was far from welcoming and I was teetering on the verge of running away as Martha knocked for admittance. We discovered our relatives living in unimaginable poverty, struggling to find even the barest necessities of life. They did not own the tumbled-down tenement in which they dwelt but rented the first floor, where they existed within the close confines of three small, cramped rooms. The first contained a tiny stove and kitchen table; the second, my aunt, uncle, and their sons, Bertie and Phillip as well as Baby Anne; whilst in the third room, a double bed housed the remaining daughters who slept side by side, head to toe. For this wretched, almost uninhabitable accommodation, the family parted with a third of their weekly income

Uncle Henry maintained the family's chimney sweeping business, a London institution since my four times great grandfather George Fearn's day. My uncle was proud of being a London sweep and always donned the sweep's top hat, something the Fearn men had done since being granted the privilege by King George. Legend has it that a sweep saved the King's life and by way of thanks he declared all sweeps to be lucky and granted them the honour of wearing top hats in an era where only the gentry and royalty wore them.

Aunt Elizabeth was our uncle's second wife and she welcomed us with a warmth and kindness beyond all expectation. Her eldest daughter, the fifteen-year-old Lottie, sat huddled by the fire as we entered and made no effort to greet us. Later in the day, we would discover that Lottie was with child, having been taken advantage of by the foreman in the factory where she worked. Dismissed without pay, she now worked long and exhausting hours in her mother's home laundry. Despite her sister's experience, another daughter Hettie, three years younger, continued to work at the same factory, for the family could ill afford to have two children out of work. Though only twelve years old, she worked from six in the morning until six at night for the tiny sum of four shillings a day.

Escaping the wretched conditions experienced by her sisters, ten-year-old Minnie spent her days selling small posies to passing toffs and their fancy ladies at Covent Garden. Though so young, she knew the benefit of presenting herself well and took great pains each morning with her grooming. She possessed two stylish work dresses, a pretty bonnet, and a shawl, keeping them all impeccably clean and in good repair.

Aunt Elizabeth also borne Uncle Henry three fine sons to follow him into the family business. Young Alfie would have been thirteen by now had his life not tragically been cut short only days after his eleventh birthday. Trapped in a chimney for several hours, he slowly suffocated as attempts were made to rescue him. Just a few months later, another son, Phillip, slipped and fell, shattering several bones in his left leg. His crippling injury was a double blow for the family. Left with a permanently deformed ankle, crutches now aided movement.

I was continually astounded by the pluck of my young cousin who showed a great deal of spirit and courage. Disinclined to part with his cherished top hat, he would continue to don it each morning and kissing his mother, would head out whistling merrily. With tears in her eyes, Aunt Elizabeth would watch her son, her face filled with pride. At seven years old, Phillip was a cheeky young thing and he haggled with the other young boys of London for a prime piece of real estate upon Piccadilly. He didn't own the property, but instead, the right to sweep it. From one kind of sweep to another, he kept the roads free from mud and horse manure, the nobility, including the Duke of Devonshire and Lord Willoughby, paying him for his trouble. As well-dressed ladies appeared, Phillip would sweep a clean passage for them and see them safely across the road. At other times, he would hold the reins whilst a horse's owner was otherwise employed. He didn't always get paid but he received enough to make his efforts worthwhile. His wit and charm made him a personal favourite of many who unofficially employed him, expecting him to be there each day to assist them.

Bertie, the final son, was now in his third year as a sweep and had blessedly managed to stay safe and uninjured during this time. There was a four-year gap between Bertie and the bairn of the family, Anne. In the interim, Aunt Elizabeth and Uncle Henry lost two children, Charley at six months with smallpox, and Flora at eighteen months from influenza. I could not imagine what Aunt Elizabeth suffered losing these bairns, her grief being intensified by the necessity of a pauper's funeral.

Our cousins were not fazed by our intrusion and went about their daily chores as though the addition of two extra bodies caused no hindrance at all. They were generous and tender. They never complained about their lot, though they had so much to weary them. By contrast, Martha and I took quite some time to adapt to life in St. Giles. The poverty we witnessed on the streets was something with which it was hard to be reconciled. I will never forget a tiny child that we came across huddled by a saloop stall, during the early days of our residency. Emaciated, her eyes bulging from her head, she sat fixated upon those who bought the warming drink. Eventually, a woman noticed the tiny child and handed her the remnants of the saloop in her mug. The child snatched the mug, consuming its contents ravenously. The woman bent again and gave the child a coin before moving on.

'Poor little thing,' Martha said.

Martha loved children and moved towards the child. Whilst I hovered a little way off, she went down upon her haunches to speak to her. The child remained silent but was quick enough to grab the penny Martha offered her. Rising to her feet again, Martha turned to me.

'I wish we could do more.'

'And if we did,' I replied, 'what about all the others?'

There were many such children on the streets of London, indeed, everywhere my eyes turned, children were crawling or sitting in the filth. Their cries of hunger echoed from the tiny shops and tenements, no one being willing or able to alleviate their suffering. Although begging was punishable by imprisonment, the problem was so huge, that such punishment did little to reduce the number of beggars. Tragically, after a few more dismal weeks, their numbers no longer astounded me. With hundreds of calamities surrounding us each day, these children often faded into the shadows, and I began to pass them by as though they were not there at all.

Initially, our residency in St. Giles was meant to be of a short duration, a roof over our heads whilst we sought new employment. Obtaining work, however, was easier said than done and all we could initially find was some piece work. Martha also continued working with the Chartists, her friends not forsaking her. More than ever, she realized the importance of their fight to get the vote and representation. If the worker's voice could be heard, the plight of the people we now called neighbours could change forever.

I discovered her one day standing in the communal yard, her feet sinking into the mud. She had gone to fetch some water from the tenement pump but stood there crying instead. Her general lethargy since arriving in St. Giles was becoming more pronounced. I feared for my sister. She could find no respite and very little to cheer her, doomed as we were to remain trapped in this living horror. Nothing pained me more than to see my sister suffer. It was country air and Granny's hearty home cooking she needed to restore her failing appetite. She was fading away to nothing.

'Why don't you go home to Granny?' I suggested. 'This is no place for you. Nothing is keeping you here.'

'I've told you that we cannot go home, Hannah. Whilst we are making a little money and can pay our way, we'll stay. I'll be alright. It's just so wretched. I could never have imagined people lived in such poverty and squalor. My heart aches for Aunt Elizabeth and the children.'

As children, Martha and I took so much for granted. Now we realized how lucky we had been. At *Sweep's Farm,* the roof never leaked.

We ate simple but nourishing fare. Fresh was the air we breathed; clean the water we drank. We ran free, paddled in the river, picked flowers, and cuddled our animals. I remembered how I used to complain when the water in our wash stands froze overnight. At least we had water, for this precious commodity was not so easily possessed in St. Giles. Our innocent, girlish dreams were now replaced by dreams about having enough money to buy the things we needed, not luxury items, but the bare necessities. Money to put food on the table and clothes on our backs. Though my family was always poor, we never knew what it was like to go without. Our parents sacrificed a lot so that we could be provided for. St. Giles taught me harsh lessons about the cold and hunger people suffered.

On Sundays, our cousins went mud larking on the banks of the Thames, a river that I once longed to see. Down by Waterloo Bridge, the muddy banks emitted a stench sufficient to induce nausea in the hardiest of souls. During low tide, the children searched for things they could sell. Whilst the girls contained their search to the river banks, the boys were game enough to search further afield. It was stomach-churning to think that one of their favourite items to collect was dog faeces, which they could sell quite profitably to the tanneries at Bermondsey. The girls took their discoveries to the Saturday market each week, erecting a small stall and touting for business from the passersby. The money made from selling these 'treasures' was supplemented by a trade in small bundles of watercress. Given straight to their mother, the few shillings they earned helped to pay the rent, a payment always due on Monday.

Rent day was dubbed by the inhabitants of our rookery, "Black Monday". Every rent day, Aunt Elizabeth struggled to find enough money to keep the rent man from evicting the family, as almost two-thirds of the family's earnings were needed for food. We bought bread by the slice and tea by the spoonful, and if we were lucky, a small slice of cheese. Sometimes it was necessary to save the little food left for Uncle Henry and the boys or to go without any food and heating to keep a roof over our heads. When she could, Aunt Elizabeth managed to secure some items on tick. Whilst the shopkeepers were usually obliging, they too needed to pay their rent, and were quick to call in debts owed. I remember the day when my cousins discovered a stray chook who laid her eggs in the courtyard. With delighted squeals they came racing inside, eggs and chook in hand.

It was also a day of good fortune when the people who rented the basement room absconded during the night. Being unable to pay their rent, they vanished silently leaving behind an entire order of unfinished matchboxes. A matchbox maker was expected to produce one thousand boxes a day, and those who did could earn enough for a loaf of bread. Though requiring far more skill than either of us could have imagined, Martha and I made the most of these people's misfortune and finished the order ourselves. The money we made was instantly donated to our aunt.

In time, I learned that if one visited Petticoat Lane, you could purchase a barrow of rags to take home and work into saleable items. When there was a lull in our piecework, these rags kept Martha and I busy, our efforts managing to further subsidize the family's scant earnings. Most days we worked around sixteen hours. Our fingers often fumbled with the needle, so numbed were they by the cold. The darkness also contributed to some inferior stitching, but our aunt's grateful smile when we gave her our tiny contribution made it all worthwhile.

Attempting to eke out a meagre existence alongside this human tragedy were the poor, half-starved mongrels of London. Living amongst everyone but belonging to no one, they searched the rubbish piles and scratched at the muddied cobbles seeking any small morsel that would sustain them in their moribund state. I pitied these animals as I thought of darling Chester and the different life he knew running freely in the fields of home. I realised that Manchester was a city not so vastly different from London, and I prayed that Chester had not been brought so low.

Despite her attempts to mask it, Martha's declining health was soon noticed by Aunt Elizabeth. The cough that had plagued her over the past couple of weeks was not abating; indeed, it was getting progressively worse. Our aunt suggested that we send news home. Without informing Martha of our intentions, the two of us visited a gentleman who wrote letters for people who could not. For a small fee, we were able to dictate a message for Frederick alerting him to my sister's declining health.

Martha's beloved paid us a visit sooner than anyone could have hoped or expected. Having journeyed all day, he arrived late one evening, my uncle opening the door to a very weary traveller. He came forward, taking Martha's trembling hand in his own, bestowing a tender kiss. Martha was pale and silent that evening, though it meant everything having Frederick by her side. Residing overnight at the Chapter Coffee House, Frederick visited again the following morning bringing a basket of the choicest fruit, a delicacy of which dreams were made: purple grapes, peaches, and oranges. Ensuring that Martha was wrapped up against the elements, he conveyed her in a hackney cab to Twining's Tea Rooms on the Strand, one of the few London tea houses that admitted women. Tea, it was touted, possessed special health-giving qualities, curing all things from headaches to asthma and stomach ailments. Twinings, with its narrow aisles stacked high with exotic tins from around the world, enchanted Martha, and the morning's expedition brought some brightness back into her world. She returned home having accepted Frederick's proposal of marriage, her news bringing a rare moment of joy for the rest of us.

Frederick left us two days later, returning home to make preparations for the upcoming nuptials. He did not depart without pleading with Martha to accompany him, but sadly she lacked the strength for the journey.

Whilst we kept vigil over Martha, the arrival of Lottie's bairn crept ever closer. Life was a struggle at the best of times for my poor cousin but carrying a growing child within her emaciated body was an eternal misery. She accepted her trials patiently and never complained, though, on many nights when her head finally reached the pillow, I would hear her crying softly and my heart ached for her. Lottie would head out on her daily errands, wrapped tightly in her shawl, her eyes cast downward. She walked with haste, eager to avoid the judgmental gazes cast upon her. I volunteered to accompany my cousin on her journeys, helping to shoulder her load and provide the moral support she so needed. I would see the glances, the faces that would turn away, and the women who muttered words of shame. It was a cruel old world and Lottie now walked along the streets of her childhood labelled a sinner, cast aside and despised for carrying a child forced upon her by one of pure evil. As we reached each house, Lottie would wait outside whilst I called upon the occupants, collecting or delivering Aunt Elizabeth's laundry.

Becoming a well-known face around St. Giles, I was now all too familiar with the streets and alleyways that Dada once rejoiced his own children need never see. Across the winter months, I plied the streets with my cousin, waging a daring fight against the freezing weather. Eventually, spring arrived, then summer and Lottie's bairn was now but a month away. She was walking slower but refused to give in to the hardships and discomfort, insisting that by walking she could relieve some of the pain she felt in her back and legs. Knowing her child was so close kept her going. New challenges awaited her, but at least there would be an end to the physical torture.

Mrs. Deane's lodgings were amongst those we visited weekly. Ordinarily, I dealt with the lady of the house, our business transacted in the same manner as any other. Approaching the lodgings one June morning, however, Lottie abruptly ceased her step.

'It's him!' she cried, seizing my arm. 'It's the foreman! Please, Hannah, we mustn't be seen.'

Lottie beat a hasty retreat, though I lingered, watching Mrs. Deane and her children farewelling the foreman as he departed for work. So, that was him, my cousin's seducer. He was a short, barrel of a man whose dishevelled beard and greasy hair made me sick to the core. I was repulsed by the tenderness with which he treated his family, having abandoned my poor, inoffensive cousin to her fate. An innocent fifteen-year-old, she committed no crime other than being destitute and alone. If only his wife knew of her husband's cowardly and brutal actions. I felt so desperately sorry for my dear aunt who, in her struggle to feed her own children, did this brute's washing and that of his family. Did my aunt have any notion that in doing washing for Mrs. Deane, she was washing the clothes of her daughter's defiler? Lottie and I vowed we would keep this terrible truth a secret for Aunt Elizabeth could nil afford to lose any of her clients, no matter how wicked or corrupt they were.

With all in readiness for their wedding, Frederick soon returned to London to convey his bride-to-be home. Martha's delicate health had deteriorated further during his short absence, however, and he was distressed by the change in his beloved. The symptoms she had taken such pains to conceal, were no longer able to be hidden. We all knew that those sparkling eyes, rosy cheeks, and ruby lips were the deceptive signs of the dreaded and brutal consumption. Wasting not a moment, Frederick decided to be married in London immediately, for Martha could not travel.

'I have waited long enough,' he declared. 'All I want is to call you my own.'

Martha's sad eyes looked at the ring upon her finger. Slowly she removed it and gave it to Frederick.

'I know that my time in this world is brief. I cannot be so selfish as to bind you to a promise made in better times.'

The sob that had been knotting my throat found expression and I raced from the room. It broke my heart to think that Martha was being forced to forgo something dreamed of for so long. My sister discovered me sobbing on the bed a few minutes later.

'It's alright, Hannah,' she assured me, sitting beside me, stroking my hair. 'It's all alright. Look, the ring has been restored to my finger.

Frederick wouldn't hear of calling it off. He really is good to me. I will be blessed being his wife even for the shortest of time.'

I tightly embraced my sister and we cried together. Two days later, Frederick carried her down the aisle of St. Clement Danes, the same church where our parents were wed, and made her his wife. She was weak and sat throughout the service, resting her head upon Frederick, but she was divinely happy. There was no talk of illness or sorrow that day, just celebrations for two hearts finally united.

Frederick was now eager to take his new wife to Margate, a seaside resort that advocated sea-bathing for medicinal purposes. He wanted Martha to attend the Royal Sea Bathing Hospital, a place whose cures for consumption were touted far and wide. Understanding just how critical time was, Frederick made haste to depart the day following the wedding. No sooner had Frederick departed, than Lottie, seized with terror, realized her bairn was on its way. Whilst Lottie lay suffering in the throes of childbirth, Martha lay next door wasting away, consumed by her own excruciating pain. It was late in the evening when Lottie's bairn entered the world, a son whom she named Ezra. There was little pleasure at his arrival, for he was just another mouth to feed and Lottie was distant and cold towards her child. How horribly cruel that this young girl had been so burdened, when Martha, newly married, would never be granted the child she yearned for all her life.

From the house of sorrow, I made my escape one bright, sunny morning. Its trials of late had become suffocating, and I sought momentary refuge in the nearby gardens. I was surrounded by the great buildings of Lincoln's Inn where all the powerful legal minds of London dwelt. I was dwarfed by their might and felt more insignificant, lost, and lonely than ever. In my sorrow, my eyes suddenly lighted upon three, dear little sparrows. They flew in and landed beside me, foraging in the sunshine for their lunch. They brought an involuntary smile to my lips, and as I watched them, happiness was momentarily restored. Their visit was but fleeting, but it touched my heart. Some passersby soon frightened my little friends away and I continued my time in the gardens alone.

When the afternoon breezes started to cool the air, I deemed it time to return home. I rose and began to amble towards the western gate. That afternoon was the closest I had felt for a long time to the carefree days of my youth when I roamed the fields and sat beside my beloved Mimram. As I mused on good times past, the allure of the gardens and the setting sun was suddenly and most shockingly shattered. As I stepped to the roadside, my eyes fell upon three small bodies. There they lay, together, the sweet sparrows who moments before brought such brightness and warmth into my dismal world. They had been crushed by the wheels of a passing cart into whose path they had flown. There was finally no doubt in my mind that this city, with all its filth, darkness, and grief, would eventually extinguish all life, even that of the most inoffensive and gentle of God's creatures. It crushed the lives of the beautiful sparrows just as it was crushing the lives of my adored sister and pitiful young cousin.

To obtain the vital medicines for Martha to have a fighting chance of recovery was virtually impossible. Frederick did his best to provide for us and Granny Ravens sent what little she could spare, but medicines were expensive and needed replenishing. It had been nearly two weeks since Frederick left and I was becoming impatient for his return. Sending a message stressing the urgency of our predicament, I waited, and whilst I did so, I decided upon a plan. To seek the foreman, inform him of his child's arrival, and beg for his compassion was my main objective. I followed him therefore one evening as he left the factory. The heels of his boots clicked loudly on the cobbled streets as he walked briskly towards a local gin shop, one of the few places in this dismal city that continued to prosper. Gazing from the doorway, I saw him being greeted by a woman wearing long, scarlet boots, someone with whom he seemed much enamoured. Those within the darkened den were evidently well-plied with alcohol, their drunken voices being raised in song. It was no place to air my grievances and

I returned home to await our next encounter. It came but a few days later when I cornered him on his way to work.

'Lottie Fearn has given birth to your son. She and the bairn are poorly and would benefit from some stimulants. Will you give me some money to buy the medicines needed?'

'This is not my concern,' the foreman declared cruelly, pushing me aside.

'It's your child,' I cried, hastening after him.

The foreman paused. A brutal, self-satisfied smile crept to his lips.

'You can't prove that.'

I threatened to inform his wife, though he failed to be alarmed by my threats.

'Go ahead,' he dared me. 'You're not the first little tramp who has come begging at my door with a tale of woe. My wife has heard it all before. If she complains, she'll join the rest of you on the streets.'

Flabbergasted by his cold brutality, I was left speechless, allowing him to stride away without further haranguing. The following day my aunt had his wife's laundry ready and I was sent to deliver it. One of his children answered the door, well-dressed and gnawing on a chicken drumstick. I entered the well-lit, warm, and comfortable abode and was struck by the injustice of it all. Having slammed a few inadequate pennies into my hand, Mrs. Deane took the clothes and carried them from the room. It was then I noticed the foreman's gold watch. I had seen it previously hanging from a hook beside the mantle. It was an ornate and clearly expensive item. On the day in question, it sat within easy reach, casually discarded upon the kitchen table. With this watch, I could help Lottie and the bairn and secure the medical aid Martha desperately needed. And so, I stole it. Snatching the watch from the table, I hitched up my skirt and ran, just ran. With my hair streaming out behind me, I splashed through muddy puddles and skidded through the slimy streets. At one stage, my shawl was torn from my shoulders. I paused momentarily to swoop it from the ground.

Not daring to return home, I hurried to the Church Lane pawn-broker where I once pawned some items for Aunt Elizabeth. My heart beat wildly and I breathed deeply. Standing in the shadows opposite the pawnbroker, it took four long hours to gather enough courage to enter. It was five o'clock in the evening when I finally exchanged the watch for eight shillings. At my trial, they maintained that Mrs. Deane paid a pound for the watch. I suppose that was correct. It was certainly of greater value than the meagre sum I obtained for it. My hours of deliberation unfortunately gave Mrs. Deane time to report the theft and with the police on the lookout, I was arrested as I stepped from the pawnbroker.

Loaded into a van alongside several others, the doors closed and we were plunged into a fearful darkness. I was in utter turmoil; dizziness overcame me and I slumped down upon the carriage floor. Reaching our destination, I needed to be carried from the carriage and revived before being roughly herded through the maze of tunnels that made up the dark abyss below Clerkenwell. The way was lit by a faint, flickering lamp upon the wall and as a drop of water trickled down my forehead, I noticed the dampness of the walls and floor that imprisoned me. I instinctively drew back from the musty smell of death and disease. The sobbing of inmates and their not-so-subtle screams will haunt me forever.

There were no separate cells here and I found myself confined with two other women and nine men. The stench was enough to render me unconscious again. I knew nothing of their crimes, though I little doubted there was more than one hardened criminal amongst them. Several lingered under the effects of too much alcohol, their bodily emissions as it wore off being truly vile. In this odious cell, I remained until my trial, terrified like never before. I knew not what fate awaited me, though they hung people for less. I was therefore fortunate that when they dragged me from Clerkenwell to stand before a judge at the Old Bailey, my fate was transportation. My life, no matter how dismal it may seem, would at least be spared. I knew that my beloved parents would be watching over me from Heaven, and memories of their love would give me the strength to endure.

4

THE GARLAND GROVE

"Took our departure from the land of Old England ... not one in fifty, would ever behold again the land of birth."
Abraham Harvey, 2nd Officer

My three months of hell incarcerated in Newgate Prison finally came to an end on the 8th of September, 1842. I was woken early that morning and taken to the matron's office to have my name finally, and most blessedly, crossed off the prison's register. Several others were waiting and I wondered whether these desperate creatures were to be my shipmates over the coming months. I kept my eyes cast firmly at the floor. My elbow was suddenly seized and a guard began to manacle my hands and feet. I prayed that I would not be restricted so for the entire journey to Van Diemen's Land. We were led as a group down the steps of the gaol and into the streets of London for the last time.

I looked about me in haste and desperation, soaking in every last bit of the city. It was not long before the waiting carriage was loaded and, giving the customary jolt, was set in motion. I was well aware of the choking heat and toxic smell of these vehicles, and I waged a brave battle against the terrible nausea that took hold of me. Anxiety was my constant friend, hampering my every breath and making my heart pound wildly in my chest. Other girls fainted as we journeyed on. There was no consoling, everyone abandoned to their misery. Consumed by the darkness, we finally heard the cries of the gulls which signalled that our journey was finally nearing its end.

As we drew to a halt, noises from the bustling port of Woolwich reached our ears, as did the far more daunting sound of hecklers yelling abuse at our carriage whilst casting rocks at its side. The prison guards soon dispersed the crowd and with the door thrown open, we were ordered out. The manacles on my ankles made it difficult to walk, and I tripped more than once as I shuffled toward the wooden boat awaiting our arrival. Standing just off shore was a ship, which was surely the *Garland Grove*. Some of its crew were attracted by our arrival and they gathered upon the deck to watch us.

I was amongst the first group of women loaded into the small boat, and setting out upon water for the first time in my life, was rowed across to my home and prison for the next four months. Doctor Bland and Officer Harvey were there to meet us. These two men would be in charge of our health and welfare throughout the voyage. Officer Harvey smiled as he issued me with a sponge and piece of soap, before indicating where I could go to wash away the prison grime. It felt so good to have months of Newgate filth finally washed from my skin. I was then issued with bedding and some new clothes.

Throughout September, more women were brought onboard from prisons around the country. Whilst we awaited our departure, we were visited by some local ladies including the mayor's wife. They brought small packages for each of us containing things to keep us entertained during the long voyage: fabric, several reels of cotton, coloured threads, a thimble, needles, pins, and scissors as well as some patchwork pieces. I was pleased to have such familiar and cherished items to help while away the hours.

Granny Ravens came down to Woolwich to see me, bringing my recently arrived sisters, Harriet and Louisa, with her. My sisters sat pale and drawn, startled by every sudden noise. It devastated me to think of the distress that I had brought upon my poor family. I asked about Martha. Granny was uneasy and she hesitated before telling me that Martha's condition had deteriorated further over the past few weeks. I was assured that Martha was now being treated at the Margate hospital with Fredrick by her side. That my family chose not to tell her about my predicament greatly pleased me. It would only have brought her distress. She was told the same tale as my cousins, that I had left suddenly to secure work.

Sadly, my family's visit couldn't last forever and, when it came time for them to depart, my sisters jumped quickly to their feet. Who could blame them for wanting to leave that gruesome ship? I was as eager as they were. I took them in my arms, told them that I loved them, and made them promise to look after Granny. They sobbed and repented having to leave me. We all knew we would never see each other again. I bid them be happy and to remember me with fondness, but only in times of idleness. I was not worth their tears. Both assured me I would never be forgotten, they would think of me and pray for me every day. They were left in no doubt that I would be doing the same, though it be on the other side of the world. Then it came time to part from my beloved Granny Ravens. Taking me tightly in her arms, she whispered.

'You're a good girl, Hannah. I know why you acted as you did. Martha is suffering. You were desperate to help her. Van Diemen's Land is a young colony and must surely offer many opportunities to those willing to take their chances. Promise me you'll make the most of everything that comes your way. You can make something of yourself over there, something you would never be able to do here.'

I clung to Granny Ravens, unwilling to let her slip from my grasp. It was the last time that I would see her, and I was physically sick at the thought. How could I ever live through a parting from this dearest of souls? Noting the advancing age of my visitor, Officer Harvey stepped forward and offered his arm to assist her departure from the ship. As he did so, my fingers tightened upon Granny's coat, and I became determined never to release her. Attempting to persuade me to grant my grandmother her freedom, the officer began prising my fingers from her coat. When my last finger was released, he must have thought victory was his, but how wrong he was, for the battle started anew as I dropped to my knees and seized hold of Granny's skirt. Her soulful eyes looked down upon me.

'Hannah, my darling one, please be the sensible and brave girl I know you to be. The time has come for us to part. Show me that you accept this by letting me go, and grieving no further. It will break my heart if I am forced to part from you whilst tears are still in your eyes.'

For my grandmother's sake, I slowly released my grasp and fought to contain my sorrow. Reaching down, she gently stroked my cheek with her tender hand and stooped to kiss my forehead.

'Goodbye, my angel. May God go with you.'

I watched on helplessly as Officer Harvey aided my grandmother and sisters from the ship, my grandmother reaching her hands out to me as she was led away. All too soon my family boarded the small boat and were rowed out of my life. As soon as they were out of sight, I curled up upon the deck and sobbed until there were no more tears. My sorrow was deepened still further the evening before we were due to set sail when word was brought to me that my poor sister Martha was taken from us at eight o'clock that morning. Officer Harvey brought me the message himself and was kind enough to stay and comfort me.

'Was this the sister for whom you were trying to gain help?'

He read the surprise on my face.

'Your grandmother told me as I escorted her from the ship. She asked me to look after you and I promised to do my best.'

Try as he may, this man brought me little solace, for it was the gentle touch and kind words of Granny Ravens that I desperately needed at that moment. Aunt Elizabeth visited the quayside in an effort to convey the sad news to me personally, but being so close to our departure, she had been barred from seeing me. How it would have softened the blow had I heard the tidings from this loved relative. It broke my heart when I was informed of her kind gesture, for I thought of her tenderness and the way the authorities would have treated her.

That evening, I was numbed to the preparations being made for our departure. As I lay in my bunk staring at the darkened boards above me, others spent their time sewing, winding balls of thread, reading prayers or their last letter from home, rocking infants or simply sitting in morbid silence. As our ship pulled away from Woolwich the following morning, I was overcome by my emotions and a sickening sort of pain. There are no words to describe my utter agony. It was Sunday 2nd of October 1842 and I was sailing from England's shores forever.

I do not know whether Granny Ravens and my sisters came to watch my departure. At times, I liked to think that they did come, waving a tearful but fond farewell. At other times, I knew they did not come. Their hearts would have been too full of emotion and pain to make the journey. Dear Granny had now lost her two eldest grandchildren within a day of each other. As we made our way slowly down the Thames, I chose to lie on my bunk, silent tears streaming down my cheeks as I tried to forget the reality of what was happening to me. I thought back to when Michael and I used to dream about escaping Hertfordshire to explore the world. Neither of us could have imagined what escaping would actually mean. Transportation across the seas was the dreadful fate that had befallen both of us, and I regretted now the time wasted planning a life away from St. Paul's Walden. At that moment, I would have done anything to return and remain there for the rest of my life.

Exhausted from the day's trauma, I slept surprisingly soundly that night. I was compelled to be joyous for my darling Martha's suffering was at an end and she'd been taken home to Heaven. If I made proper atonement for my sins, I hoped that one day we would be lovingly reunited there. As to my predicament, I could blame no one but myself, and perhaps those in positions of power who did nothing to alleviate the suffering of the masses. At least the waiting was over. Newgate and the living horrors behind its walls were behind me, I breathed fresh air again, and I held Granny's words in my heart, promising myself to make the most of every opportunity my new life would bring. I was leaving so much behind, but I was certain wonderful things awaited me.

Mine were not the only tears upon departure. Many of the women were similarly distraught at leaving home and family. Others, however, showed great pleasure at our departure. They had made merry since first boarding the ship, singing and dancing, intent upon causing a disturbance. Squabbles abounded during the first few days, and several fights erupted. I decided that to survive this brutal system one needed to be tough. Any sign of weakness showed that the system was beating you down. I made up my mind on the spot. The tears I shed upon departure would be the last to stray from my eyes, or at least the last anyone would witness.

Wicked people and their wicked ways surrounded me. I was apprehensive and afraid of everything. Many of my fellow shipmates were hardened criminals. Indeed, a girl who shared my quarters poisoned an old lady. At twenty-one, she was only two years my senior, and I couldn't fathom how anyone so young could be that evil. Others made no secret of their trade as prostitutes. They spoke fondly of their past lives and encouraged others in their crime. Many of the women were foul-mouthed and used trickery to their advantage, were flirtatious and intimate with the sailors, and used the religious tracts we were given to curl their hair. Regardless of our different backgrounds, however, we were soon united as we left the safety of the Thames and fell prey to the ravages of the rolling ocean.

Whilst I cannot say I experienced the same amount of terror as some of my shipmates, I did greet the continual pounding of those massive waves with a great deal of trepidation. My fellow reprobates were stricken with sea sickness and it was impossible to clean the ship properly for the entire first week. Although I was truly thankful that I was not similarly debilitated, the ship's ceaseless creaking and moaning did slowly take command of my mind and at times I felt I would go mad. When allowed on deck, I used to gaze into the distance, across miles and miles of nothing. The tedium of the journey was broken by the graceful presence of the seabirds that I loved to watch soaring high above, then plunging into the unknown depths beneath us. I envied their freedom and longed to fly alongside them, liberated and carefree. I also saw a great many porpoises and flying fish, animals, which until that time, were unknown to me.

The first few days brought very fine sailing weather and we arrived off Madeira in a week. From here I watched as we sailed past the Canaries, St. Vincent, and Cape Verde and as we travelled onward, the weather grew ever warmer. Officer Harvey was kind enough to point out to me several things of note including the spectacular rocky islands around Martim Vez, some albatross and very pretty cape pigeons. As we neared our destination, he showed me the group of five stars known as the Southern Cross.

Two ladies of refinement accompanied us on our long voyage. The addition of these women was brought about through recent campaigning from a lady named Mrs. Fry who was fighting for better rights and improved welfare for transportees. Falling ill almost immediately, Miss McLarene was not seen on deck for the first few weeks, and the majority of our care was left to Miss Grindrod. Routine was therefore not established until well over two weeks into our voyage. From this time onwards, we would gather each morning at nine o'clock to hear Miss McLarene read from the Scriptures, before being divided according to our ability to receive instruction in reading and writing. Teaching us these skills would hopefully improve our prospects in Van Diemen's Land and gain us meaningful employment when our sentences were complete.

In all that we did we were watched over by Doctor Bland and Officer Harvey. They ensured we were well treated and nourished and gave us additional rations of food and wine for completing extra work. It was not long before I was enlisted as part of the tutelage program, being asked to share my needleworking skills. Using the material squares from the packages issued before departure, I worked with the other women in the creation of several quilts. The ones displaying the best artistry would be sold upon arrival in Van Diemen's Land. I hoped that my limited instruction would enable many of the women to generate some income and gain them a little independence.

We were just off Cape Verde when the first death occurred. They held a service on deck for the unfortunate woman at six o'clock that evening. Captain Forward read the burial service before her body slid into the sea. I shuddered as it hit the water and thought how terrible it would be to suffer the same fate. As to the doctor who had ministered to the poor woman, I would have my first real encounter with him after I became a victim of the rolling ocean and fell on deck. Seeking treatment for my wounded knees, I discovered Doctor Bland busy with several other patients and assured him I could minister to my own wounds. Looking about me, I noticed a woman lying close by in the grips of fever. Going to a barrel of water, I took the ladle hooked over the edge and poured out two cups. Helping the poor woman to drink from the first, I used the second to wipe her brow. Her name was Mary and she hailed from Birmingham where she had worked as a servant. She was joining us on this voyage having received a fifteen-year sentence for violent assault and robbery. As I sat beside her, I noticed the initials GBJJ tattooed onto her right arm, and I amused myself guessing what they meant.

I stayed beside Mary until Doctor Bland, realizing my willingness to help, asked me to minister to another. Working alongside me was an eight-year-old named Louisa who was swift on her feet and ministered tenderly as did a young boy called William who impressed Doctor Bland with his kindness. Both were children of mothers who were being transported and I wondered what their futures held. The doctor himself seemed to have little sympathy for many of the girls under his care and punished even the dying by shaving their heads. Once I heard him refer to a girl as filthy and indolent. In my opinion, he used the excuse of being at sea far too readily when explaining the loss of five nursing bairns following the deaths of their mothers. The names of these children would not be registered in the official records, though the eight other souls who met their maker during the voyage were noted.

As we ventured further into the tropics, I became greatly afflicted by their suffocating heat. It seemed strange to be surrounded by water and yet it brought no relief. I could not drink it or bathe my burning feet. Further angst was caused when the seas became wilder and we were lashed by strong winds for five days in a row. Our ship rolled terribly in the mountainous seas. At one point our sails were so full I feared they would rip and leave us abandoned. I could hear the poor terrified animals squealing on deck. The women squealed too. The adverse weather conditions soon showed their effects in the hospital, with several women becoming afflicted with eye infections. Doctor Bland treated five cases in total with a combination of eye bathing, bloodletting, cooling lotions, and in the most severe case, head shaving. Further storms near the Cape of Good Hope in the lead up to Christmas, flooded the main deck to such an extent that we were all forced to huddle together on the poop deck.

When Christmas Day finally dawned, it brought with it tears, for I had never felt lonelier. Despite our poverty, this day had always been filled with special surprises, and we celebrated together as a family in joyous love. I was now travelling thousands of miles from that warmth and protection, never to know the like again. Things on board remained as usual, though we were granted a dinner as good as it could be in the circumstances. With the celebration of New Year, we knew that our destination was near and apprehension held sway amongst the women. We did not know what to expect upon arrival, nor what sort of treatment we would receive. Rumours were rife as to what would happen to us all. We were told it was a land of promise, but the unknown forbade many of us believing it. Some of the women's spirits became so low that it affected their health. For me, the voyage was a punishment in itself, but I had learnt to feel relatively safe and secure. Now the fear and uncertainty would start all over again.

On the 12ᵗʰ of January, I caught the first glimpse of my new home. The winds became lighter and the weather modified. Over the coming days, stretches of sand and distant breakers became visible, the rugged coastline of this land was the most breathtaking sight. At times, the towering, weather-beaten cliffs looming over us reminded me of organ pipes, battered as they were by the might of the Southern Ocean. This was a mountainous country, its soaring peaks, stark against the blue sky, extended as far as the eye could see. With our ship suddenly becalmed, the crew was forced to lower some boats to tow us into the Derwent River. At half past five on the afternoon of the 20ᵗʰ of January, 1843, the ship, again under sail, was boarded by the pilot from Hobart Town. We cheered loudly. There was great excitement and relief that the end of our journey was so close.

Making our way up the river, we encountered a magnificent mountain that instantly won a place in my heart. Its lofty heights dwarfed the small settlement of Hobart Town in its shadow. The sight of this land made me forget all that I had endured during the past few months. Be it but for a short time, I could forget my banishment, the filth and wretchedness of my voyage, and the uncertainty of my future, such was the beauty to be absorbed. My lungs were filled with the sweetest of breezes, and we sailed upon crystal waters, so clear and clean. I was thousands of miles from my homeland, but I was also worlds away from the filthy streets of St. Giles. The disease, starvation, and despair was left far in my wake.

It was indeed a blessing that we reached our destination safely, and I longed to set foot on solid ground again. It was a few more days, however, before we were able to leave the ship. During this time, the authorities boarded and made detailed notes about each of us. Colour of hair and eyes, complexion, height, and any distinguishing marks. During these procedures, people came down to the ship and, in desperate voices, called out for news from home. 'Is anyone from Cornwall? Yorkshire? Somerset?'

5

KNYPERSLEY FARM

"We walked to the gate of *Knypersley* ... and so began life."
The Biddulph Tithe Survey 1840.

Despite the early hour, the summer sun already blazed upon us as we left the safety of the *Garland Grove* and marched en masse to the Cascades House of Corrections. Our legs were wobbly and we tottered, unbalanced on our sea legs. Walking slowly, our shuffling feet raised clouds of dust that stung our eyes and stifled our breathing. After only ten minutes, we were afflicted by a terrible fatigue and desperate thirst which worsened as our journey dragged on. My feet burned, trapped and aching, as they were encased in my wretched, prison-issued, excuses-for-shoes. We passed a few neat cottages along the way, many with nicely established gardens. The heavenly scent from a row of exquisite pink roses, giving me a moment's respite. Torturous though it be, trudging uphill for an hour, I was delighted that with each step I was brought ever closer to the spectacular mountain standing guardian over this settlement. Its majestic bearing enchanted me.

Once reached, the tall sandstone walls of Cascades stood by way of stark contrast, and waiting beside them for admission, I shivered, despite the January heat, at the thought of what lay within. Back in

England we were told that any child who accompanied its mother on the journey could remain with them during their time of assignment and many women anticipated happy futures with them. The authorities in Australia, however, possessed vastly different ideas. Once at Cascades, the children were immediately separated from their mothers. The younger ones would be sent to an orphan school, whilst the ones around twelve or thirteen years of age were to be apprentices for local tradesmen or trained as servants. The promise was made to the devastated mothers that their children would be returned to them once they gained their freedom and could support the child. It was a pitiful parting as mothers and children were prized apart amidst tearful screaming.

I was relieved to turn my back on the heart-wrenching scene and follow the matron to a small room in the administration building where we were divided into three classes. I was deemed eligible for assignment to the first class. The convicts in this class had exhibited good behaviour on their journey out from England. Character references were required from each ship's surgeon, and my aiding Doctor Bland was well received. My conduct during our voyage saw me recommended for immediate transfer to Doctor Bland's friend and fellow doctor, Josiah Markham. As this gentleman was led in to meet me, the matron barked,

'Stand up, girl!'

I hurried to my feet but kept my eyes cast downward at the floor. Before leaving us, she cautioned my new master.

'Be careful of this one,' she said, having clearly noted my reticence upon arrival. 'She's a surly thing.'

Her words went unanswered, my companion waiting until she departed before speaking.

'Surly, are you?' he asked in gentle, softly spoken tones that became so comforting and familiar.

I remained frozen where I stood.

'It's alright,' he counselled. 'She's gone. You can look up now.'

His tender voice commanded me and I raised my eyes to meet his own sympathetic ones. A reassuring smile briefly crossed his lips. Before me stood the most handsome man I had ever laid eyes on. I knew not that they made such men. Robed in black, he was tall with broad, strong shoulders. He wore the cravat of a gentleman, the high collar of his shirt gently caressing his finely-chiselled jaw. His nose was long and slender and his lips thin, though not so thin as to make him appear mean or cruel. His crystal blue eyes looked out enticingly from below long, dark lashes, and they spoke of kindness, sincerity, and compassion. I knew I was in the presence of someone extraordinary. A stray curl of hair escaped his perfectly groomed black locks and settled in the middle of his forehead. Many times, over the coming months, I would see him brush that curl aside, only for it to fall rebelliously again.

'Doctor Bland was impressed by you during the journey, indeed, he said that you proved invaluable to him on several occasions. Upon his recommendation, I have requested you be assigned to my care. My wife and I are expecting our fourth child in a few months' time and we require assistance within the household. Your chores will be to aid the housekeeper and look after our children.'

His words brought tears to my eyes which flowed freely down my cheeks. Doctor Markham was instantly moved to place a comforting arm around my shoulders.

'Come now,' he said soothingly. 'Surely my offer is not that unwelcome?'

Shaking my head, I wiped away the tears with the sleeve of my dress.

'It's very welcome, sir,' I assured him.

Offering me his handkerchief, he smiled again. As I dried my untapped tears, I savoured the soft, lustrous beauty of the fine linen. It seemed like a lifetime since I last handled such quality fabric.

'Let's get you out of here,' he said, as he walked towards the door, encouraging me to follow. I held out his handkerchief for reclaiming.

'Keep it,' he said. 'Hopefully, in my care, you will have no further use for it.'

Doctor Markham's tilbury and sturdy black stallion awaited us outside. I couldn't resist reaching out to stroke the magnificent beast's velvet coat.

'Do you like horses?'

I nodded, a smile coming to my lips as I remembered the sense of freedom that riding always gave me. Doctor Markham held out his hand to aide me into the carriage. As I accepted it, our eyes met and my heart gave an involuntary flutter. A warmth rose within me. He held my future in those strong hands and I had little doubt it would be bright. I would serve this man with unwavering, grateful devotion and would never do anything to jeopardize the salvation he was offering. As we slowly climbed out of the valley, I gathered enough courage to ask the name of the mountain that lay a little further along the road.

'Wellington,' the doctor declared. 'Until about twenty years ago, it was known as Table Mountain, but they changed its name following the victory at Waterloo.'

My mother often spoke about Waterloo. Her father once had business interests in Brussels and the family lived there for a short time following the declaration of peace in 1814. Her parents attended the famous Duchess of Richmond's Ball, and the family's terrifying flight from Brussels the following day remained firmly etched in her memory. I smiled. Mam and this mountain were now inextricably linked and I would think of her each time I gazed upon it.

Doctor Markham and his wife Sophia lived in New Town around three miles north of Hobart Town, or Hobarton, as the Markhams called it. It was an area of great natural beauty and fertile soils where many free settlers chose to set up home, distancing themselves from the convict settlements further south. Wealthier merchants, government officials, and professional men all lived here. The Markhams received a grant one hundred acres of land on a gentle green slope overlooking the Derwent River. The property was named *Knypersley*

Farm after the area in Staffordshire where Mrs. Markham grew up. Her father, Sir William Gresley, was one of the last generation born at *Knypersley Hall*, the Staffordshire seat of the Gresley family.

'Do you like what you see?' my new master enquired.

'It's beautiful,' I acknowledged, gazing across the river to the ragged mountains beyond.

Doctor Markham ushered me towards the front door. As we entered, a young lady appeared from a room off the hallway. The quintessential English rose with whiter than white skin, tiny ruby lips, and soft blue eyes, her blonde hair was perfectly groomed and trimmed with tiny garden flowers. Though veiling her condition with a generous shawl, she was clearly expecting to be confined within the next few months.

'What have you brought home this time?' she asked without animation.

'She's the young girl who was so helpful to William Bland. We thought that you might like to have her here to help with the children and to aide Mrs. Kennedy.'

The lady before us, who was obviously the doctor's wife, pursed her lips in a show of disinterest and retreated into the room from whence she came. Doctor Markham seemed not to notice his wife's slight. Hastening his step, he conveyed me to the kitchen where I was passed into the care of the housekeeper, Mrs. Kennedy.

'Take everything off and get in,' Mrs. Kennedy commanded as she poured the last pail of warm water into the awaiting tub.

When I hesitated, she frowned.

'Hurry up. I haven't got time to worry about your modesty.'

Mrs. Kennedy took to me with soap and warm water, my arms, back, legs, and hair never so well-scrubbed. As the filth washed from my body, I felt cleansed and knew that my time of healing had begun. My bath was concluded as a large pail of lukewarm water was tipped over my head and I was directed to step from the tub. The clothes I arrived in were gathered up by Mrs. Kennedy, taken away, and would be burnt. They were replaced by a pale blue dress, white apron and cap. Seated at the kitchen table a meal was placed before me the likes of which I had not seen for many years. With its large pieces of meat and variety of vegetables, it quickly proved too much for me. It would be a while before I could eat a proper meal again. It sustained me, however, and for the first time in a long time, I felt full and contented.

Once I was bathed and fed, Mrs. Kennedy led me back to the room where Mrs. Markham waited. Knocking, she pushed me inside. I was left alone with my new mistress. The awkward silence with which I was greeted was eventually broken when Mrs. Markham finally condescended to lay aside her needlework and look up.

'So, my husband has seen fit to bring another transported soul into my home,' she sighed.

Despite her obvious misgivings, she asked me all the expected questions and informed me of my duties. As we conversed, she bent down and scooped up a grey, fluffy cat that was rubbing against her skirt. Taking it upon her knee, she stroked it affectionately whilst it sat, ears pulled back, hissing and growling, its nasty little teeth bared in my direction. It was a horrid creature who angrily greeted Doctor Markham's arrival with a shrill screech, its five razor-sharp claws viciously lashing out at him. Again, he seemed oblivious.

'And how do you find your new helper, my love?' he asked with that warm smile of his.

'She'll do,' Mrs. Markham acknowledged curtly. 'At least she's English.'

People spoke of this country as being one where freedom and equality reigned, but I would quickly learn that the same old prejudices had been transported with the people. Many in this country continued the same aversion to the Irish I witnessed in London. Mrs. Markham was one for whom there was nothing more abhorrent than the Irish. Within the Markham household, it was Mrs. Kennedy who bore the brunt of our mistress's prejudice, for not only was she a convict, but Irish too. As I left the sitting room, Doctor Markham followed me into the hallway.

'You mustn't mind my wife's manner. You will find her a good mistress, but you must promise me that if you are ever in need of anything, you will come to me at once. I'll ensure you are well provided for.'

Thanking him with a curtsy, I quickly withdrew, returning to Mrs. Kennedy and the long list of chores awaiting me in the kitchen. My new bed was a welcome friend that evening. As my head hit the pillow, I fell asleep almost instantly. I knew that my parents had guided me to *Knypersley*, and in the worst of all possible situations, I was granted one blessing in being assigned to the Markham family. Doctor Markham was undoubtedly kind and cared for all his servants equally. We ate well, were dressed warmly, and slept in comfortable beds. Greatly admired by Mrs. Kennedy, she showed him the kind of gratitude and devotion that is rarely seen from an Irish woman towards an Englishman. She also assured me that, despite her haughty manner, Mrs. Markham was fair in all her dealings. I knew that if I must be in service, I could not be better placed than here at *Knypersley Farm*.

The next morning, I stood in the courtyard just beyond the kitchen, marvelling at the spectacular beauty of my surrounds.

'You should take a walk and explore your new home.'

The voice was one I had already learnt to trust, and it sent a tingle of joyous anticipation down my spine. I turned to be met by Doctor Markham's gentle smile.

'It's such a long trip and those hideous ships are so cramped,' he continued. 'I walked for days and days when I arrived. Go on, I'll clear it with Mrs. Kennedy.'

What an astonishing man! We were so newly acquainted and yet he would trust me to wander at will with no guarantee I would return. Rumour on my ship was that one could abscond in this colony never to be found. The valleys and caves near Mt. Wellington were full of escaped convicts. With no desire to escape from Doctor Markham's care, I headed to the river that flowed peacefully past the property. Standing on its banks, I gazed far into the distance and thought of another river thousands of miles away. The course of water between here and there was unbroken, one ocean merging into another, no barrier holding back their ebb and flow. The water that brought me here could take me home again, yet I was under no illusion that I would ever return. Whilst St. Paul's Walden and the beloved ones who dwelt there would never be forgotten, I firmly believed that I would quickly grow to love my new island home and the people within it.

Returning from my walk, I felt refreshed and was ready to meet the children who were to be entrusted into my care. These sweet little ones were around the same age as my youngest siblings and offered great comfort in my time of need. The four-year-old Georgina and three-year-old Lavinia were built in the image of their mother: pretty, blonde, and blue-eyed. At their tender ages, the prejudices of the world were yet to destroy their innocence, and they possessed a far greater inclination towards affection than I ever saw exhibited by their mother. They adored their father, thankfully something that came naturally to them, for they were never encouraged in this by Mrs. Markham. Doctor Markham was far more demonstrative than his wife and he worshipped his children, indulging them perhaps more than was good for them. Whilst he tried not to show favouritism, I could not help but notice the partiality he had for the dark-haired beauty of the family, little one-year-old Ava. He once told me that this daughter resembled his baby sister, Avyce.

'She was the light of my life. So sweet and tender. We lost her young, for she was born with a weak heart. Being doctors themselves, it almost destroyed my father and grandfather, for they could not save her, no matter how hard they tried.'

Ava's winning ways quickly captured my own heart and she would also secretly become my favourite. She was the one who most resembled her father in looks and temperament. As I carried her around, she would clasp her arms so tightly around my neck. When I laid her in her cradle each night, she would hum along as I sang to her. Kisses were always freely bestowed and she would snuggle into me with so much warmth.

The children were quick to welcome me as their carer, for children don't distinguish between rich and poor, free and servant. They bestow their love equally amongst all who are kind to them. The Markham daughters, however, were set to be raised in the same vein as their mother. They would grow to be elegant, accomplished young women, eventually becoming the wives of gentlemen from excellent families with fine fortunes.

I quickly learnt my daily routine and expected duties. As the young newcomer, Mrs. Kennedy was eager to hand over all menial tasks to me. Rising before anyone else stirred, my first chore was to light the fires needed for cooking and household warmth. Once I made the tea, I would take Doctor Markham and his wife their trays, open their curtains, and enquire whether they were breakfasting in bed or the morning room. Mrs. Markham was generally full of woe upon waking, and I knew she would be remaining in bed until noon. Once she had breakfasted, I would return to see her settled into her morning's entertainment be it embroidery, reading, or letter writing. I was never directed to bring forth her children. She was certainly not a natural mother and thought herself a martyr, producing children for her husband, as any good wife should. As her bairn's arrival crept ever closer, she showed no enthusiasm for the impending arrival, merely bemoaning the disruption to her social calendar.

Compared to his wife, Doctor Markham was always full of good cheer and warmly welcomed each new day. He never failed to enquire how I had slept and made me promise to take the daily walk that was so precious to me. He cared greatly for all those who worked for him and showed it by the little things he did like stopping for a short talk or helping to lift a heavy pail. It made our days brighter. Never dwelling long in bed, he was always dressed and in the morning room by the time breakfast was ready to be served. With breakfast over, I would report to Mrs. Kennedy to receive the list of tasks she saw fit to add on top of my work caring for the children. Once a week, I would also join her on my hands and knees, scrubbing away at the floor until my hands stung. With an aching back, I would rise, to be directed by my superior to join her outside. There we would beat the dust and dirt from the household rugs. I did rather enjoy the latter task, for I gained a certain amount of satisfaction striking those rugs as hard as I could.

My short period of rest usually came midafternoon. Doctor Markham considered it imperative that all his workers were given an hour to themselves, a time when they could walk, sleep, or simply sit and talk. By the time I served supper at nine o'clock, my chores were almost complete. Whilst the Markhams were at supper, I would place a warming pan in Mrs. Markham's bed and prepare her attire for the following morning. I was never pampered enough to enjoy the comforts of a warmed bed, and I thought how wonderful it must be to snuggle under the blankets and be lulled to sleep by such coziness. Doctor Markham never required a warmed bed as he adhered to certain medical thinking of the time that warmed beds drained the body of energy and that the noxious fumes emitted from the coals were perilous to the health. Once I saw Mrs. Markham comfortably into bed for the night, I would retire to my room seeking much-needed rest. My days were hard, though I never felt exhausted, for every task was done with a grateful heart.

The quality of Doctor Markham's medical skills and his empathic care ensured that he was always in high demand throughout Hobarton and areas well beyond. Called out at all hours of the day and night, and in some truly atrocious weather conditions, he always hastened to the suffering without any consideration for his own health, safety or wellbeing. When night calls came, it was my duty to see him safely on his journey and to be there again to greet him with a warming fire, food, and beverage upon his return. Had it been for any lesser person, I would have resented the disruption to my night's slumber, but for

Doctor Markham, I would do anything without fear, regret, or complaint. In truth, I quickly learnt that slumber was impossible for me on the nights that he was away from home, and I would fret for his welfare until his safe return. The few stolen moments the two of us would share whilst he ate his dinner were always highly anticipated. This singular gentleman had proven himself to be the greatest of all men and I was unfailingly dedicated to him.

On many a Saturday night, there would be a dance and supper held in the barn. I would join the other household staff and farm labourers, and dance merrily to the jigs and reels played on the fiddle by one of the young stable hands. On these occasions, my heart was lighter than it had been for many years. The evenings when Doctor Markham was free to join us were always the most enjoyable. No one could dance the hornpipe like him. When I was blessed to have him partner me and, though our hands would touch only briefly, it meant the world to me.

When Sunday morning arrived, I would join Mrs. Kennedy and the other servants in walking the one-and-a-half miles from the homestead to St. John's Church for services. The church contained four large fireplaces; the notable families of the district being seated beside them. The Markhams rented a private box close to the one owned by Government House. As a convict, I did not join the other members of the community but was banished upstairs to the gallery where we were separated from the male convicts. We listened to the liturgy seated upon narrow, backless benches, watched over by warders, and locked in by a securely bolted door. In the gallery opposite sat the poor, foundling children from the Orphan Schools. These unfortunate creatures sat huddled together, their eyes fixed in a trance-like stare without the slightest hint of light or life. I thanked the Lord that I was blessed with cherished memories of my loving parents that brightened and warmed even my hardest and loneliest days. These children had nothing. With no hope of freedom, their future of service and toil was already mapped out for them. Their plight was surely worse than anyone's in this colony.

By striking contrast, my own little charges at *Knypersley* were always bright and energetic, and they kept me amused for hours each day. I used to take them walking by the river where we would pick flowers, roll in the grass, and paddle in the water. The squeals of delight that would echo from their lips always gladdened my heart. I was pleased to bring some joy into their often-solitary lives. The first time Doctor Markham discovered us lying barefoot in the long grass, gazing at the birds circling high above, I was seized with terror lest his anger saw me returned to Cascades. I did him a great injustice, however, by fearing him. His nature was not to chide and punish. He only wished to bestow joy.

Joining us, he lay so close beside me that I could hear him breathing and feel the warmth radiating from his body. I was unsure of whether it was an unconscious or deliberate act, but how wildly my heart beat regardless! If I could but reach out and take his forbidden hand in my own. My growing feelings for him were a cruel temptation indeed. Eventually, the sun slipped behind the clouds and Georgina complained of being cold. With a sigh, I declared it time to return home. Accepting Doctor Markham's hand, I was aided to my feet as the children scurried around gathering their shoes and stockings. A stray leaf remained in my hair and Doctor Markham reached out to gently remove it. Ever so lightly the tips of his fingers glided across my cheek, and my skin tingled.

Fearing Mrs. Markham's disapproval, we ushered the children through the kitchen upon reaching home, a place where they could safely remove their shoes, wash dirty hands and faces, and take off any soiled clothing before entering the main house. The children were presented to their mother for a few minutes of formal chatter before she quickly tired of their presence and dismissed them. Once they were safely settled in the playroom, I returned alone to offer my mistress a little companionship. Most days I would join her in the rose garden, a place of great beauty whose exquisite blooms and heavenly scents delighted me.

Mrs. Markham was excessively fond of roses, many of her bushes grown from cuttings brought with her from her native Staffordshire. Through time spent with her, I began to see that despite her poise and self-assuredness, she was at heart a very lonely woman. In her world of isolation at *Knypersley*, there were no intimate friends, no warmth gained from her children's love, and she had placed a barrier between herself and the tenderness her husband was so willing to bestow. She was totally reliant on her maids for everything from companionship to fastening her buttons each morning. I became determined that her daughters, my lively, affectionate young charges, would not grow up simply to retreat to a similar world. They would fend for themselves. It was imperative that I teach them how to do up buttons, brush their own hair, and tie their laces and bows.

Having been happily settled at *Knypersley* for around two months, I was awoken late one evening by a terribly loud crash from the kitchen. Hurrying from the warmth of my bed, I peered into the darkened room, but the source of the disturbance was not immediately evident. Doctor Markham soon appeared in the doorway; his face illuminated by a candle.

'It's alright, Hannah,' he whispered. 'It's only me.'

As Doctor Markham came forward, his candle lit the face of Mrs. Kennedy sitting on the floor, surrounded by the household's cooking pots. Hastening to her side, we helped her to a nearby chair, Doctor Markham prising a bottle of rum from her grasp.

'Please take this to my study,' he said, passing me the bottle and his keys. 'Hide it in the top drawer of my desk.'

Having done his bidding, I quickly returned to the kitchen. My master succeeded in helping Mrs. Kennedy into bed and made her comfortable for the night. I began gathering the pots from the kitchen floor. With Mrs. Kennedy snoring loudly, Doctor Markham re-entered the kitchen.

'She'll sleep until morning now,' he assured me. 'I'm afraid that she won't be too happy when she wakes. She's harmless though, poor thing. If you would rather, you are welcome to sleep in the main house tonight.'

I assured my kind master that I was content to stay.

'You better get back to bed yourself before you catch cold. The pots can wait until morning.'

Returning to my bed, I lay awake thinking of Doctor Markham. I had felt blessed to stand by his side whilst he ministered to Mrs. Kennedy. Yes, he was terribly handsome, but it was the tender compassion of this extraordinary human being that won my admiration and awoke my heart. Left to prepare breakfast by myself the following morning, I served it as though nothing was amiss in the kitchen. Mrs. Kennedy would only suffer were Mrs. Markham to discover the truth. Following breakfast, Doctor Markham summoned me to his study where he lay before me his housekeeper's tragic tale.

'Mrs. Kennedy,' he began, 'has a fondness for the drink. It is not due to the pleasure of imbibing; she drinks to forget. She was fifty years old when she was transported, most people by then would hope to be settled for life. With eight children to feed and a husband already transported, she stole a sheep and a few potatoes and found herself banished for seven years. She appealed for leniency but was shown no mercy. Her eldest child was twenty-three, and the youngest was only eight. She knows that she will never see them again. Please help me to protect Mrs. Kennedy. If my wife discovered her weakness, she would be returned to the authorities for certain.'

Agreeing to do my utmost to mask Mrs. Kennedy's shortcomings, Doctor Markham thanked me for my discretion before holding the door open for my departure. Taking my hand as I exited, he squeezed it and smiled. He caught my resistance napping and it was truly mortifying that all I could manage by way of reply was a deep blush, before I scurried off like a frivolous girl.

'Oh, why do I love him so much!' I cried to myself upon reaching the safety of my room. Tormented tears flowed down my cheeks as I paced the floor, agonized by the pain of my unrequited and forbidden love. I scolded myself profusely for being captivated by this man and vowed that I would build better defences. As my feelings increased, this pledge ofttimes felt like an insurmountable challenge.

The place to which I'd been banished was not dissimilar to home. It was windier, there was no mistake about that, but if I closed my eyes and listened to the voices of those around me, I could well have been back on the streets of London. There were voices from all over England, Wales, Scotland and Ireland too. The rolling green hills were the same, the cold of winter was definitely the same, and yet it was not home. The streets here were well-ordered, housing bright little cottages whose gardens were full of pretty blooms, fruit, and vegetables. We were not hemmed in, having space to move. The sun reached us, beaming down from the bluest of blue skies; it was not blocked by dark, decaying tenements. I longed to write to Granny Ravens and tell of my happiness here, letting her know I was well and being looked after. If only I could let her know that I was doing as she bid, and making the most of my situation. It was strange to think that in Van Diemen's Land my life continued, whilst thousands of miles across the sea, the lives of my family continued too. I wondered if they ever spared me a thought, or whether they were too busy with their daily struggles to think of one gone from them forever.

Sadly, there is no way to tell when nightmares will come haunting. They appear at the most inexplicable moments, even when one is at their happiest. For me, the horrors of incarceration suddenly came flooding back when all else in my life was tranquil. The wretched prison stench invaded my nostrils yet again, the cold and damp chilled my bones, and the harrowing screams joined with my own as I feared suffocation in that dark, abominable world. Waking from my nightmare, I sprang up, screaming desperately to be saved from the horror. Relief came in the form of strong, warm, comforting arms, and as my screams slowly subsided, I realized that I was being held tightly by Doctor Markham. Stroking my hair, he whispered soothing words and assured me I was safe here at *Knypersley*.

'Your tiny heart races so,' he declared sympathetically. Indeed, whilst his kindness managed to calm and reassure, my heart refused to be quietened. It had been reawakened by the doctor's innocent gesture and now beat only for him. Terror had seen me cling tightly to this kind soul, and I was unwilling to release my hold. Thankfully, Doctor Markham was content to remain with me until I was soothed enough for him to lay me gently back upon my pillow, and drift slowly back to sleep. Over the coming months when my sleep was much disturbed, I would wickedly think back to the joy of being held in his comforting arms and, imagining myself held once more, would be lulled back into a blissful sleep.

The following morning, Doctor Markham appeared in the kitchen to check on my welfare and, satisfied that my spirits had returned, he left me to my work. I sighed deeply. How I loved that silent, sturdy, and stoic figure. The very sound of his voice could heighten the colour in my cheeks, and when he was near, I hardly dared raise my eyes to meet his for fear of where my emotions might lead. Yet raise my eyes I must, for the happiness of each day become dependent upon seeing him. A mere glimpse of him in the distance could raise my spirits tenfold. I knew the dangers awaiting me were my secret ever revealed, yet not seeing his wonderous face would be the greatest punishment of all. If I were to be sent away, I knew that death would be the only welcome succour.

And so, it came time for Mrs. Markham to have her child. As thunder rumbled overhead, I approached her sitting room one evening, my ears quickly met by a groaning from within. Entering, I discovered Mrs. Markham in the early throes of labour. She cried out, ordering me to fetch Doctor Bell. Following another flash of lightning, I hesitated, reluctant to journey out in the worsening storm.

'Might I ask one of the stable boys to go?' I ventured to ask.

'No!' Mrs. Markham cried out, apparently seized by another contraction. 'I can't trust them. You must go, Hannah.'

'May I take a horse?'

'Anything. Anything. Just hurry.'

As Mrs. Markham cried out again, I hurried into the stormy darkness. Bridling a horse, I climbed the rungs of its stall and mounted, riding off bareback as in former times. The thrill of feeling the horse beneath me made me momentarily forget my mission, though only briefly and I quickly set out in search of Doctor Bell. Having fought against driving rain and a howling gale, I arrived at his home, only to discover that he was attending another. Returning to *Knypersley*, I conveyed the bad news to my mistress.

'Fetch Mrs. Kennedy then,' Mrs. Markham demanded angrily.

'I cannot, Ma'am,' I replied with a quivering voice. 'She's ...'

Very close to tears, I suggested that I go in search of Doctor Markham.

'I don't want him,' she snapped. 'No, you must help me yourself.'

What else could I do? She was so very near to having the bairn, and so I helped. By the time Doctor Markham returned home, his wife was resting comfortably and I sat cradling her newborn in my arms. He came tip-toeing into the room.

'A son?' he whispered.

I nodded and smiled.

'Congratulations, sir.'

Doctor Markham bent and gently drew back the blanket in which his son was cocooned. Peering into the bairn's face for the first time, he smiled. He then looked towards his wife.

'Is she awake?' he queried in lowered tones.

'I'm awake,' came the blunt, almost angry reply from the bed.

Doctor Markham's face changed instantly. He went to his wife's side.

'Another healthy child and a son too,' he said. 'Well done, Sophia.'

Mrs. Markham did not reply and I saw her turn her face away. How could she be so cold and unfeeling towards one so loving and caring? Were I to be similarly blessed, I would not act so indifferently. With her head still turned, Mrs. Markham declared,

'You can thank Hannah that your son arrived safely. Doctor Bell was nowhere to be found. The poor girl went out in the storm all alone. As for Mrs. Kennedy, I've discovered her little secret, try as you may to hide it from me. Hannah volunteered to fetch you, but I knew that would be of little use. I preferred to take my chances with her. Without Hannah, I would have had no one.'

Doctor Markham remained a little longer by his wife's side.

'Have you chosen a name for him?'

Mrs. Markham quickly turned her face back as she snapped,

'William, of course.'

'Of course,' Doctor Markham nodded.

He turned then and with a solemn face, returned to my side.

'Don't touch the child,' Mrs. Markham called. 'He needs his rest. Hannah, put the child in its cradle and come sit beside me. I need some company.'

I hesitated. Looking at Doctor Markham's grave face, I felt as though I should be placing the child into his arms instead.

'Hannah!' Mrs. Markham growled.

Doctor Markham smiled sadly and indicated I should do as his wife bade.

'You may go now, Josiah,' she declared, and her husband was dismissed unceremoniously.

She was bright and merry now.

'William is my father's name,' she said as I drew up a chair. 'My father is such an upright, honourable man. I hope that my son grows just like him. He will be brought up as a Gresley.'

'Doctor Markham is also a very righteous man,' I ventured to suggest.

'Mm,' she agreed. 'He's also very handsome. It was those looks of his that trapped me into this lifetime of misery. Yet, if my son grows to resemble his father, I will be satisfied, though it be small compensation.'

Why Mrs. Markham was always discontent was incomprehensible. She possessed a loving husband and four healthy children. She also had the means and ability to do what she wanted, whenever she wanted. Yet, none of it seemed to matter. She spent her life bemoaning being torn from her family and friends in England and measured everything against her unsurpassable home in Staffordshire. Eventually, Mrs. Markham tired and I was dismissed. As I crept from the room, I discovered Doctor Markham sitting just outside the door.

'Is the little fellow alright?' he questioned.

I nodded with a smile and assured him that his son was perfect.

'So, you delivered him all by yourself,' Doctor Markham said with an admiring smile. 'I knew you would do good here the moment I saw you. What a brave little thing you are. I shall remain indebted to you forever.'

'There is no debt, sir. It is I who will be forever indebted to you for offering me your care and protection.'

Later that evening, baby William woke and I was summoned to remove him from his mother's room. I took the opportunity to properly introduce him to his father. Knocking at his study, I slowly opened the door and peered into the room.

'Doctor Markham,' I said gingerly, pushing the door open a little further upon seeing the dear man's smile. 'I thought that you might like some time with baby William.'

He took his son tenderly in his arms.

'What a blessing you are, Hannah. Since your arrival, I have been allowed to get to know my children. Had it not been for you, I cannot imagine how long it would have been before I was allowed to hold William.'

The coming days brought further opportunities for father and son to bond. William's sisters were also eager to greet the new arrival. With the bairn quickly entrusted into my care, he began to join us on our daily rambles, Georgina and Lavinia eager to help me push his carriage. During one such walk, the children gathered some wildflowers as a present for their mother to cheer her whilst she recovered from the recent arrival. The sweet little things were so enthusiastic and presented their bouquet with such beaming faces that it near broke my heart to see their mother accept them without the slightest animation or thanks. As their poor faces fell, they were dismissed without ceremony, Mrs. Markham asking me to remain behind.

'Take these, will you,' she said handing me the bouquet. 'Get rid of them somewhere but better not let the children see.'

Relieving her of the flowers, I hurried from the room, a tear of pity upon my cheek. Finding a vase, I placed the offering in the nursery. Georgina was the first to spy them.

'Your mother loved the flowers so very much,' I explained, 'that she felt selfish keeping them to herself. We decided to put them in here so that everyone might enjoy them.'

I could tell by the look on their faces that they didn't believe me, but they didn't question me further. They would never ask to give their mother flowers again.

As soon as she was able, Mrs. Markham resumed her social life: visits to the theatre, concerts, regattas, and horticultural shows. Not surprisingly, she did not proceed without complaint and continually lamented that the women of Van Diemen's Land were only interested in dancing. She praised Lady Franklin who made a valiant effort to introduce more evening parties, literature and art, and found it wearisome that society remained so resistant. Doctor Markham bought his wife one of the finest horses in the colony and she could ride superbly. Turned out in an expensive riding habit, she would go wherever there was action afoot, a hunt particularly appealing to her ruthless nature. Whilst deer had been specially imported for the purpose, Mrs. Markham found wallabies offered the best sport.

Doctor Markham never accompanied his wife on these expeditions and he forbade the recounting of such cruel exploits upon her return. His wife's increasingly prolonged absences gave Doctor Markham renewed freedom. First and foremost, it allowed him time to spend with his children when they would laugh and play together without restraint. Oftentimes, Doctor Markham seemed like a big child himself. The children were full of delight to have their father to themselves, and their dear, innocent faces shone with the light of pure happiness.

During Mrs. Markham's absences, her husband was quick to flout the time-honoured conventions she so cherished, and he would often take his lunch with the men in the barn, before joining Mrs. Kennedy and me in the kitchen for supper. It was due to the interest and concern my dear master showed for my welfare that at the end of one such supper, I decided to tell him about Michael. I described him as my childhood sweetheart who possessed a wild and untameable nature.

'When Michael was transported,' I admitted, 'I often wondered how anyone could sink so low. I couldn't understand how he had found himself in so much trouble. Now I have learnt that life can cheat you. Circumstances can change so quickly. Michael wasn't bad nor were many of the women on my ship. They were just poor, desperate souls whose suffering gave them no option other than to steal. They were trying to survive.'

'As were you, Hannah,' Doctor Markham smiled kindly. 'You did everything you could to help your sister. In a way, you gave your life for her. You stole to buy medicine, and in return, you lost the life you knew.'

On my behalf, Doctor Markham made inquiries about Michael. As I hovered over the dying embers of the blacksmith's fire a few weeks later, he came to my side.

'I have news about your friend Michael,' he said.

I listened intently as Doctor Markham told of what he knew. Upon arrival in Van Diemen's Land, Michael was sent north, assigned as a farm labourer on a property just outside of Deloraine. His brother Richard was sent to neighbouring Chudleigh. The brothers received high praise during their voyage to Australia, helping to foil an attempted mutiny by their fellow convicts, subsequently aiding those in authority to keep order. Their favourable placements in Van Diemen's

Land were assured through their brave actions. I would have expected nothing less from Michael and my heart swelled with pride. As far as Doctor Markham could discern, neither Michael nor his brother were married. Doctor Markham kindly offered to contact Michael for me. Strangely, I refused his offer. In the two years since I last saw Michael, I had matured almost beyond recognition. All of a sudden, he became someone I'd known in another place and time, another life. The love of a frivolous young girl. Doctor Markham told me that Michael was well, safe, and prospering. I was content.

A fiendish tear of regret appeared as Doctor Markham left me that day, and I hurriedly brushed it away, though I could no longer deny the unfulfilled desire that brought it to the surface. I knew that ours was a vengeful God. Clearly, the promised flames of damnation would not be enough to atone for my sins. In his wrath, God sent me here, placing me in the sights of all that was perfection in man. Someone with whom I felt freer to think, feel, and live than ever before. A kindred spirit whom God had seen fit to deny me and my yearning for him would never cease. Therefore, it was somewhat of a relief that over the coming months, Doctor Markham was often from home, travelling extensively throughout the colony observing how psychiatric patients were treated and housed.

Having done much work in the field before coming to Hobarton, his expertise was invaluable at a time when several colonies were looking at new ways of caring for these poor unfortunates. During an extended stay in Sydney, he helped to draft the bill which later in the year was passed as the *Dangerous Lunatics Act of 1843*. It would secure the safe custody of people of unsound mind in places other than gaols. I was immensely proud of his work towards this outcome. During this time the children and I desperately missed his bright presence amongst us, our walks being a little subdued by his absence. Mrs. Markham seemed untouched by her husband's loss; indeed, she seemed more cheerful as the days progressed.

I used his absence to begin teaching my two oldest charges the basics of embroidery. By their ages, I had already completed my second sampler, my stitches becoming more confident and decorative under the guidance of my mother. Our work inspired Mrs. Markham to begin embroidering a new pole screen, and she joined us as I guided my little charges. Although I encouraged the children to sit beside their mother as they worked, my attempt at family unity was oftentimes misguided for my charges worked slowly and diligently upon their task whilst their mother's work was poorly executed, her stitches often going in all directions. When her daughters' work proved more skilfully executed and decorative than her own, Mrs. Markham was furious. Her frustrations would often see the children banished from the room whilst I would be asked to remain to give her further instruction on ways to improve. Upon their father's return, Georgina and Lavinia each presented him with a quality sampler, embroidered with their name, age, and the year 1843, as well as some pretty birds and flowers. Doctor Markham was excessively proud of his daughters' achievements, and I received a smile of gratitude for my efforts. Mrs. Markham also brought forward her own endeavours, and displayed them with all the pride of a spoilt child. When her husband praised her work she seemed content, though a frown crossed her brow when he acknowledged the section that I had completed as the prettiest.

A few days later Mrs. Markham's mood declined still further when she received a letter from her brother. His news greatly agitated her.

'My brother Samuel is coming to Van Diemen's Land,' she declared. 'He will rue the day that he made such a rash decision.'

Mr. Gresley was the second son and youngest child of the family, and as such, had no prospect of inheriting the estate. Possessing no desire to enter the church or army, he chose to follow his sister's lead and migrate to the colonies.

'Coming to Australia will present a lot of opportunities for him,' Doctor Markham counselled, though his wife continued to view the enterprise as nothing more than a foolhardy waste of the modest settlement their father had granted him to establish himself.

Mrs. Markham declared,

'Heaven knows, I have written to him more than once urging him not to come to this godforsaken land.'

That she tried to dissuade her brother from following her to Van Diemen's Land was no surprise. I had heard her on numerous occasions lamenting that, as his wife, she was compelled to follow Doctor Markham when he emigrated from England.

'I will never forgive that man, stealing me from my family and home,' she would moan. 'I was placed on a ship, seven months pregnant, forced to endure a long and treacherous voyage, giving birth at sea. There's been nothing but misery since the moment I set foot in this wretched country. I would do anything to prevent another member of my family suffering the same fate.'

Doctor Markham would always offer a balanced judgement.

'There are wonderful chances to increase his wealth, given the proper guidance.'

His wife would naturally scoff at such suggestions, turning the discussion back to what she saw as her husband's own failure since arriving in the colony.

'You could have been a great surgeon, a position at Guy's was yours for the taking. London would have offered so much more – a beautiful house, friends, and amusements. And yet here I am, isolated in this dreadful country, wife of a small-town doctor who ministers to all and sundry. A doctor who treats the criminal class for free and brings them here to run my household.'

Her words were spoken spitefully, clearly intending to belittle and insult her husband, though thankfully he seemed immune to their impact.

Mr. Samuel Gresley, a young man whose reputation certainly preceded him, arrived in July that year. Entering the sitting room, he found Mrs. Markham bouncing baby William upon her knee. Giving a very fine impersonation of a doting mother, she smiled.

'He's a fine, strong boy. A true Gresley.'

'He's a very handsome little fellow,' Mr. Gresley agreed. 'The image of his father.'

Mrs. Markham frowned. Growing tired of petting her child, she rose and thrust him into my arms. Mr. Gresley's and my eyes now met for the first time, and he smiled by way of greeting. As he strode across the room to join his sister by the window, I was able to observe him closely. He was the breath of fresh air that *Knypersley* so badly needed. Tall and slender, his appearance was not dissimilar to his sister, though his golden hair was darker and possessed a slight wave. His big, blue, expressive eyes possessed a merry twinkle and the constant smile upon his handsome face bore evidence that life truly delighted him. There was an innocence about him that was ever so endearing, though he thought deeply and demonstrated immense compassion to those around him. I could instantly see why Doctor Markham was very fond of him. Highly educated, he was passionate about the natural world, was widely read in the field of history, and possessed a great appreciation of the arts and literature.

A grand soiree was given in honour of Mr. Gresley's arrival in the colony, and with *Knypersley* welcoming many of Hobarton's elite, Mrs. Markham was at her happiest. I watched the ease with which Mr. Gresley mingled with those gathered. Moving amongst them with his sister, he shook hands graciously, partook of a short conversation with each group, and demonstrated genuine interest in all topics raised. I wondered whether this amazing ability to feign sincerity had been inherited, was something much practised from birth, or simply came with the security of rank. Mr. Gresley first spoke to me as I cleared away later that evening.

'I am very grateful to you, Hannah. My gathering was a great success, due in no small part to your hard work.'

I smiled briefly by way of acknowledgment whilst continuing with my work. Mr. Gresley, however, was in no hurry to leave.

'It cannot be easy,' he continued, 'to be punished as you have for such a small mistake.'

'Unfortunately, it was no mistake, sir. I knew what I was doing,' I replied without looking up.

'Jos has told me all,' he replied. 'You stole to help your dying sister. I've seen what it's like to be poor in London. I've walked past that horrendous place they held you in and smelt the stench emanating from its walls. It is a miracle you came out alive. My sister is fortunate indeed that you were assigned to her. You have been an amazing asset to this household, especially when, by delivering young William, you surely saved my sister's life. You are far braver than I could ever wish to be.'

I raised my eyes to meet his own.

'My parents always taught me to accept the good and the bad things in life, and my grandmother told me to make the most of every situation. I have been extremely lucky to be assigned to the Markhams and I am happy in my work here. My only regret is that I am so far from my home and family.'

'I am very glad to hear that, Hannah.'

The voice came from behind me and I turned to see Doctor Markham smiling at me from the doorway. Against my will, the colour quickly rose in my cheeks and a smile sat upon my lips. I hurriedly returned to my work before either man noticed. I was aware Doctor Markham's eyes were still fixed upon me and, under his intense gaze, I dared not look up lest my eyes betray me. How I adored him! The coming days saw me drawn to the river more and more as I desperately searched for a way to survive my aching heart. The waters calmed me and the beauty of my surroundings could not help but brighten my spirits. In his own quest for peace and solitude, Mr. Gresley eventually discovered my place of refuge. Standing by the water's edge, I did not hear his approach.

'Impressive, isn't it?'

Mr. Gresley smiled, indicating the majestic Mt. Wellington with its towering basalt columns. I returned his smile and nodded. Finding some rocks nearby, my companion invited me to sit with him for a while. I hesitated.

'It's alright,' he assured me. 'We won't be disturbed.'

Obligation saw me remain, though I declined the offered seat. An awkward silence reigned as we soaked in the picturesque landscape, and I gathered the courage to speak.

'Doctor Markham said you are building a house.'

'That I am,' he said, pointing again towards Mt. Wellington. 'Up there, on that magnificent mountain. From the moment I saw it, I knew that there could be no greater place to build my home.'

'It is the perfect place to live,' I agreed. 'It's quite the loveliest mountain I have ever seen.'

From a small canvas bag, Mr. Gresley withdrew a sketchbook and a long stick of black charcoal, before opening to a sketch of the mighty mountain.

'Are you an artist, Mr. Gresley?' I enquired.

My companion answered me with a good-natured chuckle.

'I would like to think so,' he replied, 'though my father would beg to differ.'

'He doesn't approve?'

Mr. Gresley shook his head, though his smile remained.

'Father always hoped I would show a fondness for the law, but nothing could entice me to that calling. I attempted to meet him halfway and undertook medical studies for two years. It was then that my heart and mind yearned for a change, and in what my father viewed as a retrograde step, I transferred my efforts to Natural Philosophy. My dear mother ensured my artistic endeavours continued and secretly funded private tuition of an evening.'

Mr. Gresley often joined me on my walks from that time on and I quickly learnt that like his brother-in-law, he was a great philanthropist. In his dealings with me, he was every bit as caring and considerate as Doctor Markham, though fortune had been kinder to him. Mr. Gresley was young and carefree and his privileged upbringing allowed him to dream big dreams. Through his art and literature, he could be transported to worlds far away from life's toil and sorrow. Once when Mrs. Markham lamented the recklessness of her brother's adventure, Doctor Markham replied, 'He's happy. At least he's happy,' and I could sense in his voice and manner that he envied his brother-in-law's freedom and audacious spirit.

On the days when my chores kept me from roaming, I would gaze across the paddocks and watch Mr. Gresley heading out alone. His tread was always light, as though he walked on air, and he would whistle joyfully as he went. I knew that the canvas bag slung over his shoulder would contain his sketchbook, charcoal sticks and reading material. His would be a day spent rambling, lost in thought. When the mood took him, he would sketch by the river, or settle himself somewhere to continue studying this new land that fascinated him. Mrs. Kennedy once caught me staring and scolded me for my idleness.

'I just envy him his freedom,' I sighed.

'Continue to work hard and one day you'll have the freedom you desire. Allow the mistress to catch you watching her brother like that again and it will not bode well for you.'

Whilst in London, Mr. Gresley had been a member of both the Linnean and Zoological Societies, and he was astounded to discover that I shared his passion for the unique flora and fauna of this amazing continent. That a young lady could content herself with fossicking in leaf matter and plunging her hands into muddy river sediments was a revelation to him.

'It's a rare mind than can be enthralled by scientific pursuits as is yours,' he declared. 'My studies would be greatly benefitted by your assistance. I shall ask my sister whether she might spare you for a few hours each week.'

Her brother's request was greeted nonchalantly by Mrs. Markham, and she granted permission with a wave of her hand. I was now given the freedom to enter a world of pure fascination and joy each afternoon. It was a world I once shared with my Michael, and happy memories lingered of his dragonflies, owls, and frogs. Treated as Mr. Gresley's equal, I quickly learned to examine animal skeletons, press floral specimens, and mount insects and butterflies. My observations of the amazing living world around me were all recorded, Mr. Gresley being amply pleased with my sensitivity and skill for drawing from life.

During this time, I had the great pleasure of examining the specimens he collected in Cape Town during the *Duke of Roxburgh's* stay there on its voyage to Australia. Upon a shelf sat a striped field mouse alongside a cape sugarbird with an extraordinarily long tail, both fine examples of Mr. Gresley's skill in taxidermy. Exquisite blooms like the protea with its lengthy pink petals, and exotic animals including the geometric tortoise, baboon, and honey badger all enchanted my eyes as they burst from the pages of his sketchbook, so lifelike did they appear. I also marvelled at Mr. Gresley's rendering of the incredible flat-topped mountain that loomed over Cape Town harbour, though I thought it nowhere near as beautiful as my own Mt. Wellington.

For the purposes of his work, Mrs. Markham allowed her brother use of a room at the back of the house, a room quickly furnished with all Mr. Gresley's wonderful curiosities, its picture rails teeming with his impressive artwork. Upon arrival in Van Diemen's Land, Mr. Gresley ordered a new display cabinet from Mr. Joseph Woolley, one of the colony's foremost cabinetmakers whose work was also furnishing Government House. Made according to Mr. Gresley's specifications, the beautifully carved cabinet was made of Huon Pine, whose intoxicating, spicy aroma was a delight in itself. When opened, its double doors revealed twenty-four drawers, two abreast, each pair gradually increasing in size from top to bottom. Lined with cork they would eventually house everything from geology samples and shells to insects and animal skulls.

In October, Mr. Gresley became a founding member of the Botanical and Horticultural Society of Van Diemen's Land, formed to advance scientific exploits in the young colony. Our work now took on increased importance, as we gathered and recorded specimens unique to our new homeland: the banksias, yam daisies, saltbush, native orchids, wattles, waratahs, mountain berries, and climbing heaths. Mr. Gresley also made significant contributions with beautifully-preserved samples of the amazing wildlife including pademelons, wombats, and the incredibly strange but immensely appealing little creature they called 'The Devil'. Our endeavours and those of our like-minded citizens were rewarded the following year when the Society was renamed the Royal Society of Van Diemen's Land for Horticulture, Botany, and the Advancement of Science. Under the official patronage of our gracious Queen, it became the first Royal Society outside of London.

As the Christmas season approached that year, the weather became markedly warmer. There would be no snow which I found exceedingly strange. At *Knypersley* there was no expense spared when it came to the celebration of Christmas. Mrs. Markham, who lived exclusively for pleasure, had grand visions for the season and all the festivities of her youth were now re-enacted in Van Diemen's Land. Celebrations at *Knypersley* began on Christmas Eve and continued through to Twelfth Night, the careful planning of Mrs. Markham's wardrobe imperative. Having missed the previous year's festivities due to the expected arrival of William, she was determined to be the most stunning and merriest of all revellers. Mr. Gresley's youthful exuberance gave her added incentive and she gleefully volunteered to host the traditional Christmas Eve Ball.

Things, however, began badly for her and I found her pacing the floor one morning in a highly agitated state, with poor Doctor Markham gently attempting to soothe her. Whilst I laid morning tea,

I ascertained that an error by Mrs. Markham's seamstress meant her gown would not be completed in time for the Ball.

'Me! Sir William Gresley's daughter!' she stormed, convinced it was a deliberate slight on the part of the seamstress.

'Perhaps I could be of assistance, ma'am?' I suggested hesitantly.

'You? What possible help could you be?'

I swallowed slowly and assured her that I could piece together a garment were she to describe what she desired. At first, she scoffed and doubted my ability. When Doctor Markham assured her I was quite capable, she turned sharply upon him demanding to know how he knew of my skills. I quickly volunteered the information for Mrs. Markham.

'I was once head seamstress for Madame Le Blanc of Regent Street.'

'Regent Street! London!' Mrs. Markham exclaimed. 'Why wasn't I told of this Josiah?'

'You were, my dear,' Doctor Markham replied patiently. 'I read William Bland's letter to you. Perhaps other things were on your mind.'

'If you *were* employed until recently in London, you should be well aware of the latest fashions. Are you able to produce a garment by Christmas Eve to match the finest worn in London?'

'I could reproduce one I made for Lady Braye not long before leaving.'

Mrs. Markham allowed a small squeal of delight to escape her lips.

'Lady Braye!' she exclaimed. 'You must start today. Mrs. Kennedy will look after the children.'

'I can still look after the children,' I assured her.

'No. My gown is far too important. The children will do well enough with Mrs. Kennedy.'

Completing my work in her sitting room, Mrs. Markham sat close beside me, watching on like an excited young lady preparing for her first ball as the gown took shape. That she was to be the recipient of my endeavours thrilled her and she chatted away merrily as though we were lifelong friends. Upon her knee she nursed her cherished feline, stroking its fur with great affection. Refusing to respond with similar warmth, the wretched animal sat ready to pounce, its glowing eyes fixated on me. That it longed to lash out was obvious, though it dared not. In the rare moments of silence, I could not help but reminisce about Christmases I enjoyed as a child in St. Paul's Walden. It was always a time of special celebration when work would stop for the day and, wrapped up tightly against the Winter chills, we would travel to Codicote to spend the day in complete happiness with Granny Ravens. There was always a roaring fire around which we would gather, Dada having lit it using the Yule log we chose the previous evening. With the Christmas fire struck, Granny would allow her grandchildren to decorate the house with greenery: holly, ivy, rosemary, and of course mistletoe, something under which we all enjoyed watching Mam and Dada reaffirm their affection.

At Christmas, the smell of roasting meats was more mouth-watering than usual, whilst the glowing pudding being carried to the table was invariably met with clapping and great excitement. Making the pudding was Mam's contribution to the Christmas feast and it was a tradition in our household to make it on the last Sunday before Advent, giving it ample time to age before serving. We children would gather around Mam whilst she measured out the ingredients before we took it in turns to stir. Mam kept a special wooden spoon just for this purpose, the wood symbolizing Christ's crib. From a young age, we all knew how the ritual should proceed. We would close our eyes, make a secret wish, and stir the mixture in a clockwise direction.

Before setting out to Granny's on Christmas morning, we would have our once-a-year breakfast treat - an orange! Mam had a certain way of peeling them so that we might bite straight into the flesh. As the juice ran down our chins and fingers, the kitchen would be filled with our delighted squeals. The presents we received from Granny Ravens in the evening remained the same each year: new mittens and scarves, knitted by her, to replace the now well-worn ones bestowed the previous year. We truly loved these little indulgences.

The contrast between the magical Christmases of home and those at *Knypersley* was stark indeed. No one here was happy. Not even the children showed enthusiasm for the season. To them, it was like any other day. Mrs. Markham possessed no desire to enchant their young minds with special Christmas stories, for she was far too captivated by her desire to possess the prettiest dress, the most elaborately decorated house, and the table with the most culinary delights. Poor Doctor Markham's face wore a semi-permanent look of despair during this season. Of his wife's spending, he could say naught, and yet, it was taken for granted that he would provide the necessary funds. In a home where money was no object, it was strange to me that no one smiled, no one laughed, and there was no seasonal goodwill.

Though they struggled, Mam and Dada always smiled and never failed to instil the true meaning of Christmas into us. They often went without themselves to give us children a magical Christmas. Even in the years when Christmas found them down to their last shilling, our parents would ensure love, laughter, and good cheer. Mam always said that money could not buy happiness, and here at *Knypersley*, I saw for the first time that she was absolutely correct.

Donning her new and much-admired gown, Mrs. Markham welcomed her guests on Christmas Eve. She ordered Mr. Gresley to take her husband's place by her side. Having been shunned by his wife, Doctor Markham was no doubt pleased to be out of the limelight, and I saw him slip away quietly around an hour later. Feasting on mutton stuffed with oysters and dancing until four the following morning, Mrs. Markham welcomed in Christmas. Her goodwill, however, evaporated by the time she finally stirred on the holy day itself, and she chose to remain comfortably settled in bed. As the dinner hour approached, I seated the children at the dining table, something of a novelty for them, and waited until they were joined by their father and uncle. With Mrs. Markham keeping to her room, the atmosphere was light-hearted amongst those present, and I left them the jolliest I had yet seen.

Having already generously provided his servants with some delicious Christmas fare, Doctor Markham appeared amongst us on Boxing Day to present our Christmas boxes. A lovely new day cap with lace trim was bestowed upon Mrs. Kennedy, whilst I received several yards of a quality cream fabric possessing a delicate floral print.

'I thought you may like to make a dress for yourself. Something to keep as Sunday best.'

I thanked him from the bottom of my heart, astounded by his generosity. Never would I have expected such kindness from a master towards his servants. Mrs. Kennedy assured him that this yearly gift was something she always looked forward to and cherished. With this, she departed and Doctor Markham headed towards the door. Suddenly, however, he turned back.

'I almost forgot,' he said, plunging his hand into his pocket. 'This is also for you. I thought that it would match the blue of your eyes and look pretty in your hair.'

He handed me a gorgeous royal blue ribbon and I smiled my thanks once more.

Early in the New Year, the finishing touches were added to Mr. Gresley's new home, and he prepared to leave us. Mrs. Markham renewed her objections to her brother's venture, and the closer his departure crept, the louder her protests became.

'It is one thing to set up your own establishment, a young man in your situation should have a home to call his own, but must it be so far away? You know you could stay here at *Knypersley*. There's plenty of land to build upon.'

Mr. Gresley would take his sister's criticisms with the good humour as became the gentleman he was, whilst Doctor Markham continued to encourage his wife's acceptance of her brother's youthful dreams and ambition, his eagerness for adventure and independence.

'If he fails,' Doctor Markham would counsel, 'he will have learnt a valuable lesson. But what if we stop him from trying? He'll bounce back from failure but not from the suppression of his dreams. Your brother is an intelligent man. I believe his venture will be a great success and he will prosper in his new home.'

'Hmph,' Mrs. Markham scoffed. 'His naivety will be his downfall along with my father's money.'

At the thought of Mr. Gresley's departure, I became as selfish as his sister in not wanting him to leave. His joyful presence would be greatly missed and I worked alongside him in a somewhat sombre manner as I dwelt upon how soon I would lose this valued companion. From within this self-indulgent world of misery and despair, I was suddenly shaken one evening as an almighty thud echoed through the room. Looking up, I was quick to discern the tumbled bookcase, its contents smashed upon the floor, but most horrifyingly, the faint cries of baby William came from beneath it. Mr. Gresley rushed to extract his tiny nephew from the rubble. Placed in my arms, his screams increased as I desperately scoured his delicate little body for injuries. Curiosity over their son's distress brought his parents racing to the room, Mrs. Markham's screams matching his own upon discovery of the scene. For a woman who rarely demonstrated any motherly affection, she was extremely quick to accuse me of neglect.

'I won't ask what you were doing to effect such gross negligence.'

'It all happened so quickly,' I sobbed. 'I can't understand it. I left him safely in the nursery.'

Mr. Gresley placed a comforting arm around my shoulders.

'It's true,' he declared. 'I saw her settle him there myself. The girls must have let him out. Little ones move so quickly.'

'Well, thankfully he's taken no harm from it,' Doctor Markham calmly assured us. 'Just a nasty fright. Hannah's comforting arms will soon console him.'

Mrs. Markham frowned.

'Hannah! I will see you in my sitting room in ten minutes.'

Ignoring her trembling bairn still sobbing broken heartedly in my arms, she stormed off leaving me dreading the punishment about to be meted out.

Ten minutes later, I stood before Mrs. Markham. She was now composed and sat calmly embroidering by the fire. Dr Markham sat at a small writing desk in the corner, his head held in his hands. Mrs. Markham looked up and without emotion informed me,

'It appears that your time with us is coming to an end, Hannah. I have received papers today confirming your transfer to a new master.'

'A new master!' I cried as my heart began to break. 'No! Please don't send me away. I beg you for a second chance. What happened to William was a complete accident.'

My eyes flew to Doctor Markham seeking support but he remained unmoved, his face hidden from view.

'Are you not satisfied with my work, Mrs. Markham?'

'My wife and I have been very satisfied with you, Hannah,' Doctor Markham assured me as he shifted uncomfortably in his chair, his voice barely discernible. 'We would very much like to keep you.'

'My husband would very much like to keep you,' Mrs. Markham snarled. 'I, though, am not ruled by my emotions, and I understand that someone else has a greater need of you than we do.'

Having spoken, she looked beyond me for the first time and I turned to see that Mr. Gresley had been a silent witness to our discussion. He now came forward and spoke.

'As you know, my new home is now ready and I'll be leaving here in a few days. Yet, I have no one to take care of me or my home. I would very much like it if you were to take on that role. You would also be a great asset to me during my continued scientific endeavours. You would be helper, companion, and colleague. Would you like that, Hannah?'

My astonishment rendered me speechless and a simple nod was all I could manage.

'Very well then,' declared Mrs. Markham. 'That's settled.'

Unceremoniously dismissed, I walked slowly towards the door. Mine was such a heavy heart. Though I knew I would be happy working for Mr. Gresley and would be treated kindly, the knowledge that I was to leave the Markhams was almost too much for me to bear. As tears began to flow, I hurried to the safety of my room and broke my heart. Later in the day, Mr. Gresley came gently to my side.

'I couldn't help but see your sorrow at the thought of leaving *Knypersley*. If it would bring you happiness, I will forgo the pleasure of your company. I would do anything rather than make you unhappy.'

That he would consider my feelings, an assigned convict maid, was truly remarkable. I assured him of the delight I felt at joining his staff. When he assured me that his brother-in-law and the children would be invited to visit regularly, I was overjoyed. Mr. Gresley was clearly under no illusion his sister would ever grace his home with her presence.

Whilst in all her dealings with me, Mrs. Markham appeared unmoved by my transfer, in reality, she was never completely reconciled to my leaving *Knypersley*. I overheard her complaining bitterly to Doctor Markham one evening, her husband doing his best to console her.

'Sam admittedly knows very little about farming and Hannah has grown up on the land. Her knowledge and skills will be invaluable.'

'Well, it's still of great inconvenience to me.'

My final evening at *Knypersley* arrived long before I wished, and having gathered together my few belongings, I went to tuck my little charges into bed for the last time. Georgina was solemn, Lavinia defiant, and sweet Ava shockingly forlorn. That baby William was too young to fully understand his sisters' disquiet was a blessing, for the three sets of tears accompanying my own were more than sufficient for me to handle. When their tiny heads were finally at peace, I returned to my room. Lacking the heart to do anything more, I climbed into bed, my heart as heavy as it had ever been. Barely half an hour passed before Doctor Markham's gentle voice greeted my ears.

'Hannah, are you awake?'

Hurrying to the door, I discovered the anguished face of Doctor Markham. He took my hand tightly in his own.

'I wanted to bid you a proper farewell, for heaven knows, I won't get the chance tomorrow.'

I thanked him with all my heart for everything he had done for me, and assured him that he most certainly saved my life. He seemed not to hear.

'Do you know what this house will be like without you, Hannah? We will return to being walking shadows, retreating into a world of silence. The children and I will become our old reticent selves again, and my wife will flourish on our misery.'

I could not help but be moved by the dear man's suffering, and reaching out I placed my other hand on those already joined. His eyes fell upon our hands, and he quickly raised them to his heart. Clutching them there, the true nature of his torment became evident.

'You've changed my world and shown me that sweetness and light still exist. Why must we now be parted? Why must my children be denied the happiness you bring them? Surely it is not wrong of me to wish them a life free from sorrow and pain.'

'The children are older now,' I counselled. 'They will not shy away from life so easily. They have found their voices. In time, they will blossom, find new interests, and I will be forgotten.'

'Never!' Doctor Markham exclaimed, suddenly clasping me in his arms. 'You will *never* be forgotten. You may forget us, happy as you will be in your new home, but we will never forget you.'

'I could not forget you!' I cried.

Doctor Markham looked at me. He still held me tightly in his arms. Barely able to breathe, I yearned for this man more than anything else in my life.

'Call me by my name ... just once,' he urged softly.

I whispered it.

'Jos.'

He closed his eyes as though he were absorbing it. His battle to control his emotions was all too clear. Once he was able, he drew a deep breath and slowly opening his eyes, released me.

'I so sorry,' he sighed. 'That was unforgiveable. But I had to hold you, just once. You have given me a treasured memory for when we are parted. Thoughts of you will sustain me and see me through many violent storms to come.'

'And memories of you will sustain me too,' I declared hurrying to the small box that I kept by my bedside. Drawing out my cherished blue ribbon, I said, 'You gave me this ribbon as something pretty for my hair, but it means ever so much more. When we are parted, wearing it will remind me of you.'

'You must promise that if you are ever in need, ever find yourself wanting a friend or protector, then you will call on me.'

'I promise,' I agreed. 'If I am ever in need of your help, I will send you this ribbon as a sign.'

As Doctor Markham left me that evening, it was our great misfortune to discover Mr. Gresley in the hallway.

'Jos!' he exclaimed, upon sight of his brother-in-law.

At that moment, Doctor Markham's demeanour was so downcast I feared he would betray us.

'I have a bad headache,' I quickly declared. 'Doctor Markham has kindly given me something to relieve it.'

Mr. Gresley smiled.

'You do look pale, Hannah. Is there anything I can do to help?'

I thanked him for his kindness and assured him that a good sleep would set me to rights. He seemed satisfied and wishing me goodnight, went on his way. I quickly closed the door as the tears welling in my eyes started streaming down my cheeks. Perhaps it was all for the best that I was leaving *Knypersley*. My tormented heart could stand no more. Returning to the dark, coldness of my bed, I cried myself to sleep. Weary and bleary-eyed, I was summoned before Mrs. Markham just a few hours later for a farewell appearance. Entering the sitting room, I discovered her reclining upon the chaise longue, the children strategically placed around her. Upon seeing me, they attempted to hurry to my side but were recalled sharply by their mother. Their father's tortured face watched on from where he stood by the mantle, a beaming Mr. Gresley stood beside him.

'So,' she murmured with indifference, 'the time has come for you to desert me.'

I gave a short curtsy by way of reply.

'It is no secret that my brother has very little notion of how to run a proper establishment. I expect you to serve him as you have served me, and not take advantage of the situation. I've seen the way you look at him, but I warn you, if I ever hear of any improper behaviour, I will have no hesitation in removing you from his care and returning you to the government.'

She then looked lackadaisically upon her mournful children.

'Very well,' she sighed. 'You may bid her farewell now.'

In parting from me, the children showed far more affection than their mother would have liked. Under her watchful eye, Georgina was the most formal in her adieus, her swollen eyes, however, betrayed far deeper feelings. With all her confidence intact, Lavinia marched forward and embraced me tightly, declaring that she intended to come and stay with us once we were settled. One look at the scowl upon her mother's face quickly assured me that the planned visit would never come to fruition. When it came to little Ava's turn to say goodbye, she remained seated, shrugging off her father's gentle attempt to coax her forward. For a child whose face never worn a frown, she now sat pouting as the most spoilt and unloving of children. When her mother tried to scold her with, 'No daughter of mine shall be permitted to show such rudeness,' little Ava simply buried her face into the end of the chaise longue and sobbed. With his sister otherwise distracted, William took the opportunity to toddle forward. In his hand, he held a bouquet of the wild flowers we used to pick together, and he proudly offered it to me.

'He insisted upon picking those for you,' Doctor Markham informed me with his gentle smile. 'I took him to where I knew the best ones grew.'

I smiled my thanks through tearful eyes and embraced William tightly. Without demonstrating the least affection when parting from her brother, Mrs. Markham declared it time for us to depart.

'I am sure that mountain roads can be dangerous to traverse,' she proclaimed. 'You'll be wanting to be safely at the house by nightfall.'

She wished Mr. Gresley luck in all his ventures and turned her cheek for him to kiss. With unfeeling, grasping arms around her children, she ensured that as Doctor Markham ushered Mr. Gresley and I to our awaiting cart, they remained beside her. As we reached the front verandah, however, the sitting room door was thrown open and little Ava came racing into the hallway. Despite her mother's angry cries demanding she return, Ava ran to me, and throwing her tiny arms around my neck, clung to me as tightly as she was able. Whilst she continued to sob, her father reached out, his face sorrowful upon seeing such grief in one of his dear children, and gently stroked her hair.

Mr. Gresley appeared impatient with his niece and the delay she was causing, and he urged his brother-in-law to take the child from my arms. The scene was pitiful as Doctor Markham tried to draw poor Ava away from me. Her sobs turned to screams of desperation and she thrashed out at her father and uncle, frantically clawing at me to remain in my embrace. Eventually, Mrs. Kennedy appeared, having been sent by Mrs. Markham to retrieve her errant daughter. The fearsome Irishwoman succeeded where the men failed and managed to prise sweet Ava from my arms, carrying her quickly away. Doctor Markham, ever sensitive to the feelings of those around him, knew how much my heart was aching at parting from the children. He promised to be especially diligent with their care over the coming days, knowing they would be missing my loving embraces, my life and my vigour. I hoped he understood just how much he would be missed, so terribly that the thought of not seeing him each day was slowly tearing me apart.

When the dreaded time finally arrived to part from this dear man, Doctor Markham threw caution to the wind and taking me tightly in his arms, bestowed a kiss upon my cheek.

'Sam cares a great deal for you and he'll look after you,' he whispered. 'You'll be happy in that mountain home of yours, far away from this bleak place.'

He was clearly hesitant to release me and the hands with which he helped me into the cart were trembling. As soon as Mr. Gresley was comfortably seated beside me, Doctor Markham hurried inside and we left *Knypersley Farm* without ceremony. As we drew away, it became evident that Mr. Gresley was also loath to leave Doctor Markham.

'Poor Jos,' he reflected, 'He'll be all alone again now. He's such a tortured soul. Stuck there in a loveless marriage, with a wife who belittles him, and denies him the warm embrace of his beloved children, yet he remains kind and loving to everyone. You have made him very happy, Hannah. He is extremely fond of you. You have taken a genuine interest in his children and always ensured that they were well cared for and loved. Jos has cherished your gentle spirit and the sweetness of your smile. Yes, you have been greatly admired and will be terribly missed.'

I said nothing by way of reply but clutched little William's flowers to my heart and prayed my torment would soon be at an end.

6

SASSAFRAS VALLEY

"A romantic little spot at the head of a secluded ravine immediately at the foot of the great northern buttress of Mt. Wellington."

The Hobarton Town Courier, 22nd December, 1837.

Heading west out of Hobarton, Mr. Gresley eventually turned our cart onto a narrow, unmade track full of muddy potholes, giant ferns, and low, overhanging branches. Progress was slow as we jolted along, gradually making our way up the mountainside. The first signs of life were in Providence Valley, an area named thus by an English settler whose life was spared following an attack by a gun-wielding bushranger. I prayed our lives would be similarly spared were we ever to meet with such a fate. This valley led to another known as Kangaroo Bottom, where several fine homes and orchards were springing up. This was our last stop before we reached Mr. Gresley's new home in the Sassafras Valley.

A simple post and rail fence signalled the boundary of the property, and we travelled along it until the dense bushland finally came to an end. Mr. Gresley jumped down to open the wooden gate, whilst I, taking up the reins, urged the horse forward. I caught my first glimpse of the delightful little cottage, nestled amongst the trees at the end of the drive, smoke rising gently from its chimney. The backdrop to this homely scene was the spectacular Mt. Wellington whose craggy tops and rugged scenery were still awe-inspiring for me.

Mr. Gresley's humble home stood in stark contrast to that of his sister, but setting foot upon its dark, wide floorboards for the first time, I loved it far more. To the left of the entrance lay the sitting room, Mr. Gresley's study to the right. From this study my master could enter his own private quarters, whilst a second bedroom lay directly across the hallway. Taking up the full width of the house, the kitchen and dining area lay at the end of the hallway. It may have been petite but the house was warm, cosy, and inviting. Eagerly ushered from its snugness, I was conveyed to a small, unpaved courtyard where I discovered a well for drawing water, a block for chopping wood, and some chickens already establishing their home. Keeping these chickens safely confined were newly-erected picket fences, one on either end of the courtyard. A stone barn completed the square, and Mr. Gresley took me inside to show me the large stones reserved for paving the sodden ground. The barn also contained various rooms for storage as well as a place for laundry, whilst at the far end there were stalls for Mr. Gresley's horse and the draught horse that was expected within days.

Re-entering the courtyard, Mr. Gresley pointed out a small wooden hut being erected much further down the slope, which once finished would accommodate the assignment of three male convicts he had requested to help clear and plant the land.

'Would you like to see your room?' Mr. Gresley enquired.

Nodding eagerly, I followed as he led me to the room opposite his own. Pushing the door open, he stood aside for me to enter. A sunbeam lit the room and all was bright and fresh. Walking towards the double doors that opened onto the verandah, I raised my eyes to behold my beloved mountain. Lost in a reverie, I have no notion of how long I was thus captivated before Mr. Gresley gently placed his hand upon my shoulder and spoke my name.

'I will leave you to settle in. On the bed you'll find a dress that I bought for you. There will be no uniforms here. A further bolt of cloth will arrive with the other fabrics, and you may use it to fashion another. Please join me in the study when you're ready.'

Having thanked him sincerely for his generosity, I made haste to ready myself, mindful not to keep my new master waiting. I joined Mr. Gresley in his study a short time later. He looked up and smiled upon my entry.

'Now, I suppose that you would like to know your duties,' he suggested. 'First and foremost, in my household, we live on an equal footing. In the eyes of the world, you may be bound to me as a servant, but I have no intention of treating you thus or adhering to any other expectations of the wretched penal system. I have brought you here primarily as a companion. All I ask is that you cook my meals and when I look up, I will always see that beautiful face of yours smiling back at me.'

'It will give me great pleasure to care for you and your home,' I assured him. 'I promise to work hard so that you never have cause to regret bringing me here.'

'Come,' he said, jumping to his feet. 'I want to show you something that I think will give you great pleasure.'

Whilst I tried to keep pace as he strode into the bushland, my steps were admittedly tentative. Rustling leaves both overhead and underfoot quickly alerted me that we were not alone, and I was curious as to what tiny creatures now shared my home. As I dwelt upon those who lurked just beyond my gaze, I was suddenly startled by the sound of gunfire reverberating through the silence. I came to an abrupt halt.

'It's alright,' Mr. Gresley assured me. 'It's just the cracking of the eucalypt bark.'

Since arriving in this colony, I had grown to love these magnificent trees, some of whom grew one hundred metres into the sky. The snow-like whiteness of the eucalyptus bark was only made all the more enticing by the amazingly fresh and soothing scent that emanated from the olive-green leaves. Whether it be against the blueness of a summer sky or the blackness of a storm-laden one, theirs was a beauty that never failed to enchant.

Our destination was eventually reached and Mr. Gresley was not mistaken about the delight it would bring me. Worthy of anyone's praise, it was a river whose waters were sourced from Mt. Wellington's pure mountain streams, and as it coursed past us, its volume proved that the dry summer months had scarcely made an impact. My soul was awakened. This river was wild and untameable, mirroring my own heart and spirit far better than the tranquil Mimram of my youth. Beside this river, I found peace and contented happiness again. Taking a seat beneath a shady eucalypt upon its banks, I knew it would not be long before I could plunge my feet into its icy depths. Today, however, I was content to sit beside Mr. Gresley, in a place which would eventually become 'our' place, and listen as he unveiled the name of his new home.

'I wanted to honour Mt. Wellington but feared the mundane with names like *Wellington Park*. I therefore consulted with Jos who has Welsh heritage, and he supplied the perfect one, *Brynmawr*. It means big hill.'

'*Brynmawr*,' I repeated with a smile. 'Yes, most appropriate indeed.'

Mr. Gresley then took my hand.

'Hannah,' he said. 'Your new life has now begun. You must promise me that here in my home, you will forget all the troubles of your past, and live for the joys of the present.'

I eagerly agreed, knowing full well that here at *Brynmawr*, my life would now be full of joy.

I will not soon forget the first night in this new home. A wind had sprung up upon our arrival, increasing across the afternoon. As I lay in the darkness, it continued to howl through the trees and rattle the doors to my room. Soon driving rain was also pummelling these doors, and thunder shook the house to its foundations. Here upon our mountain, we were clearly more susceptible to the wrath of the gods. Terrible imaginings took hold of my mind and I feared all kinds of dreadful happenings. Whilst infamous bushrangers such as Brady and Howe who once ruled the colony were no more, the effects of the economic depression over recent years and increased convict escapes had caused a resurgence in bushranging. I heard stories of the shocking things bushrangers did to people stranded alone in isolated places. There were tales of murder and cannibalism, of women being kidnapped and subjected to unmentionable horrors. I was petrified. Suddenly, the doors onto the verandah blew open, and I sat bolt upright in bed. Too scared to leave the safety of my blankets, I allowed the doors to bang freely in the wind. Drawn by the disturbance, Mr. Gresley soon came to my rescue, and calmly secured the wayward doors.

'I'm just across the hallway,' he assured me. 'One call and I'll be with you.'

Soothed by his gentle face and comforting words, my eyelids eventually grew heavy and sleep descended.

The following morning all was calm. Indeed, one might have been forgiven for dismissing the previous night's tempest as just a bad dream. Awoken by the pale rays of the morning sun filtering through the trees, I rose and gazed upon the surrounding bushland. The mists were rising and a group of pademelons grazed upon the green slopes close by. Yes, it was certain, *Brynmawr* was a little piece of paradise. Yet, whilst it appeared at its loveliest that morning, the fact remained that its isolation terrified me. Mr. Gresley was certainly not ignorant of the dangerous and brutal men who roamed this island and fully understood my fears.

To make our home as safe as possible became Mr. Gresley's primary focus. Visiting a property a little further north whose owner had gone to amazing lengths to secure it from attacks by bushrangers and natives, he returned home with an inventory of measures to adopt. Admittedly, architectural differences between *Brynmawr* and the other property created obstacles, but Mr. Gresley did his best to compensate for them. With new cedar shutters installed on all household doors and windows, I could withdraw to bed each evening confident in the knowledge that they were bolted securely. The height of the courtyard fences was also increased, each one topped off by six-inch spikes for extra security. With these and other changes, my slumbers became peaceful once more, our animals, stores, and lives secured against would-be assailants.

It was, of course, a sad truth that the native population no longer posed the same threat as when our northern neighbour settled. Disease and warfare had taken their toll and wiped out many of these innocent people whose land was stolen by white settlers. The last remnants of their tribes were shipped to neighbouring islands over ten years before we settled at *Brynmawr*, their demise continuing. Mr. Gresley showed me the remains of what was obviously a large group inhabiting the land around our home. By the river, there were traces of their camp, whilst stone artefacts and middens could be found along the banks. The country must have been very beautiful then and I envied them the tranquillity in which they lived. I can only guess at the despair the white invasion brought to these people. The invaders seized their land, stripped it of vegetation, and built houses, paying no heed to sacred areas and ancestral links. Had I not been favourably educated by Mr. Gresley whose benevolent nature and humanistic approach to life recognized the dignity these people deserved as humans, I suppose I would have been just as ignorant as those I now rebuked.

For the first week of our residency, we were compelled to make do with the bare necessities. The ship bringing many of the household items including rugs, wallpaper, and various fabrics, had been delayed and Mr. Gresley rejoiced when he eventually saw the requested dray making its way slowly along the mountain path towards us. Charley, Arthur, and the Irishman Regan arrived a few days later. They were Mr. Gresley's requested assignment of labourers, who, in coming from the convict ranks, joined the vast majority of shepherds, stockmen, ploughmen, and domestic servants in Van Diemen's Land. There was little doubt about how important this free labour was to the development and functioning of this country. Mr. Gresley did not enquire as to their crimes, preferring to take each one as he found them. With great faith in the goodness of human nature, he believed that if the men were treated well, given proper meals and warm lodgings, he would see the best of them. By assuring me the government would not have sent anyone dangerous, Mr. Gresley did his best to allay my fears and reservations.

The men's first task was to help with the establishment of the garden, pastures, and outbuildings. The land around *Brynmawr* had never been ploughed and there were problems across every acre of the rocky, root-laden ground. Van Diemen's Land possessed a strong seasonal cycle and the extremes in weather could have done much to dampen enthusiasm, yet Mr. Gresley's labourers proved themselves to be robust and willing workers. I watched with joy as the fences were eventually finished and the livestock began arriving. Astride the horse I was given, I was on hand to help muster the cattle and drive them out to their pastures. Mr. Gresley's cattle were born and bred in these mountains and the management of them was unforgiving if taken on by a novice.

For his advice and assistance, Mr. Gresley was in the debt of our nearest neighbour, Mr. Cuthbertson. A free immigrant from Wiltshire, Mr. Cuthbertson was the perfect example of how people could prosper in this new land. Born into a life of service back in England, he was and would have remained a footman all his life. Since arriving in Van Diemen's Land ten years ago, however, he had worked hard and saved enough money to buy himself the farm upon which he now resided. He understood how to run mountain cattle and whilst keeping a few close for milk and beef, he encouraged Mr. Gresley to set the remainder free to roam until winter.

Mr. Cuthbertson's wife gave me hope for my own prosperous future. Having likewise received a seven-year sentence for larceny, she arrived in Hobarton nine years ago. Serving her sentence, she then married Mr. Cuthbertson and was now blessed with two small children. She lived free and contented on the mountain, her life far better than any she could have expected back home in England. I knew that with hard work I too could have a bright future, and whilst the men worked tough, laborious hours in the fields, I set about conquering the household chores.

First and foremost, my master and his three workers needed to be nutritionally fed. In my dear little kitchen, I brought to life the cherished flavours of home once more. The preserves, breads, pies, and soups my mother, Granny Ravens, and generations of Hertford-shire women before them had baked were now served in my mountain home to a very appreciative and complimentary master. There was al-ways plenty of fresh fish from the crystal-clear river, and Mr. Gresley ensured our fresh meat supply, trading with our neighbours for pota-toes and other vegetables.

Under instruction from Mrs. Cuthbertson, I soon learnt that roast wallaby compared favourably to hare and that parrot pie was not un-like one made from pigeon. In the courtyard behind the house, a cow was always at my disposal. From her milk, I made butter, cream, and cheese, some for our consumption, the rest for Mr. Gresley to sell in town. The most rewarding and enjoyable part of my work, however, remained the moments when I found myself working with the exotic fabrics placed at my disposal to make the interior of the house as com-fortable and attractive as possible. From wool moreens, silks, velvets and fine cottons, I fashioned a variety of soft furnishings, and call-ing upon the bobbin lace-making technique taught to me as a child by Granny Ravens, I created lace for doilies, tablecloths, and pillow covers. Taking a fine silk thread, I monogrammed Mr. Gresley's pillow covers with his initials, a finishing touch he found most gratifying.

Fascinated by his ongoing study of the unique flora and fauna of this country, Mr. Gresley began creating an extraordinary garden full of wonder. Whilst his sister decreed the formal gardens at *Knypersley* should reflect those of her childhood with their poplars, pines, and roses, Mr. Gresley wanted to encourage the native animals and plants, clearing only enough land to build his home, plant its small garden and graze his livestock. His garden therefore proved to be an amazing coupling of both native and introduced species, and amongst the spectacular eucalypts, silver wattles, and waratahs, grew specimen orchids and ferns, a trellised vinery, and traditional English flowers and fruit trees. As the interior neared completion, I was able to aide Mr. Gresley in the creation of this spectacular garden. Toiling alongside my master, I felt at peace and took pride in my work. Knowing that my contribution was helping to bring his dream to fruition warmed my heart.

Spending so much of his time out of doors, Mr. Gresley was extremely conscious of the damaging effects of the Australian sun, so different was it from our homeland. One could find themselves burnt in this land even when the sun was not shining. Two hats were therefore always hung at the front door. Mine was a wide-brimmed, straw bonnet with a lovely red and white check ribbon, whilst Mr. Gresley's trusty companion was a uniquely Australian creation dubbed a cabbage tree hat. When first worn during his time at *Knypersley*, it was stark by way of its newness. Wearing it constantly around his beloved Sassafras fields, however, soon saw its cream colour darken, its brim crack, and its black band fade to grey.

I worked hard in those days, but I was no stranger to hard work. In truth, I was better suited to those days of toil than Mr. Gresley. Before arriving in Van Diemen's Land, his idea of hard work had been numerous hours poring over a text in the library at Cambridge. He dreamed, and dreamed large, but the labour needed to bring these dreams to fruition was quite foreign to him. He did not renege from it, however, and as the plans for his new life began to take shape, he was driven to continue all the more.

On warm evenings, I was invited to join Mr. Gresley on the verandah. Sharing a jug of homemade lemonade, my master would often paint or read whilst I always had some form of needlework to entertain me. Even on the hottest nights, it remained cool and tranquil on our verandah, and as we gazed upon the valley and meandering river below, Mt. Wellington kept an ever-protective watch over us. As dusk descended, the pademelons would emerge and begin their evening graze whilst other creatures began turning their thoughts to home. Amongst them was a dear little wombat that in time adopted me as his companion and followed me as would a loyal dog. On the mainland, wombats were supposedly nocturnal, but here they fed at any time of the day. Like many of the other creatures on this island, they developed their own unique behaviours. Mr. Gresley was amused by the little chap who befriended me and declared his name should be Markham.

'Markham?' I queried. 'That's a funny name for a wombat.'

'He reminds me of Jos,' Mr. Gresley said. 'Gently plodding his way through life.'

The way Mr. Gresley spoke about Doctor Markham displeased me. If the good doctor was a plodder, as his brother-in-law declared, it was life that made him so. He could not follow his heart or be as adventurous as Mr. Gresley. No, Doctor Markham had a wife and children to consider. If he failed, five others would suffer. His wife demanded much and gave little. The family's money was earned through Doctor Markham's hard work, for he owned no family fortune. Having been granted a substantial dowry, Mrs. Markham guarded it closely, spending it on trinkets for her own amusement. Admittedly, small amounts were occasionally spent indulging her children though only when expectations demanded and praise would follow.

Her brother had been similarly blessed with an inheritance and the freedom to do with it as he pleased. No one else would suffer if his endeavours failed. Dr. Markham plodded honourably and I hoped he continued to do so with the same good grace and abundance of respect always afforded him for many years to come. He was my champion, the man to whom I owed my very existence, and my gratitude and esteem would see me defend him to the hilt. Mr. Gresley noted my displeasure and the discussion ceased, though little Markham retained his name.

When I was a child, time was measured by the seasons and we cared little for the months that ticked by. London shook those days of splendour from my mind. There I counted every hour and minute of the fifty-two harsh weeks that made a year so much longer than ever before. At *Brynmawr,* order was restored and my heart became light as the days now ran as they had at *Sweep's Farm.* The seasons returned to prominence and the wretched counting of hours that never seemed to pass now vanished from my life.

Sunday was always a day of rest, or as much as it could be on a bush property. Having completed the necessary tasks to ensure our animals and crops continued to thrive, Mr. Gresley would take the hours between noon and three in the afternoon for relaxation and the reception of visitors. With my Sunday best neatly worn, I would join him as requested in the sitting room. Then one Sunday, shortly after my twentieth birthday, he rose and beckoned for me to follow him to the study.

'It's time that we taught you to read and write,' he declared.

Martha had taught me to write my name and Michael showed me what little he could. Now, guided by my master, letters became words, and words became sentences. Once I scrawled my alphabet in the dirt with a stick. Now I wrote on quality parchment with a fine nib like a true lady. My inability to write had been like having my right to speak denied. I wanted to say so much, being unable to record it was something near torture. I eagerly anticipated the day when my parchment would be filled with stories of my hopes and dreams, and memories of loved ones far away across the sea, of the ones who left this world before me, and of those whom I had met during my new life here in Van Diemen's Land.

Following my lesson, our exploration of the incredible world around us continued and we collected, sketched, and preserved specimens, including my prized discovery of an intact devil skeleton. It was during one of these rambles that I looked up from my foraging to see someone approaching. The sun's glare initially hindered recognition, but once shielded, my eyes soon beheld the handsome form of Doctor Markham, and my heart skipped a beat.

'How's my dear Hannah?'

To hear his voice and see his warm smile again was truly wonderful.

'I have brought you a present,' he said, handing me a small sapling. 'It's a cutting taken from one of my wife's rose bushes. I know that you always loved sitting amongst them and thought that you might like one of your own.'

He could not have brought me a more welcome present. Inviting him inside, I saw him comfortably settled, before preparing some refreshments. Once supplied with tea and sandwiches, he remarked on the quality of the new furnishings, admiring my needlework and lacemaking skills. Joined by Mr. Gresley, the three of us chatted freely, our beautiful mountain home attracting much praise. Doctor Markham's presence warmed my heart and the afternoon was one of pure delight, spent as it was in the company of these two extraordinary men.

The following morning, Mr. Gresley placed Charley in charge of the clearing operations, and he set off with the other two labourers unsupervised for the first time. Remaining behind, I discovered Mr. Gresley shortly afterward, hard at work outside my bedroom window. Opening the doors onto the verandah, I walked out to be greeted by his ever-beaming smile. The rose gifted by Doctor Markham sat on the edge of the verandah. Mr. Gresley pointed at it.

'Now that you have a rose, we should begin your rose garden. I thought that here, outside your bedroom, would be the perfect place.'

I stepped from the verandah onto the newly turned soil.

'There in the middle,' he said, 'I'll add a bird bath for you as well.'

I was so excessively happy and there weren't enough ways to show my gratitude. Beginning to bud from the moment its root began burrowing into the mountain's rich soil, the blooms in that first season were so prolific that I excitedly anticipated what future years would bring. The delicate scent from my perfumed paradise never failed to delight me as it floated by on the gentle mountain breeze. With a vase of the exotic blooms placed in the hallway, the continuance of the enchantment inside was assured.

A few weeks later Doctor Markham came again, this time honouring the promise made upon our last parting to bring his precious children with him. Free from their mother's prohibiting eye, the Markham children arrived with their father mid-morning. Their sweet voices, raised in excitement, met my ears as the carriage approached. The horses had barely drawn to a halt before the door swung open and the children flew out, almost falling over each other to be the first in my arms. Poor little Ava was the last to reach me, but she held me the longest and tightest. It was her tiny hand I lovingly clasped as I led them inside for a morning tea comprised of things sure to delight.

It gave me the greatest pleasure to watch as they clambered up on their chairs, kneeling to access their share of the muffins, jellies, and jam turnovers. Their mother would have been horrified to see her children's serious lack of decorum though I cared nought for it. All I wanted was to see my little cherubs happy, and the brightness of their faces, so animated and alive, and the joy written on their father's face as he watched them, told me that I had succeeded. When they finished, Mr. Gresley took his nieces and nephew to see the animals, leaving me alone with their father for the first time. I thanked him for bringing the children.

'They, like me, yearn for you constantly,' he declared, his eyes so very sorrowful.

As I stepped forward to offer comfort, we were interrupted by the sudden reappearance of Mr. Gresley.

'The children are happily feeding the chickens. Hannah, could you please keep an eye on them? I'd like to take Jos to meet my workers and show him the progress we're making in the lower paddocks?'

Acknowledging it would be of great interest to see how Mr. Gresley's plans were taking shape, Doctor Markham accompanied my master whilst I joined the doctor's beloved children. They were made of his flesh and blood and I was blessed to possess their unconditional love and to love them in return. I knew that I must be content having this much, for despite being trapped in a loveless marriage, their father's unqualified love would never be mine. This blissful afternoon together, spent in perfect peace and warm affection, proved to be our last for the season as the inhospitable days of winter would soon descend upon us. As I waved them farewell that day, I mourned that it would be such a long parting.

The howling winds at *Brynmawr* were like none that I had ever experienced. Wailing through our mountain home, their destruction was ever present. With the onset of winter, these winds eventually brought snow flurries that would dance about my head as I worked in the yard. In the distance I could see Mr. Gresley and his workers looking skyward, wondering, like me, how many days, how many hours, were left before we were snowbound and cut off from the rest of the world. In many ways, I looked forward to this isolation and the extra time it would afford me to spend with Mr. Gresley.

The snows of winter in this country were not dissimilar to those I so loved in my homeland. True, no foxes frolicked here, but the native birds still fossicked and the pademelons, their coats covered in snow, reached up to nibble the bottom leaves off trees and shrubs. Markham the Wombat continued his daily pilgrimage to my door, though if truth be told, he didn't trundle very far, having adopted the little bed I made for him on our verandah. Like so many of the other animals on this island, he had developed a thicker coat of fur than his counterparts on the mainland, for the temperatures here could drop below freezing. Despite his thick fur, he appreciated the wicker basket and old blanket I supplied.

Winter was a difficult time for my little animal friends upon the mountain. With heavy snow covering the ground, there were often meagre pickings for them, and I did what I perhaps ought not to in leaving food out for them. Mr. Gresley did likewise for those of us under his care, ensuring we did not suffer through our isolation. Warming fires were kept burning within the main rooms of the house, and the men were permitted to build bonfires around which we would gather of an evening. Each man was issued with a dram of whiskey or mug of cider to warm them, a grateful Regan toasting the master with 'Sláinte', whilst Charlie and Arthur drank to his health.

Gradually the frozen world of winter melted away and the delights of Spring burst forth. Spring on this island brought wild and unpredictable weather, especially for those of us who lived upon the mountain. The rain and sun, however, yielded fresh shoots of green, and I watched on with joy as my tiny animal friends began to feed once more. As the weather became warmer, we found ourselves blessed by the occasional sighting of a tiny furry creature known in these parts as a platypus, a strange creature, with webbed feet and a duck-like bill. Three times heavier than its mainland cousins and with no large predator to worry them, the platypus wandered freely on our island, sunning themselves upon the rocks of the river, and walking overland between streams. Mr. Gresley was much enamoured by the platypus and made a study of the creature during his time at the Linnean Society in London.

He explained that despite its docile appearance, the male of the species possesses poisonous spurs behind its back legs which can inflict a great deal of pain upon anyone so wounded. Mr. Gresley met a man in London who had been attacked by one in New South Wales with such ferocity that it would not release its spurs until killed. The man suffered agonizing inflammation of his entire arm, and it took nine weeks for him to recover the full use of his hand. Far more enchanting for me was the mother devil who proudly introduced us to her four young offspring during early September.

Devils make the ghastliest sound, and upon arrival on this island, their screams of otherworldly proportions were the bane of my existence. I slowly become accustomed to their eerie squeals and sinister growls, yet, although I studied their skeletons and examined sketches, they were an elusive creature and I was yet to see one in the wild. It therefore gave me great pleasure to hear Mr. Gresley confirm shortly after our arrival, that a devil had built her den under our verandah. During August, it became clear that there were young afoot, and their mother went about her work, busily topping up her den to keep her bairns warm. And then came the momentous day that mother and bairns crept from beneath the verandah for the first time. Two were more adventurous than their siblings and set out to explore their new surrounds, whilst their mother kept an ever-watchful eye, her other two bairns riding piggyback along with her.

I was besotted by these adorable creatures, and highly amused when their mother would run off with a carcass she brought home, the four wee bairns chasing after her, round and round. The young ones used to feed, hissing and growling at each other, ripping their food and crunching the leftover bones, the devil bite being the most powerful in the natural world. Their feeding habits and the violence of their shrieks certainly belie the true beauty of this animal. Over time, a mutual respect developed between the mother devil and me, and whilst I never approached her or her bairns, she would sometimes sun herself close beside me, allowing me to gently stroke her head. Her adventurous young as yet knew no fear of humans, and as I sat sketching them upon the front steps, they would tumble and play at my feet, tugging and hiding under my skirt. Their mother seemed to understand that I posed no threat.

As Christmas approached that year, there was every expectation that Mr. Gresley would be spending the main days with his sister and her family at *Knypersley*. I thought of his sister and the preparations that would be underway at a frenetic pace. Things would be utter chaos, everyone would be overtaxed, stressed, and angry. At *Brynmawr*, the true peace and joy of the season reigned, and wishing to make some Christmas memories of his own, Mr. Gresley chose to remain with us. On the blessed day itself, he joined Charley, Arthur, Regan, and me, to partake of the feast I prepared with love.

Earlier in the day, he aided me in the kitchen, peeling and chopping vegetables with all the enthusiasm of a child. At dinner, he carved the meat and filled the men's glasses as he would his closest friends. He shared everything with us, begrudging us nothing. He joined in our laughter, sang, and danced as though we were his equals. For the four of us granted the honour of working for him, he left us constantly amazed by his capacity to love and care. As the sun descended upon Christmas Day, I joined him as usual upon the verandah. Pointing to a rectangular parcel wrapped in brown paper, he suggested I may find joy in opening it. Hurrying to where my gift stood leaning against the wall, I went down upon my knees and carefully drew the paper aside. It revealed a painting, so exquisitely executed, that it simply took my breath away.

'What do you think of my amateur brush strokes?'

Turning to him, words escaped me, and I prayed that my beaming smile did enough to express the effect the artwork had upon me.

'You're pleased with it then?' he queried. 'I thought that it would look well hanging in your room.'

'It's one of the most precious gifts I have ever received,' I managed to stammer, before turning my eyes back to the alluring beauty of Mt. Wellington that I now held lovingly in my hands. Noticing the figure of a woman standing upon a grassy bank in the foreground, I looked closer. Caught by the wind, her dress blew wildly, her long, brown unfastened hair falling freely to her waist. The bonnet she held casually in her hand bore a red and white check ribbon. I looked up at Mr. Gresley.

'It's you,' he assured me with a smile. 'As I painted, I was thinking only of you. You allowed me to paint like never before.'

Hung at the foot of my bed, the painting joined Doctor Markham's blue ribbon to become my two most cherished possessions. It was the first thing my eyes saw in the morning and the last thing they saw at night. Now, with Mr. Gresley's masterpiece watching over me, surely my slumbers would always be peaceful. And they were, until one terrible night when I was awoken by the sound of approaching horses. Springing from bed, I hastened to the door from whence I could hear Mr. Gresley speaking with two others. The heavy tread of boots soon echoed through the hallway, quickly followed by the clinking of glasses and raucous laughter. Suddenly, the handle upon which my hand rested turned and I jumped back as the door slowly opened. With a finger to his lips, Mr. Gresley stood hesitantly in the doorway.

'Remain here,' he whispered. 'Hide under the bed until I come for you.'

'But ...' I began, though my attempted protest fell on deaf ears as Mr. Gresley vanished.

It was not in my nature to cower in fear, and I certainly wasn't going to hide when Mr. Gresley was in trouble. No, I would be there by his side to share in whatever fate may come. Slipping a dress over my nightgown, I sneaked across the hall to Mr. Gresley's room. I knew he kept a small handgun in his bedside drawer, and after secreting it away in the pocket of my skirt, I headed to the drawing room. It did not take long for the intruders to spy me.

'Well now, things are certainly looking up!' exclaimed the younger of the pair.

A horrified Mr. Gresley spun round, his face upon seeing me said everything.

'Ah,' he said, in a desperate struggle to maintain composure. 'Here's my wife.'

Coming to my side, the look in his eyes and the firmness with which he grasped my hand, told me at once of his gratitude. We would face this peril together. I looked at the ruffians as they happily guzzled Mr. Gresley's finest whiskey. Both possessing bushy beards, they wore open-neck shirts and roughly sewn jackets. Despite being indoors, their heads were crowned with hats so beaten, that I seriously questioned their usefulness. One attempted to mask his hat's condition with a wide, bright red ribbon, the frayed ends of which dangled beside his right cheek. The other had taken no such pains, nor did he attempted to conceal the fact that much of his attire appeared to be the remnants of prison garb.

'Hannah, darling,' Mr. Gresley said, 'would you please prepare some dinner for our guests? Perhaps some of your lovely soup, and a little bread. They'll be staying in the barn tonight.'

I hesitated, but Mr. Gresley gave me an encouraging nod, assuring me all would be well. With complete faith in my master, I scurried to the kitchen and began preparing the requested meal. Quickly joining me, the men sat at the table and I lay the meal before them. They ate like the swine they were, consuming the food with rapidity and oaf-like manners. I watched them eat in silence, my hand firmly grasping the gun in my pocket. With the meal complete, the one in prison clothes belched loudly and stretched. Wiping some juice from his chin with his sleeve, he pushed his chair back noisily on the slate floor and came to my side.

'You haven't said anything all night.'

I maintained my silence. He came closer, his foul breath, hot upon my cheek.

'Do I scare you?' he asked with a kind of self-satisfied triumph.

'No!' I snapped, holding my head higher, my hand tightening upon the gun.

He noticed the motion.

'What have you got hidden away there?' he asked, rummaging through the folds of my skirt.

'Get away from me!' I cried, trying to escape his grasp, but his quest continued with increased momentum.

'That's enough now, Luke. Leave her alone,' cautioned his companion.

'I beg you to listen to your friend,' pleaded Mr. Gresley. 'I'll give you anything, but please don't hurt her.'

The fiend looked at me.

'Don't worry, my beauty. I won't hurt you.'

Repulsed, a shiver ran through me. Sheer terror gave rise to a secret, inner courage, and with renewed strength I finally extracted myself from his arms. Drawing the gun from my pocket, I aimed it at his heart with a steady hand.

'Come now, little lady,' he said, 'You shouldn't play with dangerous things.'

As he reached out to disarm me, I cocked the hammer and raised the pistol to the level of his eyes. He backed away.

'I didn't mean no harm,' he whimpered, clearly in fear of his life. 'I'm sorry, missus. You're such a pretty thing. I just wanted a little fun. Please missus, spare me.'

His stony-faced companion turned to Mr. Gresley.

'We didn't come here to cause no trouble. Luke done wrong threatening her.'

Mr. Gresley nodded.

'We are all tired and our nerves are frayed. Perhaps we should retire. The barn, gentlemen, is at your disposal.'

Our 'guests' acknowledged their gratitude and withdrew, leaving Mr. Gresley and I alone. Finally lowering the gun, I looked at my master and he smiled.

'You were extremely brave tonight, Hannah. I couldn't have held a pistol so steady.'

Despite his praise, knowing that two law evaders slept only metres away made it impossible for me to force a smile. Mr. Gresley instantly read my hesitation.

'If you are agreeable, I would prefer it if we slept in the same room tonight,' he declared. 'My mind would be easier knowing that you were near and safe.'

His suggestion could not have been more welcome, for I feared sleeping alone that night, more than any other in my life. Tucking me safely back under the blankets, he lay beside me, head to toe, his own bedding keeping him warm. Rising early the following morning, Mr. Gresley gathered some supplies for the intruders, before seeing them on their way. Watching on, I marvelled at the depth of human kindness that ran through his veins. It was something I was blessed to benefit from daily, and later that evening as the sun slipped below the horizon, I would again be grateful for Mr. Gresley's compassion. With the dreaded bedtime hour approaching, my fear and loathing of being left alone returned.

'Would you like me to stay with you again?' Mr. Gresley asked as I loitered hesitantly beside the fireplace's dying embers.

Accepting his proposal with gratitude, I lay resting my head upon his outstretched arm, his handsome face smiling comfortingly at me from the pillow next to mine. I was instantly soothed by his tenderness and felt the same peace as when I was a child in Mam's arms. On the third night, there was no question, no hesitation, only a mutual, unspoken consent that we would withdraw together. That night Mr. Gresley, now my Sam, joined me in the cosy warmth under the blankets for the first time. Kissing me on the forehead, he bid me goodnight and we fell asleep together in complete happiness. From that day onwards, I was never left to sleep alone and tormented again.

Whilst I knew that Granny Ravens would never be convinced what I did was justified, that I slept alongside my master was of little consequence in this country. Things were so different here compared to England. It was not uncommon for women and men separated from husbands and wives back home to live together without being united in marriage. Others did so after having the government reject their application to marry. My banishment broke my heart, but somehow, I learnt to keep living. My pain eased and some happiness was restored when I met Doctor Markham. Horror had now driven me into Sam's arms and I found my true love there.

Having never thought of Sam in any other capacity than as a gentle, kind, and protective master, I quickly realized how willingly blind I once was concerning my actual affections. When he held me tightly in his arms, I realized I had loved him since that first night when he was kind to me at his sister's party. We walked in the fields, gazed upon Mt. Wellington, and spoke as equals. Yes, I loved him all that time, but my burning affection for Doctor Markham had veiled my true feelings. Nowadays, as I lay beside my Sam, watched him at work in the fields, and cooked his dinner each evening, I found joy in musing upon just how much he really meant to me. Yes, we had vastly different upbringings but we both possessed the same untameable heart that longed for liberty and adventure. We were ousted as the "black sheep" of our respective families, but we had found each other. Together in our mountain home, our affection grew daily, united as we were by our shared love of the freedom it gave us, the amazing flora that we studied, and the beautiful animals with whom we lived in harmony

'You know,' he said, holding me in his arms. 'My sister is far more responsible for our union than she will ever know. When you failed to deny her accusation that she caught you watching me with admiration, it gave me hope. I allowed myself to dream that one day I might call you my own.'

'It's true, I did watch you,' I admitted honestly. 'I admired your zest for life and ability to dream. In happier times, I used to dream too.'

'Promise me that you will again,' he said, squeezing me tighter. 'Dream with me about our future together, about the wonderful life we can have in this bright new land.'

That I was ever as young and naïve as I was during those blessed, happy days is now hard to believe. The excessive heat of summer soon passed and I appreciated the slightly cooler days and nights. I reached my twenty-first birthday and with Sam by my side, I could forget every trouble, every sorrow, that had ever come my way. Indeed, I was so far removed from reality in this paradise, I even failed to notice critical changes in my own body. It was April and by now I was carrying Sam's child but it took a chance visit from the much-practiced eyes of Doctor Markham for it to be noted. I was declared to be at least three months along in my journey.

Devastation doesn't even come close to the feelings that consumed me upon discovering my condition. Mam had warned me, but I failed to heed her advice. I emphatically declared I would never end up like my friend, Doritie Bell, unmarried and pregnant in the workhouse. Now I faced the same prospect far away from family, indeed, on the opposite side of the world. I wanted Mam by my side, but that could never be and I had no one except Sam and Doctor Markham to support and comfort me. I was terrified and the burden of my sin weighed heavily on me. The thought of bringing a child into the world outside of wedlock previously never crossed my mind. To say that I started to cry the moment I was informed about my condition would be an understatement. I sobbed and sobbed so desperately that neither Sam nor Doctor Markham knew how best to console me.

'Hannah, my darling, don't cry so,' Sam pleaded, holding me in his arms.

Doctor Markham came forward with a sip of brandy and he offered it for medicinal purposes.

'I have done such wrong,' I cried. 'My parents would be ashamed. They raised me to be so much better.'

'It's a beautiful thing to carry a little life within you,' Doctor Markham counselled. 'You're going to be a mother, Hannah. It should be celebrated. A new life will signal a new beginning for you.'

I placed my hand upon the belly where I knew Sam's and my child now grew. It was all at once a strange and exhilarating feeling to know I was carrying a bairn.

'Now look after her well, Sam,' Doctor Markham warned, as he made ready to depart. 'Having a baby is a dangerous thing at the best of times, let alone out here in the bush.'

Doctor Markham took my hand in his own.

'You're an intelligent girl, Hannah, and I'm not going to hide anything from you.'

I assured him that I knew the risk, after all, I saw my own mother die in childbirth. The good doctor nodded grimly.

'I only wish I could have saved you from this misfortune,' he declared. 'But what's done is done.'

Sam escorted Doctor Markham to his carriage, neither man aware that I could hear their somewhat terse exchange.

'How could you do such a thing?' Doctor Markham scolded. 'You know the precarious predicament this puts Hannah in. The Government could take her away. I've seen it before. It's the factory for girls like her. Surely, you don't want to see Hannah suffer like that?'

'Of course not,' Sam replied angrily. 'She will *never* be left to that fate. I would die rather than see her suffer. We will be wed as soon as possible.'

'Well, just make sure that you are or I'll take Hannah back with me.'

Without another word, Doctor Markham departed, and from that day onwards, it was sad to note a distinct cooling in the friendship between the two men. I was the cause and I felt immensely sorry for it. With Doctor Markham's departure, Sam returned to me, and we stared at one another in stunned silence. He eventually found his voice.

'A baby,' he said gently, his face glowing with happiness.

I nodded and he came forward to embrace me, assuring me of his undying love and thankfulness that our union had been so blessed.

The shock over my expected bairn did not soon dissipate, though as time progressed, I regretted less my mistake. I became proud of my expanding waistline, and when I caressed my little bump, I could not help but feel elated by my condition. Sam was an exceptionally proud father-to-be and was enthralled by each new phase.

'Hannah, you know this child of ours will be counted as special, one amongst the first generation of children born in this new nation. It will be born free and have a life full of opportunity, so much better than either of ours have been.'

It warmed my heart to know that I would be the mother of such a child and as we sat holding hands under our eucalypt a few days later,

Sam made my joy complete with his much-anticipated proposal of marriage. He requested one of the Gresley family rings for me, but his sister refused him, and it disappointed him to bestow one he believed inferior. I assured him I would cherish it all the more because it was of his own choosing. Despite Sam being a free and upright citizen of the colony, my status as a convict meant we needed to obtain permission from the Lieutenant-Governor before we could marry. Sam wrote instantly to this gentleman, seeking at the same time a ticket-of-leave for me from the Colonial Secretary. If granted, I would be guaranteed a certain amount of freedom from the penal system. It took but five days for the request to be approved. Sam brought me the announcement in the *Hobarton Guardian*, and sitting beside me, read each word slowly so that I could follow.

'His Excellency the Lieutenant-Governor has been pleased to grant a ticket-of-leave to the under mentioned convicts ...'

From the list of names printed, I was able to recognize my own and that of my ship. Pointing to them, I read,

'Fearn, Hannah, *Garland Grove*.'

Sam put his arm around my shoulders and pulled me close.

'That's it, my darling,' he said.

My life was more wonderful than I ever could have imagined. My beloved was a man of integrity, highly educated, and an enthusiast of the arts. He was gentle and loving and treated me as his queen. Together we made a home full of tranquillity, beauty, and love. Within me grew the seed of our love, its daily expansion bringing me contentment and fulfilment like never before. My ticket-of-leave meant I could remain with him without fearing the authorities and forced removal from *Brynmawr* any longer. I awaited but the approval for our marriage to make my world complete. It came as I reached my fifth month. By this time, I had done some substantial growing, and was proud of my new figure that could no longer be hidden amidst the folds of my skirts. I also began to feel my bairn moving within me for the first time. With the little tumbles and flutters increasing my joy, Sam came to me.

'Sweetheart, I think it is time we applied to have our banns read.'

It was to Bishop Nixon, the incumbent at St. David's Cathedral in Hobarton, that we therefore made application. The good bishop and his wife Anna arrived in Hobarton aboard the *Duke of Roxburgh*, the same ship that brought my beloved to this country. Sam and the Nixon family struck up a friendship over their mutual delight in and skill for producing landscape sketches and watercolours.

Visiting his residence in Upper Davey Street, we discovered a gentleman with deep-set, piercing black eyes, seated behind a large mahogany desk. Upon sighting Sam, he rose and extended a well-manicured, gentleman's hand, and they shook hands heartily. Sam explained the purpose of our visit. Bishop Nixon ran his fingers through the thick curls that crowned his head and smiled. As he filled out the required paperwork, he acknowledged how pleased he was that Sam had found love and the life he had always dreamed of was finally coming to fruition. When completed, Sam signed the paperwork, before the bishop handed me the pen. Pointing to a section under Sam's signature, he said,

'You can make your mark here, Hannah. A simple X will do.'

I stood holding the pen, cut to the very core by the bishop's words. He meant no harm, but the presumption that I was illiterate stung me. I put so much endeavour into bettering myself, learning to read and write, and yet, it seemed to have been in vain. I could not let it be so. I refused to let the convict stain mark me forever. I therefore held my head high, clutched the pen tightly, and reaching down wrote, in big, bold letters, just as Martha once taught me,

Hannah Jane Fearn.

The bishop nodded.

'A very fine hand,' he assured me. 'I'm sorry to have presumed.'

A brief smile of acknowledgement was my only reply. Our banns would be read over three successive Sundays, our marriage to take place on the twentieth day of September, Sam's twenty-fifth birthday.

The rumour of an expected niece or nephew saw Mrs. Markham finally venture to our mountain home for the first time the following month. Having complained bitterly about the journey and the roads she had been forced to endure, she observed my six-month bloom and sighed,

'So, it's true. I hoped it was a mistake.'

She turned angrily upon Sam.

'I cannot pretend to approve of this, Samuel. You're a Gresley and have certain expectations to live up to. What *were* you thinking? Heaven knows what Father would say.'

Mrs. Markham, who until now had been pacing the floor, fell into a nearby armchair and held her head. Sam spoke softly.

'We have been over all of this before, Sophia. You know that I'm in love with Hannah,' he declared.

His sister scoffed and waving her hand angrily at me growled,

'The evidence of *that* is clear enough. Why? *Why?* She's a convicted thief!'

'The only thing she's stolen is my heart,' Sam replied as sternly as he knew how.

'Well, she's been exceptionally clever, whatever she is, conceiving a child so that you're bound to marry her.'

She then turned to me.

'I am willing to give you a handsome settlement, Hannah, if you agree to release my brother from this obligation. I will find a good family to take in your child, and you can make a fresh start, perhaps somewhere up north.'

Utterly flabbergasted, I was speechless. Sam was not.

'Hannah and I will be married in St. David's Cathedral on my birthday,' he declared with resolve. 'It would give us great pleasure if you were both there.'

Serious disquiet consumed Mrs. Markham's face. Her husband thankfully read her mood superbly, and as she opened her mouth for another tirade, he quickly intervened.

'I think that's quite enough now, Sophia. It's best to stop before you say something in anger that you will later regret.'

Mrs. Markham did not argue, but merely frowned at her husband and turned her face away.

'You were always very fond of Hannah,' Sam reminded her. 'You were certainly angry enough with me when I took her away from you.'

'That's right,' Doctor Markham chimed in. 'You once said that you would not trust our children with anyone else.'

'That's all true,' Mrs. Markham acknowledged, having calmed down slightly. 'She was a very good servant. That is very different, though, to carrying my brother's child. A Gresley child.'

'Well, things are as they are,' Doctor Markham counselled. 'Your brother is engaged to the woman he loves, and in three months they will be blessed with a child. Isn't your brother's happiness more important than anything? You love him, or you wouldn't be so worried about him. Can't you trust that he has chosen wisely and will be extremely happy?'

Mrs. Markham did not answer her husband immediately but instead rose to her feet and began buttoning her travelling jacket.

'Perhaps you're right, Josiah,' she finally agreed. 'I apologize if I have offended you Samuel and wish you joy.'

I wondered how she could be so cold towards her brother. She then turned to me.

'I will do as my husband bids and be thankful my brother is so happy. I cannot deny that it is you who has brought him this joy, and for that I thank you. I wish you many blessings as you carry your child, and pray that you will be delivered safely.'

I thanked her for her words and she turned to her husband.

'Come, Josiah, we are leaving.'

Sam sprung forward and tried to stop his sister's departure.

'Sophia, don't leave in such haste, you haven't even taken refreshments.'

'I am quite determined, Samuel. I am leaving.'

'Perhaps I should examine Hannah whilst I'm here,' Doctor Markham suggested.

'She doesn't need you, Josiah. She's the picture of health, practically glowing. Little wonder why the two of you can't keep your eyes off her.'

'But ...' Doctor Markham began by way of protest, only to have his arm viciously snatched up by his wife.

'For heaven's sake, Josiah,' she growled in angry undertones. 'The girl is six months pregnant with my brother's child. Surely even you would have to admit the impossibility of having her now.'

Mrs. Markham turned and stormed from the room, heading immediately to her carriage. His wife's sudden departure caught Doctor Markham by surprise. Quickly grabbing both my hands in his own, he looked deeply into my eyes and spoke with great meaning,

'Take good care of yourself, Hannah. If ever you need anything, know that I'm always there for you.'

With this, he bent forward and kissed me on the cheek, before turning to shake hands with Sam. A further impatient call from his wife saw Doctor Markham hurry from the room and their carriage pulled away as quickly as it had arrived. Sadly, unbeknownst to any of us at the time, Sam and his sister would never meet again.

Without doubt, I loved the isolation of my mountain home and as the snows of winter returned and began to take hold, I loved it all the more. Once again cut off from the rest of the world, there could be no intrusions into my paradise. I remained in my own little world of happiness with dearest Sam – loved, protected, and blessed. Each evening, I would take my place by the fire, Sam seated at my feet, his head resting upon my knee. One evening as I tenderly ran my fingers through the soft waves of his hair, I sighed contentedly and wished that everything would stay exactly as it was at that moment.

'If things always remained the same,' Sam replied with a tender smile, 'Then there would be no more precious moments to make into memories.'

I immediately retracted my wish for I wanted a lifetime full of special moments to hold as cherished memories. Over the winter months, Sam's outdoor activities were curtailed somewhat and he turned his attention to things that needed completing around the house. Each afternoon he would disappear into the barn on some secret business with Charley, assuring me that everything would be revealed in time.

Concerned for my wellbeing and that of my unborn bairn, Doctor Markham braved the treacherous journey to *Brynmawr* well before the rains and snow of Winter had fully left us. Forever indebted to him for such tender ministering, I spoke of my discomfort and fatigue but assured him of my contentment. Having confirmed that my bairn and I were progressing well, he made an uncharacteristic hasty retreat.

He called again a week later though not to see me, but rather to speak of a great injustice just befallen him. Summoned before the Government's Medical Board he received an official warning over his generosity to convicts and the increased rations that he supplied to those to whom he ministered. Being reprimanded for his kindness and compassion all but broke the poor man and my heart ached for him. It was so unjust. Consumed by a fit of hysteria upon hearing the news, Mrs. Markham was apparently of the firm belief she would never be able to show her face in Hobarton again, all prospects for social advancement in the colony having evaporated. Naturally, she placed the blame squarely at her husband's feet. As Doctor Markham left us that afternoon, he took me into his arms and held me tightly.

'God bless you, my dear one,' he said. 'I may not be able to visit you again for a while, at least not until this controversy settles down. Promise me though, that when your time comes, you will send for me. You know I would do anything for you. No matter what the obstacle, I will find a way to get here.'

That evening, saddened by Doctor Markham's news, Sam placed his arm around my shoulders and we took a revitalizing walk to our river. The melting snows of winter had combined with recent flood waters and the river was high, its water raging through the gorge with great strength and rapidity. Sam and I stood in awe at its might. In their weakened state, trees whose roots had been loosened by the recent drought were no match for the power of the storms. Many toppled, and those that had grown riverside were quickly claimed by the torrent. We watched as the waters now transported them downstream as though feathers.

Eventually, Spring dawned and the blooms that came with it were matched by my own blossoming. There were now just nineteen more sleeps until my beloved and I were finally united as husband and wife, and our love increased each day. Our bairn's arrival in just over a month's time would make our lives complete. Winter's demise also saw the cessation of Sam and Charley's secret work in the barn and the proud father-to-be presented me with a finely-crafted wooden crib. Made with his own hands under the guidance of Charley, he was so proud to bestow it, whilst I was deeply touched by the amount of love and effort applied to his work. I adored it just as I did the man who so tenderly made it. We placed it at the foot of our bed in preparation for our bairn, and I was impatient to see our child lying there.

The morning of September the fifteenth dawned more brightly than any we had seen for many months past. Sam rose early and readied himself for a journey to Hobarton where he would meet with Bishop Nixon to discuss final wedding preparations. Remaining at *Brynmawr*, I spent the morning putting the finishing touches to my wedding attire; an elegant pale-yellow brocade dress that would be paired with a pretty new bonnet that Sam gave me to mark the occasion. Mid-morning Sam returned home in high spirits. Whilst in Hobarton he collected some newly arrived post from England, a letter from his mother leaving him truly exhilarated.

'Such great news, Hannah,' he declared, waving the letter at me as he hurriedly readied himself to join the men in the lower paddocks. 'Great news indeed. I will tell you all this evening.'

Kissing me, he thrust the letter into his coat pocket and was gone. I watched him as he headed down the path toward the lower paddocks. His tread was so light that it seemed like he floated. Whatever news that blessed letter contained, it had brought him great joy and I waited eagerly for its contents to be revealed to me that evening. Therefore, as the shadows began to lengthen and the golden glory of the afternoon sun reflected upon the eucalypt leaves, I wandered outside to my garden in anticipation of Sam's return. Spring brought great beauty to our cherished sanctuary and as I waited, I took delight in examining the fresh, new growth; the buds that would soon burst forth in a sea of vibrant colour.

Looking up from the blooms that I was tending, I suddenly caught sight of Charley running towards me. The anguish upon his face said everything. I looked beyond him to see the other three men coming slowly towards us, two of the men carrying the third. Charley hurried on and gently took hold of my shoulders, trying to turn me towards the house.

'Come inside now, Hannah,' he whispered.

'Sam,' I cried, instinctively knowing that my beloved was in peril. Pulling away from Charley, I tried to run but he quickly blocked me.

'He'll be here soon enough,' he said.

They carried Sam inside and laid him on the bed, Arthur quickly dispatched to fetch Doctor Markham. It had been one of the mighty eucalypts that Sam and I loved so well. Its roots, like those we watched being tossed upon the river a few weeks earlier, had been undermined by the effects of drought and without warning the tree crashed to the ground, crushing Sam beneath it. My beloved drifted in and out of consciousness as we awaited Doctor Markham, every minute seeming like an hour. Sam gently squeezed my hand in his own as I sat beside him, and encouraged me not to grieve. It was so typical that in his hour of need, Sam's only thought was of me.

Arthur eventually returned having failed in his mission to find Doctor Markham. The hard-hearted doctor who came in his place took but a fleeting glance at my dear boy before declaring that there was nothing to be done.

'How can you be so certain when you have hardly examined him?' Charley questioned angrily.

'It's a crush injury. In these cases, we just have to pray that it's quick. I have given him some pain relief.'

'Where is Doctor Markham?' I queried. 'I sent for Doctor Markham.'

'Doctor Markham was unavailable,' was his blunt reply.

'Doctor Markham is Mr. Gresley's brother-in-law,' Charley assured him. 'He would want to be here.'

The doctor shrugged and brushed past me.

'Is it a matter of money?' I called after him. 'We have enough to pay for any service necessary.'

'No amount of money can save him now,' the doctor called callously over his shoulder as he exited, leaving us alone to watch over darling Sam as he slowly succumbed to his injuries.

'Don't cry, my love,' my brave one said, trying to soothe me with a smile. 'My only regret is that I am leaving you and our child. Live on Hannah and raise our little one knowing that I am watching over you. You will be taken care of.'

Sam then asked me to look in his top pocket for the letter he received that morning.

'It's from my mother, she knows all. Everything will be alright. Take the letter to Jos and he will help you.'

Stretching his arm out as he did each night, he asked that I lie with him as usual. Acceding to his request, I climbed up beside him, kissed him, and lay my head upon his shoulder. Sam closed his arm around me, his other hand caressing the child within me. In that way, we fell asleep, Sam, to an eternal sleep. My beloved was just five days shy of his twenty-fifth birthday; five days short of becoming my husband. Sometime during the night, someone placed a blanket over me and I awoke cozy and warm, still snuggled up to my Sam. It did not take me long, however, to realize this would be the last time I was to have that privilege.

I had thought we were at the beginning of our life together. We were making such grand plans, had so many expectations, and happiness in abundance. Now suddenly all that was at an end. I had never felt so empty. Until this time, even in my darkest days, I always found hope. So many times, I clawed my way back from adversity, and found something to spur me on, but this new abyss was one from which I could never rise. My world was completely shattered. In my beautifully rounded belly, our bairn had never leaped with such vigour. In less than a month this tiny orphaned bairn would join me in this harsh, cruel world. I would do everything in my power to shield it from life's destructive forces.

We buried Sam beside the river, underneath the eucalypt that we always called our own. It was not consecrated ground, but I believed that God knew where Sam lay and would take his soul into Heaven. Upon his grave I lay a bouquet of the wildflowers he loved, the bright red of early blooming waratahs, perfectly offset by the soft white fluffiness of snow gums. Charley fashioned a wooden cross bearing my beloved's name, and I laid a single red rose from my garden at its foot. I remained by Sam's grave until it was almost dark, my three companions keeping a silent vigil before accompanying me home. That night I lay in my cold, empty bed, my eyes lingering upon Sam's cherished painting until the candle burnt itself out. Sam's great dream, all that he hoped for and worked so hard towards, was now at a sudden and tragic end. Its demise would accompany my own and it would be a long time before my life witnessed any brightness or hope again.

7

CASCADES

Colonial Times, 10th March, 1840

Those of us who were left at *Brynmawr* were under no illusion, and we fully understood that the doctor who visited would have reported Sam's imminent death to the authorities. We would be marked down as unsupervised lawbreakers, eager to use their newly found freedom to become fugitives from justice. We did not know how long it would take, but we knew the authorities would soon come for us. During our anxious wait, it was a great testament to the way Sam cared for his workers that no one tried to run. At first, Regan encouraged me to take flight in order to escape the fate he knew awaited me. Admittedly, I was sorely tempted, for I knew my doom was the wretched misery of Cascades, a place where my bairn would be fiendishly snatched from my arms and neither of us could ever hope to see the outside world again. But then I thought of Sam. He had been the most righteous person I ever knew, and I owed it to his memory and to his unborn child to be the same. I would remain at the homestead and await my fate bravely. To abscond now was unthinkable. When I stayed, the others stayed by my side.

'Don't worry, we will not leave you alone,' Charley assured me. 'Mr. Gresley treated us as equals, never speaking down to us or mistreating us. He loved you very much and we will stay with you and look after you for as long as we are able. It's our way of repaying him.'

I was extremely grateful for the kind protection of these friends and I assured them that once Doctor Markham learnt of our predicament, he would be certain to help us. It was with this belief firmly planted in my mind, that when the authorities finally came, I could greet them with composure.

'Mr. Gresley's brother-in-law, Doctor Josiah Markham, was my previous master. I'm sure that he would like to know what has happened here and would be willing to help us.'

'We know about Doctor Markham,' one of the men declared as he seized my arm tightly. 'He won't be helping you. He and his family are currently on their way home to England.'

The words hit me like a bolt of lightning striking deep at my heart.

'That can't be true!' I cried, as my legs all but gave way beneath me. 'He wouldn't have left without saying goodbye. You must be mistaken.'

'No mistake,' the man replied gruffly as he jerked me forward. 'I have a magistrate's warrant to remove you, and that's exactly what I'll do.'

I cried out in grief-stricken agony.

'Take care!' exclaimed Charley as he rushed forward and pulled me away from the man who held me. 'Her bairn is due any day.'

Charley aided me to a nearby chair and consoled me whilst Arthur and Regan stood guard. My dear protectors would not allow the authorities to remove me until they were certain my health and that of my bairn were not in danger. My mind was numb. I had been abandoned by Doctor Markham, the one man apart from Sam who I trusted would always be there for me. Why had he deserted me? Following Sam's death, I hid my beautiful engagement ring and some important documents, including the letter from Sam's mother, behind a loose brick in the barn. Whilst tempted to hide Doctor Markham's blue ribbon similarly, I was unwilling to part with the cherished gift and therefore sewed it into the lining of my petticoat in an effort to keep it near. I thought of it now, and of my promise to send it to Doctor Markham if I was ever in need. What was the use of that now? He was on a ship sailing for England, and I would never see him again.

Eventually, the authorities became impatient and tried reclaiming my arm. Charley angrily brushed their hands away.

'I will help the lady,' he declared.

His strength, height, and determination made the men hesitant to overpower him and they allowed him to see me safely into the cart. Just before I took my seat, Charley embraced me.

'God bless you, sweetest Hannah,' he said. 'Take care of yourself.'

With this, he stepped back from the cart and was dragged away. The enduring image of my last moments at *Brynmawr* was seeing Charley, dear, gentle, kind Charley, being placed in irons and taken away at gunpoint. With a crack of the whip, the horse lurched forward and the cart stirred into motion. My beloved home where I had been so loved and happy, soon faded into the distance.

Traversing the country roads as we headed towards Hobarton, the driver took little care to dodge the ruts and I desperately clasped hold of the cart to stop myself from being thrown off the thin wooden seat. As I expected, our destination was the terrifying hell known as Cascades. Nestled in a cold, damp valley below Mt. Wellington, it was devoid of sunlight for around a quarter of the year and completely lacking in warmth of any kind. Looking down from the cart, I saw a small rivulet flowing quickly along opposite the front gates. The waters of this rivulet once flowed fresh and clean from their source upon Mt. Wellington but by the time they flooded the into the yards of Cascades they were a contaminated, foul mess which we were forced to trudge through. Moisture seeped into the buildings which were generally damp underfoot, and in the air, disease waited impatiently for its next victim. Sadly, Mt. Wellington would no longer be a thing of wonder for me, but a menace, blocking out the sun's warming rays, casting shadows over the already frozen inmates.

Cascades had once been home to a whiskey distillery but now was unfit to house anything, let alone human beings. But we were not looked upon as human, only as the undesirable filth that England banished from its shores. As I walked from Cascades on that magical day with Doctor Markham, I had sworn I would never return to this dismal place. Now, there was no other option. Despite having gained my ticket-of-leave, I was still at the mercy of the authorities. When I was discovered to be with child and having no possible means of support, my ticket was quickly withdrawn. Once more, I was a prisoner. This time, however, I was sentenced to six months hard labour and assigned to the Crime Class, a large yellow C placed on my back, sleeve, and petticoat. Having a child within the convict system was against the rules and I was to be severely punished for breaking them. I was labelled and treated as a common prostitute.

Removed from the cart, I was relieved to be at the end of a very painful journey. Feeling quite unwell, I took a few tentative steps, barely able to place one foot in front of the other. Stumbling, I fell to my knees. There was no Charley to help me this time, only a stranger who ordered me to stand up. I remained where I fall. With tears, I pleaded,

'I cannot.'

The woman repeated her command, and when I again failed to obey, the driver of the cart was summoned to drag me inside. Taken to a dimly lit room, the woman stood before me. A pile of clothing lay ready for issuing to newcomers. She pointed to the washtub in the corner and I washed before returning to the table.

'Put these on,' she barked, handing me a bundle of clothing.

Now dressed as all the other inmates, I wore a gown and jacket fashioned from rough, dark brown serge, an apron, and white mop cap. That serge was tough and durable I had no doubt, which is why it made wonderful coats and military uniforms. It was not, however, for daily attire and it rubbed and itched my skin, threatening to drive me insane.

My fellow inmates thought of me as yet another victim of the assignment system. They believed that my bairn had been forced upon me by a wicked master who later abandoned me, sending me back here as punishment for his own misdeeds. I let them think what they wanted; it was easier than explaining, indeed, easier than speaking at all. I heard in later years that terrible trauma can leave one mute, and that's exactly what happened to me. It was not of the conscious kind, for I certainly didn't plan to remain in a world of silence. Silence, however, overpowered me and it became easier than finding the heart and energy to speak. Silence masked my broken heart and shattered dreams. I had once been consumed by a sense of optimism and adventure. But what was there now? Nothing.

As my hard labour sentence would not begin until my bairn was weaned, and in consideration of my advanced condition, I was initially put to work carding wool. Seated on low, backless benches our work began at six o'clock in the morning, and we would work a full two hours before a breakfast of bread and gruel was served. Following prayers, we would labour on until sunset with only a brief dinner break at noon where soup now replaced the gruel. Each evening, I would return to my dormitory completely exhausted. The skin on my hands was red and irritated, and my back ached excessively. In the tiny bed that was mine, I could find no comfort and I tossed and turned in pain most nights. When I felt my bairn move within me, there was no longer any joy. With its father dead and its mother having been returned to prison, my poor bairn would have been better off not being expected at all.

Alone in this friendless world, there was no one to calm and reassure me, no one to love me or even care whether I lived or died. Some nights I succeeded in imagining that I was once again being held in Sam's arms, and the memory of his warm embrace and tender kisses, lulled me to sleep. On these occasions, my slumbers would be peaceful, though only horror awaited me in the morning.

Some of the women incarcerated alongside me were habitual lawbreakers and were no sooner assigned a new master than they were returned and declared unsuitable. Others were returned, like me, expecting a child. For some, motherhood had been a choice, for others it had been forced upon them. Both suffered the same cruel fate whilst the men involved escaped without any kind of penitence. It was as though we miraculously conjured our pregnancies all by ourselves. Whilst those of us who had fallen pregnant were serving one of the harsher sentences of six months, the women who worked beside us were sentenced to varying lengths of imprisonment.

Being absent without leave earned one woman a three-month sentence whilst using obscene language saw another sentenced for a month. Several women were serving a six-week term for behaving disrespectfully, an offence clearly concocted to crush any sign of spirit amongst these women. My fellow inmates continued to breach the rules of silence with songs and friendly chatter, the sharing of jokes, and the mocking of the authorities who kept us prisoner. An amazing number had some kind of record for drunkenness, which in all honesty wasn't so surprising, for it was no mystery that alcohol could momentarily deaden the pain and blot out past lives, injustices, and adversity.

Three days into my residency, there dawned the day that once would have brought such utter delight, but now could only be dreaded: the twentieth of September. Waking from another fitful sleep, my mind was tortured by the knowledge that this should have been my wedding day. Increasing our joy would have been the celebration of Sam's twenty-fifth birthday. I would have woken in his arms, before rising to prepare for our nuptials. At two o'clock, we would have stood before Bishop Nixon and become man and wife. My thoughts were simply too much to bear. They paralysed me and I could not rise from bed. When the matron could not rouse me, the doctor was summoned, the medic dumbfounded by my state, awake though exhibiting every sign of being comatose. Allowed a rare day of rest, I was left alone in my moribund state, my mind persecuted by agonizing thoughts of what could have been. The following morning, I once more joined the throng, crawling from bed in my somnambulist-like state, completing my assigned tasks without thought or care.

With one day dragging slowly into the next, my mundane existence at Cascades never changed. Then one day in early October as I rose following another long, tedious morning's work, I realized that my bairn was on its way. I had felt the first pangs of my child's arrival earlier that morning but being my first bairn, was unsure of what was happening and I kept working. Summoning the matron, the task mistress aided me to the room where I was first received into this establishment.

Loaded into a cart, I was conveyed across the rivulet and about half a mile down the road to Dynnyrne House. It was a place where over the past four years, the women of Cascades gave birth, a change affected by the high infant mortality rate at Cascades. Accompanied by the matron on the short but tedious journey, she sat brooding over the fact that the task mistress failed in her duty to send me before the onset of labour. Once deposited at Dynnyrne, I was taken to a room where my labour would progress, my terror at what was to come allayed by no one. Pacing the floor, desperate to find some relief, I began to think that I, like a woman the previous week, would not make it through.

Eventually, after what seemed an eternity, a contraction like no other seized me. Clasping hold of the bed, my agonized cry brought the midwife to my side for the first time. A fellow convict, she was a rough, ignorant woman, who was accompanied by another in the same mould. I was quickly lifted onto the bed and directed to push down with each new pain that gripped me. I tried, but nothing seemed to be happening.

'I can't do it!' I cried.

'Your baby will come,' the midwife declared. 'But you must do what you are told.'

It wasn't easy. I was petrified and alone. In my agony, I cried out for Sam. Things would have been so different if my beloved was by my side. The midwife and her companion remained as hard and distant as ever. Eventually, I knew that I could hold my bairn back no longer. With another scream, the bairn's head appeared, and the midwife gave me a cold, unfeeling word of encouragement. With one final push, my bairn entered the world, and I fell back exhausted. At first, the bairn failed to cry and I feared the worst. A slap from the midwife broke the silence, and my bairn, a tiny little girl, proved she was born with very powerful lungs. With the bairn placed into my arms to feed and comfort, I was quickly left alone again.

The room was far too dark to see my bairn's face properly, though I could feel soft lips, a little button nose, and most importantly ten fingers and toes. I kissed her forehead and whispered her name, the name that Sam and I had chosen for our daughter, Kezia. All at once, it was the happiest and saddest day of my life. As I held the tiny miracle that had grown within me, I listened to her soft breathing. I had never felt love like it. She was the one thing that was truly mine, yet in this abhorrent world, I knew she could be stolen from me at any moment. My grief cut deep into my heart.

In the early light of dawn, the following morning, I gazed upon Kezia's beautiful face for the first time. She was so tiny and lay there in her father's image, with porcelain-like skin, rosy cheeks, and dark blue eyes. In those first moments spent together, I instinctively knew I would do anything to protect this precious bairn. I would give my life for her. Midway through the morning, we were moved to one of the twenty rooms that masqueraded as nurseries and they came to take particulars for my bairn's registration. Kezia Jane Fearn was registered as being born on 5th of October, 1846, daughter of Hannah Fearn. It broke my heart to see that under 'Rank', my bairn was recorded as 'Convict's Child.'

I thought it a great tragedy that Kezia was born inside prison walls. She was an innocent child, the daughter of an upright and virtuous man. Sam dreamed of such wonderful things for her. She was going to have everything the world could offer. I thought of the beautiful little crib her father made with such love. It was where she should be resting and yet she lay in a hot, overcrowded dormitory where no effort was made to clean or keep order. This was *my* punishment, the shame that *I* had to endure for having a child out of wedlock. That Kezia was forced to endure the same devastated me. My spirit was completely crushed, the tears streamed from my eyes untapped, and gone was my resolve to hide my pain from the world. Whilst I had carried Kezia, she was protected from all danger. Now I could protect her no more. My poor, fatherless child was vulnerable to two great evils: the menacing authorities and their brutal regime, as well as the diseases that ran rampant in this netherworld, and I was powerless to stop either one.

Soon after our arrival in the nursery, I was deeply distressed by the death of a young boy who could not have been more than four months old. Having not progressed far past his birth weight, he had been a sickly, weak child. The mother who watched over him was herself a gaunt shadow of former times. She brought two other children with her from England, though both were seized and taken to the orphan school upon arrival. The poor woman had hoped that this bairn, despite being forced upon her by a violent master, would partly fill the terrible void left by the loss of the others. When the child became ill, the doctor was summoned, though he passed it off as teething and no relief was given to the poor child or his grieving mother. The boy's health declined further over the coming days until he could barely suckle from his mother, the little he did manage to sup passing straight through him. The poor boy was in a highly fevered state by the time the doctor condescended to return and lay limply in his mother's arms. He died still clutched in her arms later that night. His would not be the last death, his mother would not be the last to grieve.

The findings of the inquest into his death produced little change. Life at its best was fleeting but for those doomed to this wretched place, where the children slept four to a cot with no distinction made between the healthy and the ailing, it was a precious commodity indeed. Cradling Kezia in my arms just a little tighter each day, I cherished the beauty of her innocence, the sweetness of her nature, and the little flutters of pride and joy that consumed me each time I was with her. Sadly though, I was under no misapprehension, for I knew that Kezia's and my time together would be short. I would bide in this dismal place just long enough for Kezia to be weaned and then she would be taken from me, and I would be returned to Cascades to serve my six months hard labour.

During the intervening months, I was put to work mending garments belonging to the free settlers of the colony. To me it was easy work, and though repetitive, it allowed me time to muse upon happier memories. I thought about Sam, Doctor Markham and the children, as well as my own cherished family. I wondered whether any of them ever spared me a thought, and I longed to tell them about the exquisite little life to whom I had given birth. Each evening, I would return to my precious cherub and gaze upon her gorgeous features, amazed that I could have produced something so perfect. My most cherished dream remained that one day Kezia and I would escape this cruel system and live forever free from misery and fear. I was determined to keep out of trouble for I could nil afford to have my punishment extended, and eagerly counted the days until my sentence expired.

Best laid plans, however, can be destroyed in a matter of seconds. It happened shortly after my twenty-second birthday when the matron appeared menacingly before me as I fed Kezia. Now, mine had never been a passionate nature, indeed I was rather mild mannered, but when I realized that she had come to take Kezia from me, I turned into something resembling a wild cat. Surely even the gentlest mother would fight to the death to protect her child, and I was no exception. There was no sign of warmth or compassion as the matron delivered her much practised speech assuring me that Kezia would receive the benefit of a good Christian education in morals and faith, something that I, as a fallen woman, was unable to give her. No matter how hard I tried I could see nothing Christian about snatching a child from its mother.

As the matron reached down to relieve me of my bairn, I kicked and screamed, clasping Kezia tighter than ever. Suddenly there seemed to be hands coming from everywhere to steal my child and I slapped all the invaders away. Sweet Kezia began to cry as I fought for possession, tears which turned to screams as she was finally ripped from my arms. Though so young, she seemed to sense that bad was about to befall both of us. Her screams were matched by my own as I pleaded for her release, desperately chasing after her, wildly grabbing at her clothing. I fell, cutting my knees, but I felt nothing as I fought on. Lashing out at everyone who tried to stop me, I inadvertently managed to slap the matron across the face. She stood before me in all her terrifying fury, looking to her co-conspirators for assistance. The superintendent and doctor rushed forward and with superior strength swiftly subdued me. Kezia was taken away and I listened until I could hear her cries no longer.

When the rescue of my child was no longer a possibility, I was released from the vice-like grip that detained me and I collapsed to my knees, barely able to breathe through my sobbing. Kezia was the last thing Sam had given me, my only possession, my only love. That I would never see her again, never hold her close, was something far too terrible to contemplate but I knew that in all likelihood this was my exact fate. Raised into the superintendent's arms, I was carried to the awaiting carriage and conveyed back to Cascades. Kezia stayed behind in the nursery to be cared for by a series of other nursing mothers, before being sent to the Queen's Orphan School upon turning three. Without me Kezia would probably not live beyond her first birthday let alone reach her third. If by some miracle she did make it through, it would be for no purpose other than to be sent out into domestic service.

My inability to save my child from this fate all but suffocated me, and barely conscious, the journey back to Cascades was undertaken in near delirium. For my efforts, I was sentenced to seven day's solitary confinement and, as they slammed the door in my face, life flowed back into my body. I charged like a mad thing towards the door, pummelling upon it until my hands bled. I screamed and screamed, though I knew no one could hear. Emotion eventually overwhelmed me and I collapsed, exhausted, onto the cold stone floor.

From the moment we women entered this penal system, we not only lost our freedom but also our right to be treated with any sort of dignity. Those in charge treated us as if we were not human. I shared my fellow inmates' anger that, as women, we were exiled more readily for minor crimes than our male counterparts. We were being used as pawns in the government's attempt to even up the gender imbalance and bring a civilizing influence to the colony. Why then punish us further, and far more brutally, by stealing our children? For a woman to have carried a child, brought it into the world, and nurtured it for several months, it was something worse than death to have the motherly bonds shattered by a monstrously cruel system.

I have no idea of how long I lay there; it may have been hours; it may have been days. In a cell where I was barely able to stand upright, I was issued with a bucket for use as a privy and another for water. One did not live in this world of pitch darkness, they existed, and as I lay on the damp floor, my nostrils were relentlessly filled with the offensive odour of decay. Once a day, a tiny hatch would open and a small ration of bread would be hurriedly passed through. The worst thing, however, was the silence. At home, I used to relish silence and the accompanying time for contemplation. Sitting beside the bubbling Mimram, I would be one with the birds and gentle breeze. With the sun's warming rays upon my face, I would close my eyes and float away with my dreams. This silence was different. It was vicious. Eating away at your thoughts, consuming you with choking self-doubt. I little wondered why soon after my initial arrival in Cascades, a young woman who was only my age, succumbed to the crushing oppression of the solitary cells and died before being released.

When my seven-day sentence expired, the guards came to release me. It was then that I discovered the true toll of my imprisonment and the torments surrounding it, for I was unable to stand or even move when approached. One of the guards asked the other whether they thought me dead. To discover the truth, the second guard entered and nudged me with his foot. When I gave a tiny moan, they were satisfied that I lived, and dragging me to my feet, pulled me from the cell. Taken to the infirmary, they did little to relieve the fever that consumed me and I lay there insensible to the world. In my more lucid moments, I knew that I must live for my daughter, yet in those early days of my illness, I failed to remember that I even had a child.

Eventually, my strong constitution pulled me through, and as I lay recovering, I reflected upon my predicament. I had dared to fight back against the terrible cruelty, and the authorities here in the valley of death thought that by starving me and trying to rob me of my faculties, they would reform me. Through this ruthless treatment, they believed my spirit would be broken, and I would forget the child I had once clasped close to my breast. Well, they would not break me. They could mete out any punishment they wanted, but I would never give up the fight for Kezia, the purest and sweetest thing in my life. The poor, innocent lamb had no father here on earth, so I needed to find the strength and courage of both father and mother. I must dedicate myself to saving my daughter from the ferocity of this evil system, for I owed it to my darling Sam to raise our child in the best possible manner, knowing her father watched over her with love and pride from Heaven.

As soon as I was able to stand without buckling at the knees, my six months hard labour began, and I was put to work at the wooden wash tubs that ran the full length of the long factory walls. Issued with a wooden bucket, my day began as I drew the first of at least sixteen buckets of water from the well. With arms barely strong enough to carry these exceptionally heavy buckets, my work was slow and tedious. Once readied, the tubs were filled with our assigned loads. I always dreaded the huge pile of sheets that was generally my lot. My hands were often numb, the harshness of the soap drying and splitting the skin. Once I would have bemoaned the loss of my pretty, soft hands. Now I worked without care for my hands or anything else.

When the rivulet flooded in front of the factory, my toil was completed in ankle-deep ice-cold water. Submersed in this rancid overflow, the one thing that surpassed the agony of my frozen feet was the chill that gnawed away at my bones. My woollen dress failed to protect me, for it soaked up every drop of water that spilled from the tub and was never completely dry. Nighttime was the worst, however, for despite the monotony of the days, whilst there was a task to perform and a timeframe in which to complete it, there was no time to dwell. Sadly, my unfriendly bed offered no such distraction, and each evening as I lay in the darkness, thoughts of my darling bairn would consume my mind. Without her by my side, utter desolation consumed me. They told me upon my recovery that I was one of the lucky ones, but I often believed those who succumbed were luckier. Whilst they would be doomed to eternity in a pauper's grave, un-mourned and forgotten, they would at least be free of Cascades and the cruel system that banished people there.

Burying my head in the putrid, rock-hard pillow, I would try to mask my nocturnal tears, though they were soon discovered. Having arrived in the colony as a free settler, an older lady whose bed adjoined mine, found herself banished to Cascades for six weeks hard labour after falling upon hard times. Hearing my distress, she tried her best to comfort me.

'Let her go, love. It's for the best. She'd only have been a burden. What could you possibly have done with a young child in tow? People aren't going to help the likes of us. Your child will be better off, believe me.'

Although a kind attempt to console me, the woman's words only succeeded in heightening my sorrow. Kezia could never be a burden to me, and there was no way in Heaven she would be better off incarcerated at the orphan school than with her mother.

At the end of my six months, the matron informed me my new 'home' would be at a coaching inn, a terrifying forty miles from Hobarton. At once, I found the courage to attempt another rescue of my beloved bairn. Appealing to her better nature as a mother who had suffered the loss of six of her own children, I pleaded for Kezia to accompany me. The answer, bluntly told, was no. Yet, I could not leave her to the fate I knew awaited her. In desperation, I enquired whether a nice family might be found to adopt her. Although I knew that adoption would see my heart broken irreparably, if it meant she would be safe, I would somehow find the strength to bear it. The matron, however, refused to listen to my pleas. Until I was in the position to take the child and support her myself, she would remain imprisoned within the walls of that wretched institution. Until that blessed time, thoughts of her would give me a reason to live, a reason to fight on. I only prayed that in the meantime she would be strong and healthy enough to survive the disease and malnutrition that would be part of her daily existence. I hoped that somehow, she would still feel my love despite the distance between us, and that the magical mother daughter bond would sustain her until I returned to reclaim her.

8

BOAR'S HEAD INN

"The Colony's Best Coaching Inn."
Seamus Moloney, 1847

Hearing I was to be assigned to a coaching inn brought to mind memories of the *White Hart* in Welwyn. I was pleased I would be working in such a lively and constantly changing environment. Preferring not to be assigned to another family, for unfavourable comparison with my beloved Markhams was inevitable, I also prayed there were no young children at the inn. Watching them happily at play whilst my Kezia was held hostage at Dynnyrne, would only break my heart anew.

The stableman who was sent to collect me was more creature than man. Short, bald, and terribly pockmarked, his grin was that of a simpleton, and I was horrified to see the black gums and missing teeth it displayed. He said very little, the few words he muttered being barely distinguishable such was the thickness of his Irish accent. An assigned convict himself, he was clearly determined to treat me with disdain and hatred, for I was an English woman, a native of the country so many Irish viewed as a murdering invader. It did not bode well for me, therefore, when part way to the inn it started to rain. Whilst the stableman possessed a large hat and waterproof cape to keep him dry, I

157

had naught but my thin shawl, and nothing further was offered. With my drenching came the saturation of the roads we traversed and it was not long before our buggy became stuck fast in the mud. The stableman jumped down and indicated for me to do likewise. Still without speaking, he clearly conveyed that I was to help push the buggy from its resting place, before walking alongside it to lighten the load.

With the mishaps along the way, we reached the inn long after everybody had retired. Gathering my bundle, I followed the stableman to a door at the back of the inn. Throwing it open, he entered, leaving me alone in the yard. Deciding to follow, I discovered myself in a room where the fire's dying embers were the only light. The stableman quickly busied himself with some leftover dinner, guzzling it down with a pint of beer. Setting my bundle down, I went forward seeking some warmth from the fire, but found only chilling fear as I encountered the landlord for the first time.

'She 'ere?' he queried, emerging from the darkness.

The stableman pointed in my direction and the man staggered closer, squinting at me through the fire's pale glow.

'Yer a mess,' he said by way of greeting.

I remained silent.

Seeing that the stableman still lingered, the landlord shooed him from the room in a manner best befitting the wildest beast.

'There,' he said, turning his attention back to me and pointing to a small alcove at the far end of the kitchen. 'Dat's where ye'll sleep. Get changed.'

Pulling back the flimsy, filthy curtain that divided the alcove from the kitchen, I discovered an area just large enough to contain a bed. On closer inspection, the so-called bed proved to be a converted window seat where a thin mattress sat upon a single wooden plank. There was just enough room underneath it for my small bundle of belongings, but nothing else. As the wind howled through the broken window pane, my hope for some relief at the end of my long, cold journey was completely dashed. No comfort was to be garnered here, of that, I was sure.

Once changed, I cautiously peered out from behind the curtain. Seeing nobody was about, I again crept towards the fire so as to dry my hair. My steps, however, were instantly halted by the sudden appearance of a snarling, brutish creature whose yellow eyes glowed in the firelight. As it came menacingly towards me, I slowly backed away. My thoughts instantly flew to a hill near my childhood home and the terrifying apparition that was said to haunt it. On stormy nights, Granny Ravens used to gather us by the fire, and in answer to our pleas, would tell us the story of the villainous hound. As with all good ghost stories, she would begin,

'It was on a night just like this, dark and stormy, in a place that had been a burial ground for witches across the centuries.'

The story would continue and we would listen with bated breath to hear about the night when a massive storm rolled through the countryside, a bolt of lightning striking the gibbet atop Galley Hill. Rising from the fire as the gibbet split in two, came the apparition of a huge black dog who howled a devilish howl and danced amidst the flames. The people who gathered watched in terror as the hideous beast continued to leap about until only embers remained. It was then and only then that the dog gave one final, haunting howl and vanished. Those who witnessed it, and those who have told of it since, know this dog was sent by an evil force to gather the souls of condemned men. Many have seen the beast since that night, its glowing red eyes and fearsome howl haunting them forever. Reports abound of travellers who have been menaced by this beast who barred their passage on the roads. Those who are deemed wise and good will be turned back, but those who are unrighteous will be lured to travel onward to vanish forever from this earth.

As a child, I both loved and feared this story. Now, in the midst of a raging storm, and with the Galley Hill hound reincarnated before me, I was paralysed with terror. Suddenly I heard a deep, short laugh, and looking up, I saw the landlord leaning upon the mantle.

'He'll get used to ye in time,' he declared. 'Until then, be on yer guard. He's killed before.'

I swallowed slowly and remained anchored to the spot. The landlord whistled.

'Musket, come 'ere boy.'

Thankfully the hound, who bore such an ominous name, obeyed his master and instantly left my side. Picking up a plate, the landlord dipped a ladle into the large pot hanging over the fire and dished up some stew. All but throwing it on the table in front of me he told me to sit and eat. When I finished the meagre offering, the landlord, who had been watching me broodingly, cocked his head towards the small alcove where my bed lay and snapped,

'Go on, get out of me sight. Make sure ye rise early. We don't be wastin' no time 'ere.'

Returning to my alcove, I stood for a moment simply staring at the bed. Hesitantly reaching out, I touched the mattress. Hard and damp, it was covered with black mould, and the whole alcove smelt awfully musty. There were no sheets and the only covering was a small, tattered blanket rolled up on the end. As I sat upon the mattress to remove my boots, thick, spear-like straw broke through the worn hessian piercing my legs. Once readied for bed, I took a cloth from the kitchen and stuffed it in the broken window before wrapping myself in the thin blanket as though in a cocoon. In this way, I gained a little warmth and some protection from the hostile prickles and tiny predators that I was certain slept alongside me. As a drop of water trickled down my forehead, darkness and sorrow consumed me. Withdrawing Doctor Markham's cherished blue ribbon from its hiding place, I pressed it firmly against my cheek. How I did long for this one-time protector to rescue me now. Oh, why did he abandon me? The very thought of it brought tears to my eyes, tears that became torrents as

I remembered my similarly abandoned bairn at Dynnyrne. Unfortunately, the landlord heard my sobbing.

'Ye can stop that howlin',' he bellowed. 'Ye won't get no sympathy 'ere.'

Fighting back my tears, Granny Ravens' words suddenly came to me,

'Promise me that you'll make the most of everything that comes your way. You can make something of yourself over there, something you would never be able to do here.'

How could I possibly make the most of this terrible situation? Life was extinguished here. Yet, I knew if I could survive the *Boar's Head*, I could survive anything. It became my resolve to find strength from my struggles here, and to see out life's journey with courage and determination. Uplifted, I eventually fell asleep, dreaming that my bairn's soft cheek was once more against my own.

With the tempest of the previous evening ceasing, sunshine greeted me upon rising the following morning. Dressing, I went in search of the landlord to receive a list of my duties, but he was nowhere to be found. Fearing reprisals should I start anything without his permission, I took it upon myself to explore the environs of the inn. Located on the outskirts of town, the rolling plains surrounding it were sun-scorched and brown, settlers having denuded large swathes of the land for farming and livestock. With darker and thinner trunks, the eucalypts here paled in comparison with the majestic gums on my mountain. Poplars and pines, so typically English in their use, were planted as fence markers, windbreaks, and shade for the animals. Being a farming community, I was familiar with the workings of this place, though visually all was completely foreign.

Roughly built, the inn itself was a strange mix of wood, stone, and tin, as though the landlord had used whatever materials were available. The walls within were roughly plastered, those in the bar and guest areas, slightly more refined than the rest. Throughout, the floors were laid of an uneven stone, the sweeping and washing of which would oftentimes prove almost impossible. The most solid part of the inn was the rear courtyard surrounded as it was by a high brick wall that protected the stables, water well, and kitchen area. A beautiful river flowed alongside the inn, and I felt blessed, for I knew these waters would bring me much solace. In time, I would also discover that the landlord used its banks to house his illegal still.

'What ye doin'?'

Startled, I froze when I saw the landlord hovering just outside the front door.

'I couldn't find you,' I managed to stammer.

'So, ye do speak. That's grand to know. Thought they'd sent me a mute.'

I was mute once more.

'It's alright,' he urged. 'Ye can look. Things often appear better in the light, ye certainly do.'

I unfortunately made my abhorrence far too apparent.

'Don't worry,' he snarled. 'I won't touch ye. It takes more than that.'

Storming off, the landlord left me alone and I sat upon a tree stump, mourning my terrible plight. A regime of punishments awaited me if I committed wrong whilst on assignment, and I could not afford to abscond or rebel in any way. To secure the release of my bairn, I must work hard and obey even the most obtuse of masters. Being a diligent worker since childhood, I knew that I would try hard to please my new master, no matter how difficult the task. Evidently, this man possessed a short and violent temper, and I would do anything rather than attract his wrath.

'Do ye like what ye see?' he asked, having composed himself whilst awaiting my return.

Hesitant to enter discourse with this man, I merely nodded. Noting his fearful frown, however, I quickly found my voice.

'It's in a very pretty setting,' I assured him.

'Sure, I reckon it is,' he agreed. 'The inside could do with some tartin' up though. They told me that you could sew. Is that right? And don't go noddin'!'

'I can sew,' I acknowledged.

'Curtains and things?'

'Yes.'

The landlord finally seemed pleased.

'And what might they have sent ye out 'ere for?' he asked.

'I stole a watch.'

A calculating smile crossed his face.

'Ye might come in 'andy yet,' he said. 'I weren't no good as a thief meself.'

As I lowered my eyes to avoid his scrutinizing gaze, I noticed the awful scars on this man's wrists. He was quick to observe where my eyes rested.

'Horrify ye, do they?' he asked, proudly holding out his wrists.

'No,' I replied honestly.

'Them English pigs done this to me. I toiled from dawn to dusk, shackled in chains, 'til me skin was raw. The wounds cut deep, almost to the bone.'

'I was forced to wear them too,' I admitted, clasping my left wrist with the memory of the pain they caused.

'There ye are now,' the man proclaimed. 'If they be puttin' a mousy wee thing like yerself in cuffs, just be thinkin' what they done to me. I once tried to remove 'em and got six dozen lashes.'

I quickly withdrew my eyes from the terrible wounds. Ordered to take a seat, I listened as the landlord proudly recounted the crime that brought him to Australia. Born in County Wicklow, Ireland, Seamus Moloney was sentenced to death for murdering his wife and unborn bairn. By questioning his wife's mental state, and claiming that he killed in self-defence, his death sentence was commuted to transportation for life. Working through three masters and twelve years hard labour, he finally obtained his current limited freedom. Now in his early fifties, he used his ticket-of-leave status to establish this small country inn.

'What were ye doin' in Cascades?' he asked. 'I thought only naughty girls got sent there.'

'My last master died,' was all I was prepared to volunteer.

'Kill 'im, did ye?' he asked with an awful grin.

I frowned my displeasure at such a suggestion. He roared with laughter. At that moment the stableman came sauntering in.

'What do ye want?' Moloney snapped.

The stableman pointed to a plate of dry bread and dripping that lay on the table. Moloney waved him on. Pointing at this hungry servant, Moloney questioned me.

'Can ye guess why 'e was transported?'

Terrified, I tried to leave the table, but Moloney barred my way. Catching me by the wrist, he laughed the villainous laugh I would come to dread.

'Come on, do ye know?'

I shook my head.

'Should we tell 'er, O'Dwyer?' he asked jovially.

The stableman nodded, his face wearing its usual evil, toothless grin. An even deeper, more sinister laugh than his master's escaped his lips. Bringing his face flush with mine, Moloney whispered,

'He raped an English woman.'

I shuddered.

'Done the same to his master's wife in Hobarton. She was English too. Ye went to Port Arthur for that one, didn't you, O'Dwyer.'

Maintaining his simpleton's grin, O'Dwyer, who was seemingly enjoying Moloney's revelations, nodded with another chuckle. Doctor Markham once spoke of Port Arthur. It was a place where they sent the incorrigibles, the worst of the worst. Doctor Markham said that there was no way to escape, the narrow neck of land leading to the settlement being guarded by a line of attack dogs, ready to tear apart anyone who passed their way. I understood that I was in the hands of two very dangerous men, and dreaded the thought of being here all alone and unprotected.

Moloney established his inn between two important coaching towns, Green Ponds and Tunbridge, in the hope of cornering the business of coaches who didn't stop at the first and couldn't make it to the second. His inn, however, was set back from the road and offered none of the genteel accommodations and facilities the others did. In reality, very few coaches ever stopped at the inn, its clientele mostly local men, ex-convicts and ticket-of-leave holders, all of whom were passionate about drinking, brawling, and taunting me. Women rarely visited the inn, those who did were of the commonest kind, and only there to gain what advantage they could from the sordid underworld of felons who gathered each night. Moloney believed it was part of my role to act as civilizer of this wretched and desolate place, and whilst O'Dwyer acted as boot catcher in front of the inn, removing and cleaning the customers' boots, I was required to cook, pour spirits, quell skirmishes and endure unwanted advances and innuendos. I did my best to run the inn efficiently, though with Moloney it was a losing battle.

Encouraging dishonesty at every opportunity, his favourite customer was one in a hurry, who would have to pay regardless of whether they received service or not. I was expected to take a long time preparing their meals, before serving them food too hot to eat, subsequently rehashing the abandoned food for the next innocent soul who ordered. Moloney taught me to substitute expensive ingredients with things like ground roots and dried leaves; the spirits served at the inn were also diluted.

My work began before sunrise and took me through to the inn's unofficial closing time at ten o'clock each night. It was nothing unusual for one or two men to have drunk themselves into a state of semi-consciousness, and I would discover them slouched in their chairs, their heads upon the table. Though incapable of staggering the short distance home, Moloney forbade their lingering. O'Dwyer would therefore be summoned to drag the revellers outside, where they were thrown upon the hay beside the pigs and chickens. I would then go to work, rummaging through each man's pockets, taking as much money as I could without it looking as if he had been robbed. If questioned in the morning, I was trained to acknowledge taking enough to pay for accommodation but nothing more. I knew it was wrong to pilfer from these men, but what other option did I have? If I protested, who knows what fate might have awaited me? I was a thief and Moloney knew it. He was determined to use my light fingers to his advantage and profit from them.

Before falling exhausted into bed, my last duty was to secure the inn for the night. Moloney didn't trust O'Dwyer to lock up properly, and, having rendered himself incapable through some generous imbibing, left it to me to bolt the front door, secure the windows, and stable the horses, before finally locking the courtyard gate leading to the road.

Part of Moloney's charade to retain his ticket-of-leave was played out each Sunday at Mr. Ashton's home, the place where the Catholics of Green Ponds attended mass whilst awaiting the building of their own church. Eager to show off his new 'possession,' he insisted upon my attendance and dressed me to impress all who saw me by his side. Kept safely guarded during the week, my clothes were only released into my hands for a limited number of hours each Sunday, and I was tutored on how to act and what to say if approached. No one must ever know that I was an assigned convict. Moloney worried in vain, for no one ever spoke to us despite Moloney greeting everyone we encountered. Condemning all who slighted him, he swore under his breath and vowed vengeance.

In residency just over a week, I managed to avoid conflict with Moloney by learning quickly, keeping my mouth shut, and obeying his orders. My cooking was by no means legendary but the humble fare I was able to churn out seemed to satisfy Moloney and his resident miscreants. Sadly, I was only human and liable to make mistakes no matter how hard I tried. My first blunder came one evening as I cleared away the dinner plates. Having scraped all the leftovers into the dog's bowl, I placed it in front of him as I was accustomed to doing for the dogs at home. Suddenly, the horsewhip that Moloney always carried, came smashing down on the table beside me.

'What's the dog eatin'?' he asked angrily.

I explained that they were the scraps from the inn.

'Musket don't eat no scraps,' he replied, snatching the bowl away from the dog. 'He eats the same as me.'

Chastened, I apologized for the mistake and assured him that in future I would feed the dog as I fed myself. I inquired as to his wish for the scraps in the future and was told to put them in a bowl for O'Dwyer. Peering from my alcove, I had already watched the stable-man sneaking in once all were in bed. Salvaging what little he could for his dinner, he would sit at the darkened table eating with his fingers, the gravy soaked up with the single piece of stale bread Moloney allowed him. One luxury permitted was a tankard of porter to wash down the loathsome fare. It was clear he savoured that drink, the one enjoyable thing in his life. I could only feel pity for this man, such was the abominable treatment he received.

Sometimes this treatment was extended to me, and I regretted that Moloney had observed the terror his horsewhip could produce. Cunningly using it to his advantage, he often toyed with me, lightly tapping it on his thigh as we spoke, and he found great joy in whipping the back of my skirt when I least expected it, laughing raucously at my distress. If I made the slightest mistake, that vile man and his hideous whip would await me.

In forging a relationship with the local police constable, Moloney discovered someone who was willing to accept bribes whilst turning a blind eye to dubious dealings. Corruption was rife amongst government officials in the colony, something I witnessed firsthand at Cascades where the warders allowed women to traffic meat, rum, tobacco, and brandy with the outside world. At the *Boar's Head*, Constable Hoare's corrupt dealings soon became blatantly obvious through his steadfast protection of Moloney who conducted a very lucrative homebrewing business despite it being illegal in Van Diemen's Land. Hoare was richly rewarded for ensuring that Moloney's still never came under suspicion, receiving a share in the profits, an unlimited supply of the produce, and a promise to hand over any escaped convict seeking refuge at the inn.

Moloney was shown at his sadistic best whilst fulfilling the latter promise, and many were the poor, unsuspecting escapees whose tongues were loosened through his liberal supply of alcohol. Their fate would be sealed once they admitted to absconding, Hoare being quickly summoned to rearrest the wayward soul. Some of the saddest victims of Moloney and Hoare's collusion were the women who absconded from service, desperate to find their lost children. Quickly ensnared in the web of deceit, I couldn't help but sympathize with them whilst understanding the foolhardiness of their endeavours.

Of all the despairing mortals who walked through our door, one young mother remains vividly etched in my memory. Granted the rare treat by her master of visiting her bairns at the Orphan School, she had been unable to find transport any further than Green Ponds and was travelling home on foot when she stopped for refreshments. Pouring her a cooling lemonade, we sat together discussing her cherished bairns as well as my own sweet one being held at Dynnyrne. Sadly though, this woman attracted the black-hearted Moloney's attention and, as soon as her glass was empty, he swiftly refilled it with rum. Imploring her to leave, I demanded that Moloney desist from his wickedness. My pleas, however, fell on deaf ears and I watched despairingly as he and other fiends plied her with drink. Like so many desperate creatures before her, she sought solace in drink, alcoholism in this colony being a major challenge for the authorities. No help was ever given to them other than returning those afflicted to the gaols and factories for punishment, before reassigning them for the cycle to begin all over again. Having drunk herself to near delirium, Moloney's victim staggered to her feet.

'Please,' I begged him. 'Let her stay for the night. You could tell her master that she was unwell and we took her in to rest. If she leaves now, she'll only end up in trouble.'

Moloney frowned.

'Me inn isn't a refuge for wayward women,' he declared coldly.

'Just one night,' I pleaded.

'Alright,' Moloney agreed with terrifying serenity, 'but I have me price. Sleep with me and she may have yer bed.'

I shook my head at his callousness.

'You're heartless,' I sobbed. 'How can you ask such a thing when all I want to do is help her?'

'These are me terms.'

His cruelty rendered me speechless and turning from him, I placed my arm around the woman and aided her to the door. As I sneaked a few coins into her hand, I wondered why Moloney was content to observe me so quietly without issuing a sanction. The reason for his reticence became all too evident as I opened the door to discover Constable Hoare in all his terrifying might.

'Constable Hoare,' Moloney proclaimed, 'we've got a runaway on our hands.'

'No!' I cried, pushing the woman back inside.

'Hannah!' Moloney bellowed wildly, angrily seizing a clump of my hair.

Forced to relinquish my protective hold, the woman quickly fell prey to the constable who easily cuffed her, prising the coins from her fingers. I will never forget her eyes as she was led away, it was as though all life, all hope ceased to exist. Pummelling into Moloney's chest, I screamed at him.

'That was wretched! Wretched!'

Dragging me to the kitchen, he threw me to the floor, slapping my face to subdue me.

'Finished?' he queried once I was silent. 'Yer certainly a feisty wee thing. Quite arousing actually.'

I sat pouting at him. He merely laughed.

'Right,' he said, reaching down to grab my wrist. 'Ye can get up from there now. I need ye to do a task for me.'

Slapping his hand away, I remained defiantly on the floor.

'Please yerself,' he declared, 'but your little piece of trickery has earned ye a night in one of the guest rooms. I have accepted a handsome offer for you to entertain one of me gentleman friends.'

My heart stopped. Spend the night with one of those debauched animals!

'Never!' I snapped. 'I would rather die.'

'Ye don't have no say,' he growled as he made another grab for my arm. 'Ye belong to me to do with as I please. Two pounds is a lot of money and I won't let that slip through me fingers.'

With a squeal, I retracted my arm.

'What's the problem? Ye convict whores have all done it before. I know *ye* have. Can't get knapped by yerself.'

'You know nothing about me,' I cried, my voice broken by a sob.

'Lord! Don't start that again,' Moloney sighed. 'I know enough to know ye have a bairn and I don't see no fella linin' up to marry ye.'

Sobbing was my only answer. Taking a seat at the kitchen table, Moloney stared at me as though in a quandary as to what he should do.

'Yer right,' he finally declared. 'Strangers shouldn't touch me lovely possessions. Why should I share me pretty things? And ye are mine, ye know. One day I'll show ye exactly what bein' mine really means.'

Bending forward, he kissed me. Repulsed by the touch of his lips, I cried out, slapping his face. With an otherworldly roar, he again grabbed my hair, and using both hands, hauled me to my feet.

'O'Dwyer!'

Bellowing for his stableman, he dragged me to the courtyard where I was thrown into a muddy puddle just outside the back door.

O'Dwyer appeared and my tormentor pointed an accusing finger at me.

'She's all yours,' he declared. 'You've tamed wild beasts before. Tame 'er.'

As Moloney stormed off, O'Dwyer lifted me effortlessly from the mud and carried me to his room. Fetching a towel, he began wiping the mud from my legs. Unwilling to have this beast touch me, I snatched the towel from him. Grunting, he walked to a nearby table and poured two small glasses of spirits. Skolling his own, he pushed the other towards me. I left it where it sat.

'You won't drink?' he asked, nudging the glass a little closer.

I shook my head and we sat in silence, though I could tell from his twitching fingers that he longed to reach out and touch me. Averting my gaze, I searched for a means of escape, but nothing presented itself. I was trapped in the foul-smelling room.

'Moloney treats you all wrong,' O'Dwyer mumbled. 'I wish I owned a lass half as pretty as you.'

I was horrified.

'I don't belong to Moloney,' I snapped. 'He doesn't own me. There's nothing between us and never will be. I'm an assigned servant exactly like you.'

O'Dwyer looked doubtful but said no more and silence reigned again. Eventually, the chill got too much and I gave an involuntary shiver. O'Dwyer noticed and rose to gather a blanket. Placing it around my shoulders, he managed to draw a grateful smile from me. Although slight, it was all the encouragement he needed to sweep me into his arms and attempt to kiss me. O'Dwyer's brawn gave him the advantage and his grasp tightened the more desperately I fought for freedom. As he forced me towards the bed, I was blessed indeed to spy a ceramic jug lying just within reach on the bedside table. With O'Dwyer finally stealing his longed-for kiss, my fingers seized the jug and I smashed it over his head. Instantly recoiling to clasp his wounded skull, O'Dwyer released me and I scurried from the room.

Bursting into the kitchen moments later, I discovered Moloney by the fire. He said nothing. Even Musket who lay at his feet, failed to stir. When the wounded O'Dwyer followed shortly after, however, Moloney rocked with laughter.

'It looks like she's tamed you instead.'

Miraculously, nothing more was ever said and our lives carried on as before. That I had fallen prey to the roving eyes and wandering hands of Moloney and O'Dwyer was no great surprise. Over the coming months their unsolicited advances and innuendoes continued, the duo frequently joined in their foul play by the other cretins who frequented the inn. But, no matter how great the temptation was to escape, memories of that poor young mother being led away by Constable Hoare forced me to bide a while longer. The road to regaining Kezia was already long and fraught with obstacles, an extended sentence could destroy all hope of ever holding her again.

With the rapid pace of progress in the colony, convict road gangs were often completing public works in our vicinity. Sometimes they would be brought to the inn for a rest and feed, and I would watch as Moloney secretly conversed with those from his native land, encouraging violence and revolt. Being a staunch supporter of any revolutionary minded Irishman, he also gave food and asylum to Ribbonmen and political prisoners, and always sheltered them from the law. These self-proclaimed 'wild geese' were often in conflict with our other patrons, though thankfully always avoided me, the 'daughter' of their oppressors. For one of their number, however, the temptation of a conquest was apparently too hard to resist, and creeping up behind me one evening, he seized me in his arms. Quickly snatching up the poker from the fireside, I spun around and pressed it firmly into the fiend's throat.

'Use that and you'll hang,' he snarled.

'I don't fear dying,' I declared. 'I'd sooner hang than be sullied by your kind.'

'Brave words from one whose life is in my hands.'

I pushed the poker harder into his throat, his words failing to intimidate me. Reaching out, he wrapped his thick, brutish fingers around my neck, slowly tightening them in an effort to squeeze the life from me. Without flinching, I stared coldly at my aggressor. Drawing nearer, he stood over me, the stench from his clothing and rotting teeth making my stomach churn. He tightened his fingers still further. I refused to let him see even the slightest quiver. His chest heaved as he stared silently into my unblinking eyes. He let out a furious roar and, shaking me violently, released his hold. Failing in his mission, he spat at my feet and retreated from the kitchen without another word. Hours later, Moloney appeared. Walking to the fireside he picked up the poker that I had restored to its rightful place.

'I hear that ye threatened one of me patrons,' he said calmly.

'He threatened me first,' I replied bluntly.

'Ye impressed him with yer courage. He said that ye feared nothin'. That true?'

I remained silent. Moloney slammed the poker onto the table where I sat. I barely moved.

'He was right,' Moloney declared, casting the poker aside. Grabbing my shoulders, he stooped and kissed my neck. I shuddered at his touch.

'Ah,' he declared sarcastically. 'Perhaps there is somethin' that ye fear.'

With a satisfied chuckle, he withdrew, leaving me with the loathsome memory of his touch. When I first arrived at the *Boar's Head*, I used to question why the government would allow a young, single woman like myself to be assigned to Moloney. The inn was a den of iniquity, its owner and his assistant, men of ill repute whose records spoke of violence, brutality, and hatred. Now I realized the government did not care. Women like me were expendable. They brought us here to serve, for the colony needed workers and there were no better workers than the ones who came free of charge. Convicts were the slaves of the island. If we succumbed, there were always others to take our place.

The loneliness I suffered at the *Boar's Head* is indescribable. With no one to whom I could turn, and no one to care, my life seemed meaningless. I worked, tears filling my eyes, ready at any moment to burst forth. They would flow in torrents as soon as I lay my head down for another fitful sleep. Having cried out the woes of the day, my thoughts would always turn to Kezia and her sweet, innocent face. The soothing sound of her breathing close beside me would return to my ears, and I would be calmed. Some nights, however, the obstacles seemed insurmountable and I would wake in the middle of the night, melancholy thoughts consuming my mind. On these nights, I could not be so easily pacified, and my tears would turn to choking sobs, thoughts of yet another day of entrapment lying ahead suffocating me.

When September eventually dawned, my mind reminisced on events from the previous spring. Comfort and love had been mine, the strong arms of my adored Sam always there to guide and protect me. How could twelve months bring such drastic change? Defenceless and alone, I was the reluctant co-conspirator to all of Moloney's immoral schemes, and knew never to question his motives. And so, one evening when he ordered me to slip on my Sunday best, I obeyed without the slightest curiosity or doubt and waited for instructions. Coming forward, Moloney seized my wrist so tightly that it throbbed and he hurriedly whispered his plan.

'There's a man out there who must be encouraged to bide 'ere a while.'

'What do you want me to do with him?' I ventured to ask.

'Nothin. We leave this one alone. He can do me a great deal of good. Make sure we give him a generous donation before he leaves.'

I frowned, confused by his sudden generosity. Moloney was too busy to notice. Clearing the table, he replaced my utensils with the inn's best crockery and glassware, the smelly tallow candle by which I worked, snuffed out in favour of a bright, white, and far less pungent whale oil one. With all in readiness, Moloney ushered in his guest, Father Timothy O'Malley. Travelling from Launceston to Hobarton, lameness in his horse's foreleg forced the poor man to seek refuge at our less than reputable inn.

I found the priest far more amicable than his Irish compatriots, and whilst he partook of the meagre feast I prepared, he told enthralling tales of his travels. Following supper, Moloney invited Father O'Malley to sit fireside, issuing him with some spirits upon which to sip. I was then called upon to bring forth 'the good book.' Guided by Moloney's outstretched hand, I approached the small shelf beside the fireplace and picking up the only volume there, followed my master's instructions and gave it to the priest.

'Will ye read to us, Father?' Moloney asked feigning piety.

'Do you have a favourite passage, Hannah?' Father O'Malley asked, his kind eyes smiling at me.

Moloney's horror was all too obvious, yet I was not perturbed and I told the priest of a passage from Corinthians. It was the one that would have been read at Sam's and my wedding, and the priest read it now.

'Love is patient, love is kind. It does not envy, it does not boast, it is not proud. It does not dishonour others, it is not self-seeking, it is not easily angered, it keeps no record of wrongs. Love does not delight in evil but rejoices with the truth. It always protects, always trusts, always hopes, always perseveres. Love never fails.'

Wiping away a tear, I thanked him, and he placed a tender, comforting hand on my own. Quickly jumping to his feet, Moloney volunteered to show Father O'Malley to his room. The room where the priest rested that evening rarely housed one so virtuous, more commonly rented out at an hourly rate to the rabble who drank at the inn and the women they chose to liaise with; women who swore heartily, smoked a great deal of tobacco, and drank too much rum. Employed by Moloney to service his customers, they received a mere pittance of the substantial sum paid to him. Often taking one of the women to his own bed, their squeals and laughter would penetrate the walls, keeping me awake until the early hours.

Whilst I was destined to remain in this dismal place for the foreseeable future, I was resolved that my endeavours to better myself would not cease. Dearest Sam taught me my alphabet and I became determined to practice it every day. With neither pen nor paper, I decided that just as I had once used the earth as parchment, whilst at the inn I would use the leftover flour sprinkled on the table. During the long, solitary hours I spent alone in the kitchen, my endeavours became a godsend, something to distract me from the darkness of the world that was trying to consume me. I hoped that in time I would be able to use my knowledge to create a better life for myself, and the thought seemed to lessen the tedium of my days. One evening, Moloney discovered me hard at work. Initially ignoring me, his mood suddenly changed as he approached to warm himself by the miserable fire.

'What's all this then?' he demanded, indicating my letters scrawled in the flour.

I remained silent.

'They didn't tell me ye could write.'

My continued silence enraged him and he suddenly grabbed me by the elbow, pulling me roughly from the bench.

'Answer me, girl!' he bellowed, shaking me furiously. 'I'll 'ave none of this, do ye understand? None!'

As he hollered, he thrashed about on the table, wildly brushing away my letters, and everything else in his path. Even Musket cowered at his anger.

'If I ever catch ye doin' that again, I'll chop off yer hands.'

Instinctively hiding both hands behind my back, I watched in terror as he stormed from the room. That such an innocent act could generate such rage was a shocking reminder that I must be extra vigilant and not antagonize him any further.

Like those who once guarded Moloney and O'Dwyer at Port Arthur, here at the inn I had my own attack dog watching over me. Devil dog that he was, Moloney maintained his beloved pet once torn a man to pieces. Whilst I seriously doubted his claims, I tragically possessed no similar doubt when it came to the toll Musket took on the native wildlife population. His first victim during my residency was a sweet furry creature, known as a bandicoot. I discovered Musket toying with this poor animal as I entered the kitchen one morning, and though injured, it was still very much alive. Without thinking, I rushed forward, screaming at the dog to stop. Musket looked up, baring his teeth ferociously. Grabbing a jug of water from the table, I threw it over the bandicoot's assailant, allowing the unfortunate creature to make a momentary escape. Its bid for freedom, however, was futile and Musket pounced again. Crying out, I raced in search of Moloney, begging him to come to my aid.

'A worthless bandicoot!' he exclaimed angrily. 'Ye interrupted me for this!'

'Please,' I pleaded, unwittingly clutching his arm with my hand. 'Please help it.'

Frowning at me, Moloney picked up the shovel from beside the fireplace. Instinctively knowing what was to come, I withdrew slightly, hoping beyond hope that I misread his intentions. I urged him again.

'Please!'

'Very well,' he replied with a sinister grin, and the shovel was quickly brought to rest upon the dear creature's head.

Covering my eyes, I screamed and turned from the dreadful scene.

'How could you?' I cried.

'Ye can clean it up now,' Moloney ordered as he threw the blood-covered shovel back on the hearth.

Refusing to go near the morbid scene, I scurried to my alcove and drew the curtain against the world. Cursing his luck at possessing a servant like me, Moloney marched to the backdoor and bellowed impatiently for O'Dwyer, the stableman cleaning up the poor creature's remains without flinching.

Survival at the *Boar's Head* meant keeping track of every day; each day survived bringing me closer to freedom. There were but two years of my sentence left, and regardless of circumstances, I knew that these years would eventually pass, and I would be free. Yet, be that as it may, when the sun-drenched morning of October the fifth finally dawned, bringing with it Kezia's first birthday, it was almost impossible to find the courage to fight on. It was the most perfect spring day imaginable, and from the moment I woke, I thought only of Kezia. I thought too of the woman who would now be holding her in my place. So very bitter were the feelings consuming me, that despite the brightness of the morning, my mood as I prepared breakfast was extremely dark indeed.

'She'll be well cared for,' Moloney assured me bluntly, attempting to dismiss my distress.

'They'll have her trapped in that deplorable nursery, in all its suffocating heat, when she should be outside in this beautiful sunshine.'

'Ye could bring 'er 'ere.'

'What!' Moloney's words astonished me.

'Come out of that hidey-hole of yers and be mine. All I ask is that you give me three or four bairns of me own. Who knows, one day I might even decide to marry ye. That's all it would take. Agree, and yer bairn may join us 'ere at the *Boar's Head*.'

All I lived for was to have Kezia by my side again. Yet, no matter how desperate I was, I could never agree to Moloney's terms. When I subsequently recoiled from his attempt at a tender touch, he crashed his fist onto the table with a rising, infuriated growl.

'Damn it, Hannah! What do I 'ave to do? What? Yer more than infuriating.'

Hastening from the room, he returned moments later with his best hunting knife and began sharpening it by the fire. Having ground away at the appalling object, he examined it closely, all the while holding it almost flush with my cheek. Anxiously awaiting the anticipated terror, my heart pounded, though I was determined that no outward sign of my fear would be visible. With no cowering victim at his mercy, the knife lost its appeal and Moloney stabbed it violently into the table to be forgotten in favour of other vices.

Once the inn finally fell silent later that evening, Moloney joined me again. Dishing up some dinner, he sat quietly at the table. I took up some needlework and we dwelt in silence for a time. Sensing that Moloney watched me intently, I eventually looked up. His face was so extremely calm that it frightened me. Eventually, with dinner complete, he left me alone once more. Unnerved, I retreated to my alcove where I fell into yet another troubled sleep. Several hours later I was awoken by a light and I opened my eyes to discover Moloney, in all his nakedness, standing beside the bed.

'Y'ave foolishly failed to consider the advantages of a union between us. I'm not so blind. I know that I'd do better with a wife, and think ye'll do fine.'

An icy shiver ran down my spine. That night Moloney was not rendered insensible by drink but retained all his powers, both mental and physical. Dragging me roughly from my bed, he threw me to the floor. Seizing my wrists in his brutish hands, he pinned them above my head, holding me down.

'The first duty of a wife is to produce an 'eir,' he declared, fighting to rip my nightdress from my body.

Desperately screaming for help, I fought to escape his heinous grasp, knowing that no one would come to my aid.

'Stop it!' he bellowed, shaking me, as his devil dog edged closer.

I had not lived on the streets of London without learning a thing or two. Having seen a young girl save herself from a drunken sailor down by the Hungerford Stairs, I adopted her method and finally extracting my wrists, plunged my thumbs deep into Moloney's eyes. As he grasped his injured face, I hastened towards freedom. In my panicked state, I struggled to gain my footing, and I half crawled, half staggered across the room. At one stage Moloney caught my ankle, but I kicked him away with a power previously unknown to me. Upon reaching the back door, I threw it open and raced across the courtyard, hotly pursued by Musket. With the wretched animal snapping at my heels, I reached the gate, only to realize with absolute horror, that it was already bolted it for the night. Taking the lock in my hands, I shook it desperately, praying that it would give way, but it did not. I was trapped. As Moloney approached, I turned and braced myself for his onslaught, my trembling legs putting me in fear of collapse.

'Ye *will* be mine,' he said so calmly that it chilled me more than any threat.

Slamming me against the wall, anger took the place of passion, and he raped me. Such violence and fury were enacted upon me, that the force lifted me from the ground. My screams and sobs only served to spur him on, the thrill of victory propelling him still further. Eventually, I became limp and sank to the ground. With his fervour now waned, Moloney stood over me.

'Ye asked for that,' he declared, with hatred in his voice. 'That's what ye women do, lure unsuspecting men to their doom. Ye've tempted me to develop feelings for ye, unnatural feelin's that an Irishman shouldn't feel. Yer witchcraft succeeded in breakin' down all me resistance, but then yer cold, English heart denied me the pleasure of havin' ye. What was I meant to do? I'm only human, after all. But we'll see what this brings.'

Whilst his master spoke, Musket stood beside him. Saliva trickled onto my face from his sharp, bared fangs and the dog's blood-curdling growls subdued me still further. Dragging myself up, I crawled slowly towards the barn, Musket stalking me as if I was prey. O'Dwyer, who witnessed the final part of the attack, watched on. Looking up at him, I pleaded with him to show a little heart and help me. He remained motionless.

'That's it,' Moloney applauded. 'Leave the whore be. Come, we'll drink to me conquest.'

O'Dwyer cackled boorishly as he blindly and obediently followed Moloney and his demonic hound back to the inn. As the door slammed shut, I heard the bolts being applied with haste. Barred from the inn, and left alone in the muddied darkness, the barn would serve as my bed that night. Nothing can describe the pain that consumed me as I lay curled up in the hay, the thought of Moloney's devilish violation killing me inside. Wounded, both in body and soul, I was too distraught to sleep, yet feared that if I did not, I would not have the strength and wit to repel any further attacks. My spirit was completely broken and I yearned only for death. Try as I may, I could garner no comfort or inspiration from Granny's words, even thoughts of my dearest bairn failed to raise me. Unfastening Doctor Markham's ribbon, which I now tied in my hair each evening, I clutched it in my hand. It sadly gave little relief. Several hours then crept by before I finally succumbed to the pain and exhaustion and drifted into a nightmarish sleep.

'O'Dwyer!'

It was Moloney's bellowing that shook me from my tortured slumbers the following morning. Cautiously peering from the safety of the stables, I saw the fiends gathering their brewing implements. As they headed towards the still on the riverbank, I retied Doctor Markham's ribbon in my hair and crept from my hiding place. The morning mist was still rising and a frost blanketed the ground, numbing my bare feet as I hurried across it. All was quiet apart from the roaring of the river which, following recent heavy rains, was in full flood. Rivers had always managed to bring me great consolation, and I hoped that this one would do likewise. I gazed upon its raging torrent so fearsome and yet so enticing. How very different was the last time I stood watching such treacherous waters. With Sam's tender arm squeezing my shoulders and Kezia still safely cradled in my beautifully rounded belly, I had known nothing but happiness.

Today the river offered something new. It was calling to me, luring me down its banks into the icy depths. I waded out like a somnambulist with no other thought than that my trials were finally at an end. Swallowed up, inch by inch, my watery grave consumed my ankles, my knees, and finally my waist. Slowly, I lowered myself into the turbulent, black abyss, the freezing waters snatching my breath away. Panic suddenly seized me as I fought for air and struggled towards the bank. The river, however, was not ready to relinquish its hold and the rapid currents swept me off my feet and began dragging me down the river. Having hoped for death just a few moments ago, I quickly realized that life, no matter how shocking, was better than this icy demise. My cries must have alerted Moloney, for he came racing along the bank.

'Hannah!'

My progress down the river was swift and Moloney followed, searching for the most opportune moment to attempt a rescue. Mercifully, I arrived at a section of the river, where it slowed before trickling over a tiny waterfall. Moloney took advantage of the slackened current to wade into the water, plucking me from my fate just moments before my body would have been dashed upon the jagged rocks of the rapids. The moment I was gathered into his arms I lost consciousness and did not rejoin the world again until I was warmly wrapped in a blanket and placed beside the fire with a tankard of rum. Never before was there such a fire at the inn, nor had Moloney ever shown such genuine concern for my welfare. Instinctively I felt for my ribbon. Although clinging on by a thread, it was there. Untangling it from my hair, I held it against my lips and managed the briefest of smiles. Moloney watched on with a furrowed brow.

'He won't be waiting for ye,' he declared suddenly.

Lifting my eyes in surprise, Moloney indicated my ribbon.

'Clearly a token from a man. Yer so pathetic. He'll have forgotten ye. Moved on. You should too.'

As tears graced my cheeks, Moloney's face wore a satisfied smirk, and he rose to stir the fire. What hurt more than anything was I knew his words were true. Doctor Markham would no sooner be thinking of me at that moment than O'Dwyer.

When I felt strong enough, Moloney said I should change out of my wet clothes. I stood, but progress was hampered, as the rum, coupled with my frozen legs, rendered me incapable of walking properly. Moloney swept me once more into his arms. Carrying me to my alcove, he placed me gently upon the bed and withdrew, leaving me more astounded than ever. It was abhorrent to think that I now owed Moloney my life, but more importantly, I had been spared. My dearest Sam's dying words came to me,

'Live on, Hannah, and raise our little one knowing that I am watching over you. You will be taken care of.'

That Sam was watching over me was never more evident than that morning, and whilst my rescuer was Moloney, I knew that Sam had sent him so that I might live, reclaim our bairn, and raise her with a mother's tender love.

As evening approached, Moloney appeared beside my bed.

'You hungry?' he queried, somewhat gingerly.

I remained silent.

'D'ye need anythin'?' he tried again.

Having observed the silent shake of my head, he turned and began to walk away.

'Wait!' I cried out, and he turned back. 'Remember that poor woman who was here a few months ago? She was granted permission from her master to visit her children.'

'Yes, and look how that turned out,' Moloney replied bluntly. 'Ye'd run away too.'

'Not if you or O'Dwyer were to escort me. It wouldn't take long.'

Moloney shook his head.

'Got too much to do round 'ere to go drivin' ye round like a fine lady.'

And with this, he left me. Turning my face to the wall, silent tears streamed from my eyes until I slowly drifted off to sleep. Many hours later, when all was quiet and I believed myself to be alone, I hesitantly crept from my alcove only to discover Moloney reading by the fire.

My appearance seemed to startle him and he threw something that looked like a letter into the flames. Sensing that the letter's contents concerned me, my courage rose.

'What was that?' I asked.

'What?'

'The letter.'

Moloney shifted uncomfortably in his chair.

'Somethin' that it's better for ye not to know,' he declared.

'I beg of you,' I pleaded desperately. 'Is it about my daughter?'

Moloney frowned.

'Yes. She's no longer at Cascades.'

'Has she been adopted?'

Moloney shook his head.

'I'd hoped to save ye the pain. Yer child has died. T'was a fever, or so they say.'

I never felt grief like it.

'No,' I murmured breathlessly, staggering blindly towards the fire. 'No!' I cried loudly in torment.

Moloney came to me, steadying me in his arms.

'Tell me it isn't true,' I begged him. 'Tell me you're mistaken.'

Moloney shook his head. Hysteria consumed me, and screaming, I pummelled into his chest, whilst he fought to control my flailing limbs. Eventually, my energy was spent and my passion subsided. I stood limply in Moloney's arms, my head resting upon his shoulder. All that I could manage now was a slight whimper. As my senses slowly returned, I suddenly became aware of how very tightly Moloney held me, and of how his lips caressed my bare shoulder. Quickly drawing away, I snatched up my shawl that was lost in the commotion and fled to my alcove. The monster's devilishly raucous laughter filled the room and I hurriedly drew the curtain on his abominable face.

Lying upon my bed, staring mindlessly at the mildew on the ceiling, I refused to believe Moloney's claim. My bairn could not have died, I was certain I would have felt the loss. Mam used to say I was intuitive about these things and vowed it came from Dada's Irish connections. Whether it was true or not, I did believe a mother who felt such a strong bond to her child as I did to Kezia would have some inkling when things were wrong. When Kezia's picturesque face suddenly appeared before me, I knew this was the sign I had awaited, a message only I could fathom, and I instinctively knew, deep in my heart, that my darling girl was still alive. Her face filled me with such pure joy that it spurred me on, strengthening my resolve to escape this wretched place and find her.

Sliding silently from the bed, I had no time for dressing but quickly rolled my few belongings in a shawl. I knew I would be punished for running away, but whatever the punishment, it would eventually end. The agony of being without my beautiful bairn would not. Stepping cautiously from my alcove, I stealthily made my way across the darkened kitchen and through to the bar. It was then that my steps came to a sudden halt as the dying embers of the fire illuminated Musket lying across the door to freedom. His ears pricked up at my approach, and a deep growl came from within his throat.

Unwilling to turn my back on the fiend, I retreated slightly, reaching out for the roast beef left over from supper. Waving it slowly in front of his nose, I succeeded in luring the dog to his feet, and he trotted forward, his eyes focused upon the meat. Yet, enticing as the meat may have been, it was apparently no match for the temptation of a live kill, and as I made a dash for freedom, the dog pounced, snapping viciously at my legs. My cry alerted Moloney.

'What the 'ells goin' on?' he bellowed.

I knew that if I was caught trying to escape, I would not see morning, and I darted towards the safety of my alcove. Moloney though was waiting in the kitchen. He snatched up my wrist as I rushed past him.

'Let me go!' I sobbed, trying to shake myself free. 'Let me go!'

'Oh, no ye don't,' he growled, grabbing me tightly. 'Yer not leavin' me.'

My bundle of belongings became my weapon of choice, and I propelled it as hard as I could into his stomach. Naturally, this only served to anger him further, and he tore it from me, flinging it towards the fire. Squirming in his arms, battling for my liberty, Maloney forced me down upon the kitchen table. With his hands wrapped tightly around my throat, I feared being throttled and cried out, begging for mercy. He was deaf to my pleas. Then suddenly, something miraculous occurred as a glint in the flickering firelight drew my eyes to the hunting knife that he stabbed into the table a few evenings prior. Frantically reaching for the precious object, my quest was unintentionally aided by Moloney who, in his attempt to conquer me, propelled me further onto the table. Finally, my fingertips reached the cold metal of the blade. Bit by bit I extracted it until I finally held it in my hand. Grasping it firmly, I mustered all the strength and courage I possessed and plunged it straight into Moloney's shoulder. Squealing like a wild pig, Moloney instantly released me. Clutching his shoulder, he staggered to the back door and bellowed for O'Dwyer whilst shouting all kinds of vengeance. Scurrying to collect my belongings, I fled through the bar, out the front door, and ran for my life.

With no friend to whom I could run, I decided to seek help at *Woodville*, the private residence of Green Pond's doctor. Doctor Gorringe was a gentleman well known for his kind ministering to convict road gangs, and I prayed he would be similarly sympathetic to my own plight. Barefoot and in the dark of night, my journey was eternal, but I was spurred on by the terrifying thought that Moloney might be in pursuit. Upon reaching the doctor's front door, I pummelled upon it, only able to briefly cry for help before my legs collapsed beneath me. Doctor Gorringe opened his door to discover me lying sobbing upon the doorstep. Instantly swooping down, he gathered me into his arms and carried me inside, lowering me into an armchair by the fireside. Gently placing a shawl around my shoulders, he summoned his wife who brought me a warming drink.

Allowing me time to compose myself and rest, the necessary questions were asked, as the doctor and his wife were naturally curious about the blood on my hands and nightgown. When the atrocities of the inn were revealed to the sensitive and caring doctor, he quickly vowed to do all in his power to help me. Whilst he was obliged to return me to the authorities, Doctor Gorringe assured me my time at the inn was over and guaranteed that Moloney would be punished for his actions. When the sergeant arrived the following morning, Doctor Gorringe laid down the conditions for my handover.

'Hannah must never be returned to Seamus Moloney. She realizes she has done wrong in running away and will accept her punishment, but no crime deserves assignment to that man.'

As I was led from the safety of *Woodville* that day, I turned and thanked Doctor Gorringe with all my heart for his kindness to me. The doctor took both my hands in his own.

'I wish that I could have done more,' he declared.

'You did all and more than was expected. You have ensured that I will not return to the inn, and have therefore saved my life.'

To receive my punishment for absconding, I was dragged before a magistrate. Moloney was there, his arm worn in a sling. As he gave his testimony, I was determined not to flinch under the withering, hateful glare he cast at me. When he finally finished, the magistrate spoke.

'The prisoner's actions, I am told, were in self-defence. I have before me a signed affidavit from the doctor to whom she ran for help. It seems that your actions towards the prisoner on that day, and on several previous occasions, were reprehensible. I am therefore dropping the charge of grievous bodily harm.'

Moloney's simmering anger was obvious to all. Ignoring him, the magistrate turned to me.

'Although you found yourself in a dire situation, you did wrong by running away. The law must take its course but I intend to show leniency in my sentence. From here you will return to Cascades to serve the required three-month sentence before re-assignment. I am foregoing the usual order of hard labour. Further to this, I am making the recommendation that Doctor Gorringe, at his own request, be allowed to scrutinize all prospective placements before you are assigned in the future.'

I thanked the judge for his mercy and waited to be led away. As I did so, I had the great satisfaction of hearing the judge address Moloney again.

'Henceforth, you will not be assigned any further convicts. Your actions have seen you forfeit that right.'

The smug, self-satisfied smirk that had beset Moloney's face throughout the proceedings was at an end. A smile now danced upon my own lips instead.

'Now, about these rumours of an illegal still on your property, Seamus Moloney,' were the last words that I heard, but I was satisfied that the magistrate would see justice done. The still would be located and Moloney would finally be returned to the penal system where he belonged. Yes, it was justice indeed.

9

HOBART TOWN

"There appears to be a good deal of Society here: I heard of a Fancy Dress Ball at which 113 were present in costumes!"
Charles Darwin, 1839.

For those of us incarcerated at Cascades, Easter Sunday that year was no different from any other day. Two days later, however, I was called forth from my work and ordered to follow the matron. What followed was my very own Easter miracle and I remember the extraordinary events of that day as vividly as though they were yesterday. Marched outside, the sun almost blinded me as I stepped from my darkened surrounds. Hurrying past those busy at the tubs and through the lines of washing flapping in the breeze, I was taken to the matron's quarters. The scowl on her face said it all as she ushered me into a room and closed the door upon me. A woman's gentle voice spoke my name and I gazed mutely into the room. A vision in violet rose before me and spoke again.

'It is Hannah, isn't it?'

I nodded hesitantly. The woman's pretty face smiled. It was so long since I'd seen anyone smile. She came forward and held out a pale blue dress. Pointing to some lace work on the bodice she asked,

'Is this your work?'

I acknowledged it was and queried whether she found fault with it.

'Fault!' she exclaimed. 'Why no, quite the contrary. I thought this dress was completely ruined and yet you sent it back like new. Where did you learn such a skill?'

'From my grandmother and aunt.'

The woman looked at me.

'May I ask the circumstances surrounding your predicament? Surely someone with the sensitivity to produce such fine needlework should not be incarcerated in such a bleak place as this.'

'I ran away from my master.'

'Indeed. Why would you do that?' she queried.

'He attacked me. He ...'

I stopped short and bit my bottom lip, shuddering at the memory.

'You need say no more,' the lady acknowledged. 'I have a very good idea of why you ran. And you have been punished for this?'

I nodded slowly and the lady shook her head. She was thoughtful for a moment.

'May I ask one thing more?'

I agreed.

'The matron informed me that this is not the first time you've been here. Is that true?'

'Yes, that's true,' I replied. 'Just over a year ago, I bore a child out of wedlock. I was sentenced to hard labour at the wash tubs as punishment.'

'And the child's father abandoned you to your fate?'

I hung my head and stared at the floor. I couldn't answer her.

'So young to have been through so much,' she mused. 'Does your child live?'

I informed her that despite numerous requests, I remained ignorant of my bairn's welfare and had not seen her since she was a few months old. At eighteen months, I knew that Kezia would still be housed in the nursery, having as yet not been banished to the orphanage. The lady before me frowned with clear concern. Marching quickly towards the door, she summoned the matron and ordered that my daughter be brought to us. The matron appeared surprised by the demand and explained that because the child was at another facility, adhering to the request could take a great deal of time.

'I have no pressing engagements,' the lady declared resuming her seat. 'I shall wait.'

Clearly displeased, but in no position to refuse, the matron departed. I was wickedly pleased to see this deplorable woman humbled. The lady, who I could tell was of a very kindly disposition, signalled to me to sit beside her. She took my hand in her own.

'It appears that your child lives, Hannah,' she said with a smile. 'I should very much like to help the two of you. My name is Bronwyn Johns. My husband and I have four children, two boys and two girls. I require a lady's companion and would like to offer you the role. You would have a home with me, as would your daughter.'

Stunned by her generosity, I struggled to find words. Such warm-hearted kindness, however, could not go unacknowledged and I found enough voice to thank her from the bottom of my heart, assuring her that no offer could be more welcome. Moments later, the door opened and after months of heartache and longing, I miraculously set eyes upon my cherished bairn once more. Strangely, despite the length of our separation, I still anticipated the same tiny bundle that was torn from my arms would be returned to them. I was surprised, therefore, when a well-developed toddler with long legs and a head of golden curls was brought to me.

She was the most delightful child I had ever beheld. Prejudiced, I may have been, for she was my own child and mothers are that way inclined, but I knew that she was a beauty. There was no mistaking that Kezia was Sam's daughter, being blessed with the same soulful, blue eyes, fine features, and aura of gentle mirth. What horrified me, though, was the way she clung so tightly to the woman who carried her. I feared that by not remembering me, she may reject me and refuse my love. The woman seemed reluctant to release my bairn and it was left to Mrs. Johns to intercede.

'I believe it's time this child was given to her mother.'

As she spoke, Mrs. Johns seized Kezia under both arms and prised her away from the woman. It was obvious that Kezia was used to being handled by strangers, for though initially a little hesitant, she was transferred into my arms without fuss. There are no words to describe the feelings that consumed me. Having dreamed of this moment every day since our parting, nothing could have prepared me for the thrill of holding her close, of stroking her hair, and kissing her cheek. These wonders could not be compensated for through dreams, no matter how vivid. Life was breathed back into me, I felt warmth for the first time in months and my heart beat again. My bairn was clothed in the most basic of garments. An ill-fitting shift dress hung loosely from her shoulders, a garment whose course material was grey with age, and matched a similarly shabby cap. I had seen other children at Dynnyrne in stockings and shoes, but my little girl was brought to me barefoot, her tiny feet frozen.

'What a pretty child,' Mrs. Johns declared as she stroked her cheek gently.

Burying my face into my bairn's shoulder, her face and mine were finally united and I knew they would never be parted again. Mrs. Johns, having organized for our transfer into her care, declared it time to leave. Without looking up, I allowed myself to be led from the matron's office to Mrs. Johns' carriage. Blindly handed into my seat, I took my place beside my saviour. The dear lady was sensitive to my feelings and allowed me time to savour cradling my child once more.

The Johns family home was an elegant establishment on Hampden Road in a section of town known as Battery Point. With the magnificent Mt. Wellington watching over it, the house was situated on top of a steep incline overlooking the Derwent River. Upon the verandah as we drew up was a grey whippet. The dog lazed upon his back in the sun, wagging his tail at our approach, and we gently stepped around the sleepy creature to enter the house. As Mrs. Johns led me inside, I not only walked into a house of utter chaos and disorder but one where love flowed and happiness reigned. With their mother's arrival, excited children came from everywhere. A tall girl with long, dark hair came racing down the stairs, sliding down the banister for the last few metres.

'Mother!' she exclaimed. 'You found her!'

Apparently fully enlightened as to her mother's mission, she came forward to greet me and was introduced as the seven-year-old Angharad. Excited to see I had a bairn, she tickled Kezia's dangling foot as she sat upon my hip, and I heard my sweet child giggle for the first time. A second admirer in the form of Angharad's younger sister Eilys soon joined us and was equally enthralled by my child. The first of the boys appeared from the back of the house, rolling his hoop with a stick the full length of the hallway. When he spied his mother, Aled abandoned his hoop to embrace her. The solo hoop continued its journey along the passage until it fell heavily upon the wall. I noted the damaged walls around me and guessed that it was not the first time a hoop or similar had been cast upon them. The bairn of the family, Owain, toddled forward clutching a wooden spoon covered in cake mixture, and buried his grubby little face in his mother's skirt as she bent to bestow a kiss.

'Come,' Mrs. Johns smiled. 'I'll show you to your room.'

As we ascended the staircase, I looked back with amusement to see the boys now sitting cross legged in the middle of the hallway sharing the delights of the precious spoon. Upstairs Angharad hurried ahead and threw open the door at the end of the passage. A cat raced out with a hiss and Angharad chided it for having been inside. Mrs. Johns seemed not to notice as she ushered me into the large, bright room, so clean and comfortable. Drawing the curtains, she pointed to some nearby building works.

'They've been building St. George's ever since we arrived in this colony. Work on the tower alone has been going on for the past six years. They were required to rebuild a lot of the original structure to support its weight. It's been entertaining watching it. Hopefully, you'll find some interest too.'

Whilst I knew that watching the tower climb ever skyward would be of great interest, I was also certain my heart would surely draw my eyes in the opposite direction towards the river. The waters of the Derwent led to the lovely little inlet above whose tranquil depths lay *Knypersley Farm*. In seeing them I would always think of dear Doctor Markham and the joy I experienced in his care. I would think too of my cherished Sam and the happy times we spent sitting on the riverbank. Gazing upon them now with Mrs. Johns by my side, I felt safe and protected again, and was filled with the comforting knowledge that here in my new home, I would finally experience contentment and happiness once more.

By this time Kezia was starting to become irritable and Mrs. Johns suggested I might like to bathe her before laying her down to rest. What a delight it was to wash Dynnyrne's dirt from her little hands and feet and to see the warm water bringing life and colour back to her precious body. She was calmed and soothed by the cleansing waters. Dressing her in the lovely clean clothes generously bestowed by Mrs. Johns, I laid her in a crib that was quickly fetched from storage and placed comfortingly close beside my bed. Unable to resist the temptation of Mrs. Johns' suggestion that I join my bairn in her slumbers, I was soon resting my head upon the softest of pillows ready to drift into a blissful sleep. When I woke several hours later, my eyes instantly fell upon Mrs. Johns sitting beside my bed, Kezia in her arms. Fearing the worst, I sprung upright.

'Is she alright?'

Mrs. Johns looked up and smiled.

'She's perfect. Apart from a nasty rash and the effects of a naughty molar trying to break through, little Kezia is the picture of health.'

Laying my head back upon the pillow, I sighed contentedly. Mrs. Johns rose and laid my daughter by my side. Clasping her near, I kissed her sweet face, overwhelmed by the all-consuming love I felt for this little angel. Soon sleep claimed me once more and I dared to dream of our happy future together. With the cessation of my slumbers, I opened my eyes to discover my bairn breathing softly beside me. As my doting eyes dwelt upon her, I knew that I was truly blessed. Kezia had been returned to my side and my heartache immediately ceased. When her big blue eyes eventually opened, she gazed at me and chuckled. Seeing my child so joyous made my heart light, and I laughed too. Rolling onto her stomach, she crawled into my awaiting arms and I kissed her tenderly. Chuckling again, she placed her precious lips upon my cheek and returned my kiss. Hearing those within stirring, Mrs. Johns appeared in the doorway.

'Do you feel well enough to join us downstairs?' she queried.

Informed that I would be extremely happy to venture downstairs, she brought forward one of her own dresses and laid it on the chair beside me.

'I had your other clothes burned. It was cruel to expect any human to wear such ghastly things.'

I gasped.

'There was a ...'

'Blue ribbon,' Mrs. Johns interjected, holding up the beloved item. 'I realized its importance when I saw the way it was sewn into your petticoat.'

Returned to my possession, I quickly clasped it to my heart.

'From someone special?' she asked.

I nodded.

'From someone I will love forever.'

Once bathed and dressed, I gathered Kezia in my arms and joined Mrs. Johns downstairs. Wheeling forward Owain's old baby carriage, she offered it to me for Kezia's use. So beautiful and comfortable, I could instantly see myself walking proudly in the sunshine, my beautiful daughter breathing in the fresh, clean air she had been deprived of for so long. Yet, when Mrs. Johns suggested that I might like to place Kezia in it immediately, I could not bring myself to release her. Clutching her tighter than ever, I quickly took a seat, assuring Mrs. Johns that I was content to hold her for now. Seeing the other children at play, however, Kezia became discontent and began to grizzle, trying desperately to escape from my arms. The more she struggled, the stronger my hold became.

'Hannah, dear,' Mrs. Johns said gently, 'I think Kezia would like to join the others.'

'No,' I replied. 'She'll settle in a minute.'

Kezia though did not understand the fear I had of letting her go, and her tears began to flow.

'She will be safe,' Mrs. Johns urged, seeming to understand my hesitation. 'We're both here to watch over her.'

With Mrs. Johns' intervention, I reluctantly released my grasp on my bairn and she quickly slid from my knee, crawling to where the Johns children sat amusing themselves. My companion turned her sad eyes to me.

'I shudder to think what you must have been through to produce such weariness of the world.'

'It's still too raw to speak of,' I replied. 'But one day I should like to share my story with you. I feel that you are one person who would understand without judgement.'

Mrs. Johns reached out and squeezed my hand tenderly, as my eyes dwelt upon Kezia who I would soon learn to enjoy watching at play, and delight in every new phase she entered.

It is impossible to describe the home where I had found refuge. It was the warmest, most welcoming place that I was ever privileged to visit. Large and beautifully furnished, it was surely one of the loveliest in Hobarton, but it would have nothing without the amazing family who resided there. Mrs. Johns was the sweetest person. Totally disorganized, she was always searching for something and seemed oblivious to the pandemonium that continually surrounded her. In her husband, she had found her soulmate, and I will never forget his arrival home on that first evening. With a fine tenor voice, he sang greetings to all within, his children singing their reply before hurrying to greet him. Vying with each other to get the firmest grasp upon his hand, they also contended with an excitable little spaniel who bounded through the house, coming to a skidding halt at his master's feet. Led into the drawing room by his children, he greeted his wife with great affection before I was introduced. Mr. Johns welcomed me as an old friend. Taking my hand firmly in both of his own, he shook it and bestowed a kiss.

'Croeso, dear Hannah. Croeso,' he said jovially, greeting me in his native Welsh tongue.

Scooping two kittens from his chair, he joined us to hear all the day's adventures. My new master was an engineer who served his apprenticeship with the Thames Tunnel Company, working with Mr. Brunel and his son Isambard. Encouraged to apply for a position with the Colonial Government following the passing of the Water Act in 1835, his expertise saw him given the position of overseer for the works providing pure water for Hobarton. Arriving with his new wife the following year, his surveying and town planning skills proved invaluable in the new settlement and his current project was providing sanitation and water access to outlying towns. There was never a cross word between this fine couple and they loved each other dearly. They were content and happy in their lives, surrounded as they were by their children and music.

Hailing from Pembrokeshire in the southwest of Wales, they met when Mr. Johns called upon his wife's father, the local miller of Caerforiog, to inspect a defective water wheel. It was love at first sight and they were married a few months later, just prior to their departure for Van Diemen's Land. It was sweetness indeed when we gathered of an evening and my ears were captivated by the seraphim-like airs that resonated from Mrs. Johns's Welsh harp. Blessed with the glorious voices for which the Welsh are famous, the family would join her in song, the children being proficient in the language of their parents' homeland. Setting myself the challenge of learning the beautiful, lyrical words of this ancient language, in time I too was able to join in their song, be it though poorly.

As she grew, Kezia succeeded where I failed, and came to regard Welsh as her second language. The pride the Johns family had in their language, led me to think about a young Welsh woman named Anne who travelled with me on the *Garland Grove*. Able to write and speak fluent Welsh but lacking any English skills, one of the teachers on board labelled her defiant and meted out the harsh punishment of a bread and water diet. Her predicament sent the poor girl to the brink of madness and she made more than one attempt at suicide. Anne was one of those chosen to journey onward to Launceston upon our arrival, and I know not what happened to her. The memory of the discriminatory treatment levelled against her, however, will remain with me for the rest of my life.

Welcomed into their home with genuine warmth and affection, the happiness that I experienced under their roof, made me almost forget that I was still an assigned convict. Bronwyn and Huw, the names I was invited to call them, treated me with the kindness and friendship that had become so foreign to me of late. In fear of taking their kindhearted intentions for granted, I continually asked Bronwyn about the terms of my residency. Each time I broached the subject she would say,

'There's time enough for that later.'

My chores therefore would need to be of my own devising, and I set about tidying the house and caring for the children each morning whilst making it all appear incidental. Of an evening, I would withdraw to my bedroom where work was secretly underway to produce a new dress for Bronwyn, a gift of gratitude for my salvation. The look of pure joy upon her face when I placed it into her hands, warmed my heart and I knew I had chosen well. My life now entered a period of peace and tranquillity that would not be disturbed until Huw came to my side on the evening of 28th of January, 1849.

'Here's something to make you joyous, Hannah,' he said, handing me his newspaper.

I recognized my name and the astounding word "freedom". Huw read me the rest.

Certificates of Freedom
Issued to the undermentioned Convicts, whose sentences
are expired: -
Reg. No. 513 Hannah Fearn, at Hobart Town, on 28th ult.

My heart beat lighter as I heard the magic words that, after seven long years, I was finally free. I was forced to wait a further six months to hold the longed-for document in my hands but at last I possessed it - my Certificate of Freedom! Huw smiled like a proud father as he examined it. I knew that I must keep it with me at all times, so I folded it carefully and placed it at the bottom of my bag for safekeeping. Bronwyn took me into her arms and kissed me.

'So, what are you going to do with your newfound freedom?'

I knew that I was now free to return home, but I could nil afford such an expense. I would therefore be staying in Van Diemen's Land and making a new life for myself. Many ex-convicts had done well for themselves becoming owners of property and businesses. They lived in nice houses with space to breathe and move. They were eating well and raising strong, healthy children and found a place in society that was unimaginable in England. I wanted to join the ranks of the successful and well-respected citizens of this colony and I told my friends exactly that. I set before them an idea I had been mulling over for the past seven years: a dressmaking business of my own. My proposal was met with enthusiasm. 'But where will you conduct this business?' Bronwyn queried.

With my freedom approaching, I had begun investigating lodgings and told them of some I found in Campbell Street, near the Theatre

Royal. If I worked hard, I could just manage to pay the rent. Bronwyn's face fell. Huw looked at his wife.

'We were hoping you might consider remaining here with us,' he said.

A squeal of delight escaped my lips. I had so hoped to stay but thought it impossible.

'Then you will stay?' Bronwyn asked eagerly.

I nodded as tears of gratitude and joy streamed down my cheeks. Coming forward to embrace me, Bronwyn presented me with two small banking deposit books.

'The government wasn't going to stop me from rewarding you for your contribution to my household. By law, if a convict works, their employer is required to deposit one penny for every shilling they earn into an account at the Convict Savings Bank to claim upon their release. I adhered to the rules but also secretly placed the remainder into a separate trust account at the Derwent Bank in the name of Miss Kezia Gresley-Fearn. The proceeds from both accounts should help you to get settled into your new life very comfortably.'

'And I should like to offer you the use of the small room the previous occupant used as an office,' Huw added. 'It's light, has its own entrance, and would be perfect for conducting a business.'

What incredible friends! I was rendered speechless by their generosity. Mine was an industry where one risked earning only twelve or fifteen shillings a week, an income barely adequate to pay for food and lodgings, let alone the upkeep of a child. That I was able to live out my dream in the safety and comfort of the Johns' home was remarkable. There remained but one thing more to guarantee true fulfillment – a change of identity.

I heard that here in Van Diemen's Land, no one was judged by their convict past, only by what they made of themselves upon gaining freedom. Yet, I knew there was still fear amongst the masses that a convict stain would mark future generations. Many former convicts were doing all they could to escape the taint of past wrongdoings, the shame for me having increased twofold through unmarried motherhood. For a lot of women, the chance to start anew came following their marriage and the adoption of their husband's name. I was not so lucky. There was a name, however, that I was once promised by the most honourable of men. It was a name that would have been mine long since had fate not seen fit to intervene. Deciding that now was the right time to assume it, I declared that henceforth I would be known as the widow, Mrs. Hannah Gresley. It would have pleased my sweetest Sam to see his dear name so adopted. Fashioning myself an elegant mourning gown from lavender silk, I set forth into Hobarton society with an air of respectability.

With the generous assistance of dear Huw who installed shelving, drawers, and workbenches, my small salon was soon readied. Modelled on some of the elegant boutiques that delighted me during my time in London, I decorated the interior with the latest arrivals from that grand city. Tempting the senses with the finest quality cottons, silks, and linens, I displayed them alongside the prettiest laces, ribbons, and beads. For my supplies, Bronwyn accompanied me to Mr. Walker's fine drapery store in Liverpool Street where I discovered much to delight me. His father-in-law, Mr. Mather, owned a shop further along Liverpool Street, and between them, these two men provided me with everything that my heart could desire. Conscious that my hands, once so soft and delicate, had been roughened by my years of toil and service, I reinstated the evening ritual of cream and gloves once practised at Madame's in the hope that some beauty might be restored. With calling cards printed, I placed an advertisement in the newspaper. Bronwyn helped me with the wording and suggested I also utilize my time with Madame.

Conducted by Mrs. Gresley
(Late of Madame Le Blanc's Establishment, Regent Street, London)
Hampden Road, Battery Point
Dressmaking and Millinery

Executed in the latest styles from London
Short notice specialist. Reasonable terms.

Remembering the Markhams' friend, Mrs. Carminow, a lady of great repute who always demonstrated genuine compassion and admired my designs, I believed she might be willing to assist me now. I therefore called upon her unannounced one afternoon. Apologizing for my intrusion, I set about explaining the purpose of my visit.

'My business would greatly benefit from the kind patronage of a lady of influence. I always appreciated the trust you were willing to place in me and know that you are a woman of great style. I have come to beg your indulgence for my new venture. I would be honoured to furnish you with several outfits free of charge so that you might judge the quality of my workmanship and gauge the reaction of your acquaintances.'

'I remember your exquisite work, Hannah. I benefitted from it for too short a time. It would give me great pleasure to be your patron. My wardrobe is sadly outdated and I would be happy to place a large order to rectify the problem. You will be paid in full for every garment produced.'

True to her word, dear Mrs. Carminow became the most generous benefactress. With her support and that of the friends, I was able to continue offering the high-quality fabrics and accessories for which my establishment soon became renowned. In general, the women of Van Diemen's Land had a great desire to dress modestly and many couldn't afford the luxury of new attire, so many of my orders required reworking old dresses into modern styles. I worked hard to succeed in my little enterprise and I was granted a great deal of satisfaction.

Whilst Kezia was still a toddler, she would sit at my feet, a piece of lace or empty cotton reel keeping her entertained for hours. As she grew, she would sit alongside me creating her own designs as I sketched mine. The walls of my workshop were covered by our dual creativity. In time she developed an appreciation for fine silks, beautiful ribbons, and delicate laces that went far beyond a childhood craving for something pretty, and was eventually able to lend some very welcome and able assistance. Just as I once taught Georgina and Lavinia Markham, I now imparted the skills for sewing a sampler to my daughter. She always set about her work with diligence, her tiny fingers busily weaving needles of brightly coloured thread in and out of the fabric to produce pretty birds and flowers, as well as elegant letters and numbers. Her stitches were small and delicate and showed skill far beyond her age. Bronwyn was always astounded by her endeavour.

'She's quite a remarkable little thing,' Bronwyn remarked one day.

'She certainly is,' I agreed. 'She's her father's daughter.'

'No, Hannah, she's your daughter,' Bronwyn confirmed. 'You can take credit for everything about that sweet child.'

My friend's words cheered me and I looked upon my daughter with great pride and an adoring heart, unable to believe that something so perfect once grew within me.

At this time, the Anti-Transportation League was active in Hobarton, my friends being members since its inception. The League encouraged ladies to join and Bronwyn eagerly seized upon the rare opportunity. Soon elevated to the vital role of spokeswoman, she was chosen to make the journey to Sydney with the League's president, Mr. Cowper, to report on the recent conference held in Van Diemen's Land. Whilst an invitation was issued for me to accompany her, in truth I could not bear to be parted from Kezia. This did not mean that Bronwyn departed without my signature being added to those of eight thousand other ladies, all calling for an end to transportation. I was incredibly proud that I was able to write my name on such an extremely important document. My hesitancy to leave Kezia paid dividends just days later when she was struck down with fever and I had never been more grateful for a decision in my life.

From the time she was old enough, Kezia joined the other children playing on the street just beyond the window where I sat at work.

Watching her, I was filled with an exhilarating warmth seeing what pleasure it brought her. Then one day she was not at play. Though my eyes searched, she was nowhere to be found. Opening the door, I called to Eilys who was not far away.

'Kezia went inside,' she informed me. 'She was too tired to play.'

As I turned, ready to investigate, my eyes caught sight of my poor little bairn, curled up in a corner. Bending down, I placed my hand on her forehead and felt its burning pulse. She moaned. Crying out, I raced from the room seeking help. Moments later, Huw gathered her safely in his strong arms and carried her upstairs. As I made her comfortable, I was filled with horror to see the same bright lips and cheeks that once plagued my beloved Martha. Apart from a few sniffles, Kezia had never been sick, and it chilled me to see these ominous signs. Of late she frequently complained about a headache and sore throat. How I wished I had taken more notice. Kezia moaned again and I grasped her hand in my own, vowing that she would not be taken from me. Huw quickly summoned a doctor and I waited impatiently for relief to arrive.

I was kneeling beside the bed upon his arrival, silent tears flowing down my cheeks, clinging to my daughter's small, limp hand so firmly that Huw had his work cut out prising me away. Taken into Huw's soothing arms, I stood there sobbing. Suggesting I wait in the drawing room, Huw escorted me downstairs before returning to the doctor's side. Left alone, I wilted to the floor and resting my head upon the sofa, continued my sobbing. What a charmed life I had lived until now. Despite incarceration in some of the filthiest and most disease-ridden places on earth, I managed to escape with my life. Kezia's confinement at Dynnyrne, which caused me so much heartache and distress, was also blessedly completed without contamination. Now though, my beautiful daughter had fallen gravely ill in her own home, a place where I should have been able to protect her from harm. Having failed dismally, I was wracked with guilt.

After what seemed an eternity, Huw eventually reappeared declaring Kezia's fever broken. Jumping to my feet, I raced to embrace him. As I did so, my eyes caught sight of the doctor for the first time.

'Doctor Markham!' I exclaimed, staring at the apparition before me, doubting my senses.

The poor doctor fared little better. After an obvious struggle, he eventually found voice enough to tenderly whisper my name. I went forward and gathered his hands in my own.

'Thank you,' I whispered. 'She's my entire world.'

'Sam's child?' he queried.

I nodded.

'I thought so,' he said tenderly. 'She's the image of her father, though she would have been better blessed if she'd taken after you.'

I squeezed his hands tightly before gently releasing them.

'I must see her,' I said.

Whilst Huw escorted the kind medic to the door, I hurried to Kezia's side. As I gently brushed a stray hair from her forehead, she turned her pale face towards me.

'I love you,' she whispered.

With a cry encompassing both relief and joy, I collapsed onto the bed and clasped my bairn in my arms. When Huw returned, I showed him the terrible rash now covering her small body, and was truly thankful to hear that Doctor Markham believed it would begin to fade in around four days' time. Promising to sit by Kezia, Huw encouraged me to get some sleep. Withdrawing to my room, I tried to sleep but found that it evaded me. Yet, it was not due to fretting over Kezia, for the warm, mellifluous voice of Doctor Markham promised me that my little girl was safe, and I trusted no one more. No, it was thoughts of the doctor himself that unsettled me.

So many years had passed since I last saw him, years that brought great change to my life, but when I saw him standing there, my heart beat like never before. How desperately had I struggled to suppress my feelings, but now those soft, blue eyes met my own once more and he smiled his ever-affectionate and comforting smile. It was impossible to have a worse place or time, but my feelings could not be stifled any longer and they rose wickedly from their dormancy, all the stronger for their suppression. I lost my heart to him all over again. When my gentle friend returned later that afternoon, I was secretly overjoyed to see his handsome face again, all the more so when he assured me that Kezia was now stable. Looking upon her sleeping peacefully, Doctor Markham smiled.

'She's inherited her mother's strong constitution,' he declared, the comforting tone of his voice so soothing.

I acknowledged that at least I could be thankful for that, and he gently placed his supportive hand upon my shoulder. We stood there for a few moments in silence until Doctor Markham spoke,

'Mr. Johns seems extremely concerned about the child. Is he fond of her?'

'He thinks of her as one of his own,' I confirmed.

'And you, are you fond of him too?'

'Yes, I am. He has done so much for me.'

'Things that I longed to do for you myself,' he murmured with a heavy sigh, his head bowed. 'And now I am too late.'

Before we could say more, the object of our discussion appeared in the doorway.

'How do you find our little girl this afternoon, Doctor?' he asked good-naturedly.

Doctor Markham drew himself up and answered Huw as coolly as I ever heard him speak.

'The child is doing well enough,' he said. 'You've been blessed yet again.'

Gathering his bag, Doctor Markham hurried towards the door.

'I must be on my way,' he mumbled as he brushed past me. 'I will call again.'

He was gone and I felt astounded by his behaviour. What about Huw's appearance made this usually demonstrative man so reticent?

What did he mean by 'blessed yet again'? Had these two men known each other in the past? Was there animosity between them of which I knew nothing?

Having nursed Kezia late into the night, I was relieved by Huw in the early hours of the following morning. Utterly exhausted, I fell asleep the minute my head reached the pillow. Allowed to sleep late, I sadly missed Doctor Markham's morning visit, though I was gratified to hear that he found my darling daughter much improved, believing she would make a full recovery. Though dismayed at not seeing the dear doctor, we would not be parted long. Lured outside by the soft blue sky and gentle breeze later that afternoon, I was wandering towards the river, when my eyes were delighted by the sight of faithful Doctor Markham making his way slowly up the Hampden Road hill towards me. My steps drew to an instant halt and I watched his approach, desperately struggling to maintain my composure. As he reached my side, my heart skipped joyously.

'How are you, Hannah?' he asked with such genuine concern.

I assured him that I was well and thanked him again for the devoted attention he was giving Kezia.

'I would do anything for you and that little girl,' he declared.

I looked into his beautiful eyes. They were overflowing with kindness and sincerity.

'You have done well for yourself,' he said.

'I have been very fortunate. I have a little business of my own now which is doing rather well.'

'I'm so pleased for you, Hannah. Mr. Johns is a lucky man. *His* wife didn't place obstacles.'

As Doctor Markham reached down and took my hand in his own, I heard Huw's voice calling from the verandah.

'Hannah! Kezia's asking for you.'

Doctor Markham instantly let my hand slip from his own and stepped aside.

'You must go,' he said. 'I'll be there shortly.'

Hesitantly, I left him and returned to the house. Looking back from the verandah, the dear man cut such a lonely figure, his head and shoulders slumped forward as though he lacked the energy to stand upright any longer. Entering the house, I attended to my daughter, though knew not that Doctor Markham followed close behind. When I turned from the bed, I found him standing in the doorway, watching me closely. His face wore the same tragic look I would sometimes see burdening his countenance when his wife delighted in torturing him. That he could no longer hide his anguish clearly showed the level the abuse had now reached. Coming forward, he examined Kezia.

'I can happily say our young lady is now completely out of danger,' he assured me. 'Indeed, just a few more days and she'll be up to her old mischief again.'

With this, he gave Kezia a wink and she giggled merrily. A great wave of emotion swept over me upon hearing his blessed words. All the feelings I had kept close to my heart over the past few days burst forth, and completely overwhelmed, I fainted into Doctor Markham's arms. Rejoining the world sometime later, I awoke in my room to find Doctor Markham gently stroking my hair as he sat on the bed beside me. With his earnest face watching over me, I was quickly reassured and calmed.

'You gave me quite a scare,' he whispered, his endearing smile beaming forth.

There were no words. What could I say at being so blessed? My cherished daughter's health was restored and Doctor Markham was in my life once more. I lay there contentedly, my hand clasped in his own, a smile upon my lips.

When the necessity for his daily visits was at an end and my beautiful daughter was finally able to rise from her bed, I offered Doctor Markham a sum of money that I believed was appropriate for his diligent care. He quickly restored the money to the palm of my hand, closing my fingers around it.

'I could never take payment for treating one that I love,' he assured me. 'Kezia is my niece. What sort of man would I be if I charged for treating her?'

I thanked him from the bottom of my heart for his generous and thorough ministering. He merely smiled.

Kezia's illness signalled the beginning of a scarlet fever epidemic which would hold Hobarton in its grasp for the next two years. The disease worked its dreaded way through all the Johns children, Doctor Markham ministering to each one with the same care and devotion he had shown Kezia. Mercifully all our dear ones were spared, but many families would sadly suffer the loss of a child. A family living not far from us was devastated by the loss of four of their five children on consecutive days. When Bronwyn returned to us, she was much grieved that she was absent during her children's time of need and was indebted to Doctor Markham for his expertise and tender care.

'Now that the children are well again,' she declared, 'I should very much like to meet the famous Doctor Markham. Would you like to issue him an invitation to afternoon tea?'

Acknowledging that I should very much like that, when I led him into the sitting room the following Sunday afternoon, my heart swelled with pride. To me, he had only grown more handsome during the years of our separation. Dressed in his Sunday best, he wore the frock coat and silk cravat of former times, although I was sorry to observe that he seemed to be living in reduced circumstances, his coat now faded and the cuffs of his shirt rubbed. I wondered what had brought hard times upon him. Quickly relieving him of the top hat he twirled rather nervously in his hands, I seated him by the fire before pouring his tea. Sitting beside him, we chatted like old friends until Bronwyn joined us, apologizing for her tardiness. When Doctor Markham rose to greet her, her eyes quickly darted to mine with a look of infinite approval.

'I must thank you for the wonderful care you gave my children,' Bronwyn said by way of greeting. 'Huw has told me of your dedication, and I feel myself fortunate that you were here to minister to them in my absence.'

'Your children?' he murmured by way of reply, the poor man's face betraying deep disquiet. 'I thought Mr. Johns was a widower.'

Oblivious to the impact of her words, Bronwyn chuckled good-naturedly.

'Well, I do hope he hasn't been spreading that rumour. No, Huw is my husband. I was sadly detained in Sydney during my children's illnesses.'

As Doctor Markham's cup danced involuntarily in its saucer, he slumped, almost fell, back into his chair and his unblinking eyes desperately searched my face most peculiarly. Managing to find his voice, he whispered breathlessly,

'I thought that you ... you're not his wife?'

I quickly shook my head.

'Then ... you're not married?' he just managed to utter.

'No,' I replied, a declaration that seemed to completely overwhelm him and he sat staring blankly at the floor, almost as though he'd lost consciousness. I gently spoke his name. Starting from his reverie, he jumped to his feet.

'I must go,' he suddenly declared.

Astounded by our guest's strange behaviour, Bronwyn urged him to stay. Yet, he could not be swayed, such was his haste to depart and he quickly thanked Bronwyn for her hospitality. Fetching his hat, I handed it to him, though his trembling hands fumbled and he dropped it immediately. Scurrying after it, I placed it safely on his head. The poor man was evidently struggling, his face wearing such a strange, disturbed look. Grabbing my hand, he held it in both of his own, raising it to bestow a gentle kiss. Without another word, he rushed towards the door. Hurrying after him, I begged him to wait as I raced down the path to his side.

'Hannah,' he began. 'I have come such a long way to find you. I must speak with you.'

I smiled by way of encouraging him to speak, but before he could do so, Huw arrived home. Having been called to town on urgent business, he greeted Doctor Markham warmly.

'Doctor Markham! You're not leaving already?' he asked good naturedly as the men shook hands.

'Unfortunately, I must,' Doctor Markham replied.

Huw acknowledged his regret and expressed his hope that our guest would soon return. As Huw entered the house, Doctor Markham turned back to me and smiled sadly.

'You had something to say?' I urged, though he slowly shook his head.

'It doesn't matter. Now is not the time,' he said and hurriedly took his leave.

Thankfully Bronwyn's invitation was swiftly reissued, and Doctor Markham joined us for dinner the following Saturday. He came with humblest apologies, though any slight was quickly forgotten. When an astounded Bronwyn joined us, she discovered our guest seated with the children on the floor, having accepted their request to join them. They were all equally fond of Doctor Markham, though Kezia proudly made certain that no one forgot that he was *her* uncle. Having been granted the special privilege of staying up to greet our highly-favoured guest, the children's bedtime was now at hand. Bronwyn's children followed her obediently without complaint, whilst Kezia lingered, grizzling at me when I tried to urge her on. Naturally things were different when Doctor Markham offered his hand and promised to escort her. Seizing his hand tightly, Kezia trotted along merrily beside him, her beaming face looking adoringly up into his own.

With Kezia tucked in and settled, Doctor Markham returned downstairs, taking his seat beside me at the dining table. Following the strangeness of our last meeting, I was rendered incapable of any kind of serenity as I sat there wondering whether he would have the opportunity to broach the subject on which he had been so eager to speak the previous Sunday. Having uttered few words of any consequence throughout the evening, I knew how my seeming indifference would be perceived, and as the meal drew to a close, I finally found voice enough to speak.

'I must apologize, Doctor Markham,' I said, taking advantage of a rare pause in the evening's conversation. 'Being so consumed with Kezia's illness, I have failed to ask after your own family. How are Mrs. Markham and the children? Are they also in Hobarton?'

Doctor Markham shook his head.

'They have remained in England. Sophia and I separated not long after we arrived home.'

I know that my heart stopped upon hearing his words, and I listened breathlessly as he conveyed the rest of his story.

'Sir William arranged for a divorce and Sophia took the children to live with her father and mother on their estate. I lost most of my fortune in the divorce settlement but I worked hard and eventually made enough money for a passage back to Hobarton, a place that held such happy memories for me. It was important that I find a dear friend who I had left behind. A friend without whom life could not continue.'

'And have you found that friend?' Huw queried innocently.

'I certainly have,' Doctor Markham replied as he reached out and placed his hand upon my own resting on the table. His eyes met mine and he smiled that smile that could melt hearts.

I was barely able to breathe, such was the enormity of what had just been imparted. Bronwyn shifted excitedly in her chair and looked into my face with great meaning. For once I tried to avoid her gaze, and lowering my eyes became intent upon studying the lacework of the tablecloth. I felt a strange, draining feeling in my head, and my ears heard nothing other than the loud beating of my heart, strangely amplified. Huw was thankfully mindful of his wife's talent and passion for matchmaking and at once suggested that Doctor Markham join him in his study for a liqueur and coffee. Bronwyn fully understood that she did not enter her husband's domain when he was entertaining guests and therefore was compelled to concede defeat for the immediate present.

As the men withdrew, I was left behind with my overly enthusiastic friend, knowing full well I would not avoid discussion of Doctor Markham's newly discovered marital status. I wished that I too could escape and partake of liqueur and coffee. Bronwyn seized my hand tightly.

'Oh, Hannah! He came looking for you. After all these years and despite the distance between you, he came back. How he must love you! He can't take his eyes off you.'

'He's everything to me, except my own,' I acknowledged, my voice broken and barely audible. In truth, at that moment the impact of Doctor Markham's news had rendered me practically insensible, unable to think or act with any kind of reason.

'Poor Hannah,' Bronwyn sighed. 'You're so pale and silent.'

As Doctor Markham left me that night, he took my trembling hands in his own and whispered,

'May I call upon you?'

I nodded, and without further words, he was gone. With the warmth of his touch still caressing my skin, I closed my eyes and dwelt on his wondrous words, may I call upon you? Surely only a dream could bring such happiness. As I lingered in the hallway, an exchange between my two friends, slowly reached my ears.

'I wonder how long he managed to hide it from his wife,' Huw pondered. 'It can't have been long. His face betrays him every time she's near.'

'I've never seen such infinite love,' Bronwyn agreed. 'And our sweet Hannah looks at him with such tenderness.'

Was my love for him really so apparent? I had no notion I was betraying my feelings so utterly. Yet, there was little sense in being perturbed, for I adored him with every fibre of my being, and now with my amour no longer forbidden, I cared not who knew of my ardour.

The toll of a sleepless night was evident the following morning when a severe headache compelled my return to bed. Bronwyn crept in to check on me.

'Can I bring you anything, dearest?'

I shook my head.

'My head aches so terribly,' I replied. 'I just need to lie here for a while longer.'

A few hours later I heard the door slowly opening and I could see Bronwyn's silhouette against the light.

'Hannah dear,' she whispered. 'Are you awake?'

I assured her that I was.

'There's someone here to see you,' she informed me, stepping aside to admit my visitor before I could object. A tall figure joined her in the doorway. Bronwyn drew my curtains slightly, and my heart was instantly lighter at the sight of Doctor Markham. My dear friend came gently to my side and Bronwyn left us.

'I believe you are not well,' he said, smiling kindly.

'Merely a headache,' I swiftly informed him. 'It has eased off now.'

'May I?' he asked, indicating the side of my bed.

I nodded and Doctor Markham helped to arrange the pillows behind my back before taking a seat beside me. Sitting silently for a time, simply content to be together again, it was a while before Doctor Markham spoke.

'Are you happy here in Hobarton?'

Assuring him I cherished every moment of life, I acknowledged how sorry I was that his life had not been happy since we parted.

'Perhaps it was all for the best,' he said. 'I was content in Van Diemen's Land but convinced myself that I would be happy to see my homeland again. After my warning from the Government, Sophia felt humiliated and I was no longer fully satisfied by my work, so I thought that a trip home might help. As soon as we arrived, I realized that England was no longer the place that I left. With the terrible impact made by the Poor Laws, there's so much more poverty. I was treating a whole new range of illnesses, so many of which came from working in those wretched factories. I realized all too late what I left behind in Hobarton. Sophia wanted to return home and, as her husband, I was compelled to go with her. We no longer lived as man and wife, but in the eyes of the world, I was still a married man. I was trapped. And then there were my children, I couldn't just leave them.

Not long after our arrival, Sophia met Lord Charles Grey. He was the man of whom she had always dreamed, the man she wanted me to be. Suddenly a divorce was being organized and paid for by her father and I found myself a free man again. When she took my darling children away, I had nothing left in the world. Following this, I took time to think and reflect. I knew that there was only one person in the world that could make me happy again and so I decided to return to Australia and start my life over.

I worked hard to earn enough money for my passage and I took on a practice where four thousand poor, suffering souls were under my care. Part of my role was to minister at the workhouse where I witnessed such horrific conditions. I remember an eighteen-year-old boy, who I arrived too late to save. Lying in his coffin he was just skin and bone, having been practically starved to death by my predecessor. The inquest failed to establish guilt, and perhaps I can see why, for it was a case of mere neglect rather than deliberate torture.

The heavy workloads and high expectations now being placed on doctors mean so many cannot cope and suicide rates have soared, two of my acquaintances being among their number. Nothing could have enticed me to take my life, not when I was driven by a greater purpose. Every day I worked, I knew it brought me closer to returning to Hobarton and finding you.'

Moved by his story, I unconsciously placed my hand on his own. He took it and gently squeezed it.

'You know,' he declared, 'I have never forgiven myself for deserting you when you needed me the most.'

'Please don't blame yourself,' I pleaded. 'It was Mrs. Markham. I know that there was nothing you could have done to change things.'

'But there was,' he insisted. 'I was far too willing to defer to Sophia's demands. I am ashamed to say that I found it easier to give in rather than fight. I was even content to leave without saying goodbye to those nearest and dearest.'

'I understand ...' I began, but Doctor Markham interrupted.

'The truth is I had lost you. You were living with Sam, expecting his child, and seemed so happy. I had always hoped that one day ...'

'Don't distress yourself,' I urged. 'All is well now, and we have met again.'

He looked at me, his piercing blue eyes stirring my heart.

'Could you ever find a place in your heart for me?'

'You have had a place there since the day you rescued me from that wretched factory.'

Doctor Markham edged closer and gently kissed my lips. I could not breathe. That kiss, that incredible kiss, and now no longer forbidden.

'I didn't know that it was possible to love as I love you. When I was told of Sam's death, my thoughts instantly flew to you. I knew your advanced condition would not stop the law from taking its course, and that you would be condemned to that despicable factory. Perhaps I made my feelings a little too evident and Sophia accused me of being in love with you. It wasn't the first time that she accused me of such. I couldn't deny her accusations. I *was* in love with you ... desperately in love. I loved you from the first moment I saw you sitting there so pale and silent, in need of a good bath and feed. I simply lost my heart. Yet, I was thousands of miles from you. I didn't even know if you were still alive. I have lived six long years yearning to see your face again.'

My lips trembled.

'I have so little to give you,' he said. 'And I want to give you so much.'

'I have all that I could ever want right here,' I declared, placing my arms around his neck, holding him tightly. And I did. The mere sight of him lightened my heart and brought an end to my suffering. Doctor Markham ... no, Jos, was mine at last.

It was late in the evening a few days later and having no further clients, I sat working on my orders. Kezia was seated beside me, measuring and cutting material, ribbon, and lace, ready for my use. Soon I heard someone entering. Thinking it was a walk in off the street, I rose ready to greet them and was delighted indeed to see Jos's handsome face looking back at me.

'Look at you,' he said, his head thoughtfully tilted. 'Little Hannah Fearn. She's grown into such a fine lady and still as beautiful as ever.'

Coming forward, he took my hand in his own.

'I'm so very proud of you, Hannah. To see you happily settled makes my heart glad.'

Not to be ignored, Kezia tugged on his sleeve, pleading for an embrace from her adoring uncle.

'Noswaith dda,' he said, greeting her in Welsh.

Truly enamoured by my Welsh-speaking daughter, who preferred bara brith to scones, and whose favourite dish was the lamb stew known as cawl, he marvelled at the chance meeting that brought Kezia and me to live with the Johns family. That his niece had been brought up to understand and appreciate the language and customs of his own mother's homeland was of great delight to him. I invited him to join us for dinner and sent Kezia ahead to inform Bronwyn of our guest. Once she departed, he turned his eyes back to me.

'Did Sam ever tell you that he provided for both of you in his will? In fact, he left you his entire estate. I am the executor of the will. When I heard of Sam's death, I contacted my solicitor in Hobarton and asked him to act upon it. I received a letter shortly afterward confirming that the stock on the *Brynmawr* estate had been sold, the house boarded up, and a trust established with all available funds.

Those funds are yours now, Hannah. You may do with them as you wish.'

The enormity of what Jos was telling me, was so great, that very little sunk in at that moment other than the fact that my beloved *Brynmawr* had been boarded up. I know that the name *Brynmawr* echoed from my lips but very little else. Undaunted, Jos continued.

'I visited Sir William during my stay and ensured he knew Sam left a child. It came as a great shock to him when I spelt out my belief that the child should receive equal acknowledgement alongside his other grandchildren. The discussion became rather heated until he eventually saw sense upon a second visit. The children's eldest cousin, Edward, will inherit *Knypersley* and the Gresley title, but the other grandchildren, Kezia included, will inherit substantial wealth.'

I could hardly believe my ears, my daughter, heiress to a fortune. Yes, how very strange this new country was, in that it had thrown together two people possessing such vastly different backgrounds as Sam and I, and now our daughter stood to be a very wealthy woman. The following day, Jos suggested the perfect way in which to spend some of my newly acquired funds. Looking at Kezia, who was by now six years of age, he said,

'That child has been given an idyllic childhood. She will never want for anything, thanks to you. She has a gentle, loving, and devoted mother, a secure home, the gift of music, and the artistic skills of both her parents. She has a wonderful life ahead of her. Do you think it would be worth considering giving her some schooling to complete her education?'

Wanting to give my daughter every advantage, I quickly agreed, knowing that the money set aside by Sam for his daughter's upkeep would allow me to engage the very best of tutors. For young boys there would be no quandary, the Hutchins School offering everything one could desire. Modelled on English Grammar schools like Rugby, it possessed a wide curriculum including the Classics, Latin, and Greek. Yet there was no school equal to Hutchins that could educate young ladies. Kezia would therefore join Angharad and Eilys to be home-schooled by the formidable Welsh woman, Mrs. Ceridwen Davies. Under her tutelage, Kezia was guaranteed a well-rounded education including all the accomplishments: theory and practice of music, drawing, embroidery, French, as well as the elements of science. I was so proud to see my little girl settle so diligently to her studies. It was extremely gratifying that in her short lifetime, Kezia had already received more education than I ever would. In time, Jos also enlisted Mrs. Davies's help to further my own education, continuing the good work begun by dearest Sam.

Living alone as Jos now did, I little doubted that his ministering to the afflicted would be first and foremost in his mind, his own welfare coming a very distant second. With no one to care for him, the best way I could help was with my needle, so I decided to make him a gift of two new shirts. Despite cloth now coming in an abundance of new colours, I was adamant that Jos's shirts would still be white and made of comfortable cotton. It always told of someone's wealth and austerity when they could afford to have their shirts frequently laundered to keep their pristine, white appearance. I understood that Jos possessed no great wealth, but he did have breeding and a position to maintain in society. In bestowing the shirts, I therefore pledged to also launder them as required and to supplement their number in time.

Jos was more touched by my gift than I could ever have imagined. The sizing proved perfect and, whilst he tried them on, I took the opportunity to attach the new cuffs and collars I made for his existing shirts. The day I delivered my gift was my first visit to Jos's new home. With the elegant *Knypersley Farm* sold upon the family's departure for England, Jos now lived in an altogether different area of town. Originally built as a shop, his home lay on the corner of Campbell Street and one of the many small laneways leading off it. The wharf was just visible from its front window as were the many warehouses and factories that were being built in the area. Established in a low-lying part of town, the area was prone to flooding and possessed a reputation for danger, drunkenness, and notorious women.

The setup was not dissimilar to my own in that there were two entrances, one for the business, and the other for the dwelling behind. Jos's surgery contained everything needed to give a patient excellent medical care. As for his lodgings, it was clear from the bed, travelling trunk and washstand, that he slept in a small alcove adjacent to the surgery. There was an overwhelming sense of emptiness, the dear man cutting a very lonely figure sitting at his desk upon my arrival. Acknowledging the adjoining house was not furnished to receive visitors, he invited me to take a seat in the surgery.

When Jos produced the tea service, it saddened me to observe there was very little else in the cupboard. On the sideboard were the remains of some cheese and bread, obviously left over from his very meagre meal. I was touched by his dignity and saddened that his ex-wife left him so desolate. When it came time for my departure, Jos volunteered to escort me home.

'These parts are not safe for a lady to be roaming at night,' he assured me, and I was infinitely pleased to take his protective arm and wander home by his side. Refusing an invitation to stay a while, he waited for me to enter before retreating down Hampden Road. I thought of the miserable little dwelling to which he was returning and my heart ached for him.

The following evening, I decided to prepare a warming supper for Jos, and once Kezia was settled, I set out to surprise him. Discovering him at his desk as he entered the final few notes from that day's patients, he sat in his shirt sleeves, the rebellious black curl I so loved having fallen across his forehead. He looked up upon my entrance and smiled. Laying the tray on a nearby table, I encouraged him to rest and enjoy his supper. Taking a seat on the sofa, he held out his hand and drew me forward to sit beside him. With supper complete, Jos gently stroked my cheek with his little finger, before leaning forward to kiss me.

Over the following week, I savoured every moment spent with him, thanking God for the blessing of our reunion. Then one evening, I entered to discover him sitting on his bed, still fully clothed. His head fell limply forward as though it was impossible to hold it upright any longer. Work of late had been so hard, and the hours so long, that he sat there completely exhausted. Hurrying forward, I removed his boots, encouraging him to lie back upon the pillow. As he rested, I sat beside him, gently stroking his hair. With eyes closed, he lay there whilst I soothed him, my other hand clasped in his own. Eventually, he slept.

The serenity of the moment must have had an equally lulling effect on me, for when I woke the following morning, I realized that I too had fallen asleep, curled up beside him. Though there was no blanket to protect me from the icy morning chill, I did not shrink from its bitterness, for Jos's arm was around me and my body tingled to be held so close by the man I adored. I dared not move for fear of waking him, especially dreading that he might be angered by my stay. How grieved he would have been to discover my hesitancy, for when he finally stirred, he merely smiled, drew me closer, and kissed me.

'Don't ever leave me, Hannah,' he whispered.

'No one will ever part us again,' I assured him.

'I remember the first time that I held you?' he reminisced. 'After that terrible nightmare. You were so frightened. I held you far tighter than I should have, but I already loved you. Those few moments gave me such joy, the likes of which I had never before known.'

The following evening as I slowly undid his buttons, slid the shirt from his shoulders, and ran my hands over his strong chest and arms, it was I who experienced joy like never before. As I lay my head upon the pillow, Jos took his place beside me, and raising himself on an elbow, he looked down at me and smiled.

'How long have I waited for this moment, my darling,' he said as he kissed me.

Words cannot be found to express the feelings that consumed me as I lay with Jos that evening. Never could I have imagined the ecstasy of being made love to by my adored one, who was at once strong and passionate, gentle and romantic. I was the most fortunate of women.

Confessing my sin to Bronwyn the following morning, I was amazed at the incredible calm with which she greeted my news, indeed, there was even a certain levity about her response.

'How wonderful!' she exclaimed. 'When two people love each other as you do, they should be together.'

'But I slept with him as though a wife,' I sobbed. 'When I've finally found my place in society, I must do everything to maintain it. And now, I'm a mother too. I can't do anything that will hurt Kezia.'

'Then you better give him a little extra nudge towards that proposal,' Bronwyn declared light-heartedly.

'Oh, I could *never* trap him so!' I cried with true horror.

Bronwyn laughed.

'Hannah, you are either too innocent or completely blind. Jos is infatuated with you. There's a proposal coming, you mark my words, perhaps he just needs a little encouragement.'

'No. If what you say is true, I will wait until Jos thinks it's the right time to ask me.'

With a heart perhaps too eager to believe Bronwyn's declaration, I waited patiently whilst seeking every little distraction to momentarily take my mind off the highly anticipated proposal. One delightful diversion came by way of the Hobarton Regatta which was always a day of great celebration. We found the previous year's event rather disappointing, many of the usual young men who crewed the boats having been lured across the sea to the colony of Victoria for the gold rush just commenced. This year, however, as we gathered in splendid weather upon Mr. Kermode's hill, there were boats aplenty, many flying colourful banners from their masthead. It warmed my heart to see the new League flag being flown by the starting boat as well as many others, for an end to transportation was such a crucial thing to be achieved.

At the conclusion of the day's racing, the starting boat's flag was brought ashore, and amid cheering crowds was carried to the top of the hill. Held aloft, it was declared a symbol of peace and goodwill, representing a holy cause. The flag was subsequently paraded around Battery Point, though we only followed it as far as Captain Gardner's home, for a grand ball was to be held that night, and ready ourselves we must.

With work keeping him constantly busy, I did not expect to see Jos during the day, and I had similarly low expectations concerning his appearance at the ball. I fully understood that his quiet, evening hours were a time to rest and recover from his daily toil before the demands of a new day came flooding in. My delight, therefore, was extreme when I heard Bronwyn's magic words,

'Oh, Hannah. It's Jos!'

Standing with my back to the door, I couldn't trust myself to turn, for my body was all in a quiver.

'He's so very handsome,' Bronwyn sighed. 'But look, he's coming this way.'

Clasping hold of Bronwyn's arm, my heart beat wildly as I whispered, 'I'm going to faint,' but before I could carry out my threat, I heard his beloved voice.

'Hello, Hannah.'

His voice gave me the courage I needed, and I turned to be greeted by that beautiful smile.

'You grow lovelier every time I see you,' he said. 'And that dress! I can see from its exquisite quality that it's one of your elegant designs.'

How very much like him to take the time to recognize the intricacies of my work. In truth, my one thought whilst completing my gown, was that Jos might one day see me in it. That he saw me on its debut was the greatest delight. Enchanted by the man who now held my hand to his lips, my cheeks wore a glow of pleasure. Yet, whilst consumed by such utter joy, my voice could not find the words to speak and it was left to Bronwyn to inform Jos that my card was free for the first dance.

'Sadly, I cannot avail myself of that pleasure,' he replied. 'Protocol demands that I dance the first tonight with Mrs. MacDonald.'

'Who's Mrs. MacDonald?' Bronwyn queried.

'She's the widow of a local attorney. Sophia and she were good friends. It's not long since she lost her husband, and I felt it my duty to escort her tonight. But never fear, she's good friends with Reverend Polkinghorne and will spend most of the evening with him, leaving me free for far more pleasurable pursuits.'

Reaching down, he unhooked my dance card from my wrist and began filling it. When he did return to claim the second dance, it was all the more special, and held in his arms, I could soak in the true artistry of his face. His were looks of rare distinction. Instinctively, I reached up and stroked his cheek, the skin of which was soft as a bairn. His frock coat and crisp white shirt had been tailored by me and he lent them true elegance. Although my steps were clumsy and stilted, Jos's grace upon the dancefloor thankfully saved me from humiliation, something that was crucial, for it was our first public appearance to-gether. All eyes were on us. As we danced, his eyes twinkled with their former brightness, something I had seen slowly fade during my time at *Knypersley*. How I did celebrate its return.

'Do you remember our first dance together?' he whispered. 'In the barn with young Jonas playing his fiddle.'

'You will never know what those dances meant to me,' I replied.

'If they meant half as much to you as they did to me, then I fully understand. A moment with you always gave me courage, and I waited impatiently from one meeting until the next.'

Throughout the evening, I was approached by several gentlemen seeking my company for the next dance, and whilst my dance card was already filled by my beloved, he generously stood aside in their favour.

'You're certainly the belle of the ball,' he declared proudly as I returned to his side following one such parting. 'And rightly so.'

'I don't wish it,' I sighed, staring at the sea of unwelcome suitors. 'If only they knew there's only one person ...'

My words ended abruptly but Jos understood my meaning.

'Me?' he whispered, placing his arm around my waist and pulling me closer.

I turned to him and smiled. Seizing me tightly by the hand, he quickly ushered me outside. For a time, we walked in silence, content to absorb the beauty of the pretty lantern display, but then Jos's steps halted and he turned to me.

'It's been ten years since you first came into my life and changed it forever,' he said. 'Now you have returned to me, I feel alive again and can dream of the future I always hoped to have with you.'

'We are surely owed some happiness,' I declared. 'We have waited long enough.'

Taking me into his arms, he held me close as my head rested upon his chest and we gazed out at the moon sparkling upon the water.

Kezia was still awake when I arrived home and as I sat beside her, she begged to hear everything about the evening's entertainment.

'Was Uncle Jos there?' she asked eagerly, seemingly much pleased by the confirmation that he was.

Subsequent questions followed enthusiastically: Did you dance with him? Did he like your gown? Did he dance with anyone else? My answers seemed to give her much gratification, and she quickly snuggled under the covers, sighed a contented sigh, and fell asleep.

It was a momentous day indeed when the last ship bearing female convicts arrived in Hobarton. As the *Duchess of Northumberland* tied up at the wharf on Thursday 21st of April, 1853, I stood reminiscing. That Kezia should also witness this historic event was of vital importance to me, and she stood holding my hand as we watched. I looked upon the miserable women onboard with mixed emotions. I understood the burden under which they would be labouring and the pain in their hearts at having been wrenched from family, friends, and everything familiar. It must have been a bitter sting indeed when they realized that they would be the last ones banished. They had come so close to remaining in their homelands. Yet, what did life at home have to offer these women? Left to linger in British prisons, if they survived until release, would the world outside be any friendlier? Sorrow and toil, death and disease were the lives of so many in my homeland. Here in Hobarton, there was freedom, wide open spaces and fresh air. It was the land of opportunity. Without transportation, I would never have experienced the joy and contentment I felt every day.

The true magnitude of the day's events, however, would not be revealed until Jos arrived mid-afternoon to convey me to the foothills of Mt. Wellington in his pony trap. Gone now was his elegant tilbury of former times as well as the brilliant black steed who pulled it. In their place stood this small, wooden cart onto which was hitched a sturdy, piebald working horse Jos rescued from the knacker's yard. As if indebted to Jos for saving him from a terrible fate, the trusty little horse trotted along proudly and didn't once falter as we began the ascent up my beloved mountain. Climbing as high as the cart track would take us, we looked out over Hobarton and the glistening waters of the Derwent. Jos helped me down from the cart and as we gazed upon the beauty below, I declared it to be one of the most picturesque places I had ever been.

'I wanted this moment to be so special,' Jos acknowledged. 'That's why I brought you to this mountain of yours.'

I smiled my thanks.

'Darling,' he said, gently turning me to face him. 'These past few months have been the most wonderful in my entire life. It's impossible to think that I ever existed without you. I didn't believe I could love you more than I did at *Knypersley*, but seeing you again has proven me wrong. I love you more as the days go by.' With this, he took my hands into his own and looked at me earnestly. 'Hannah, my life will never be complete without you by my side, but I hesitate to ask for what my heart desires most. Do I have the right? I am an old, broken man, a divorcee with four children, and you, you're so young and beautiful, so full of life.'

'That life is worth nothing if it can't be spent loving you,' I assured him. 'You are neither old nor broken, but the most generous, kind, and affectionate man I have ever known.'

I reached up and lovingly stroked his poor, agonized face. His eyes, so tender and yet so apprehensive, broke my heart as they looked at me.

'Then,' he began tentatively, 'will you allow me to ask what I have dreamed of asking since the first moment I saw you? Is it too much to ask, too much to wish for, that you would do me the honour of accepting my hand in marriage?'

'Oh, Jos,' I sighed contentedly as I threw my arms around his neck. 'Yes. Yes, I will.'

It was all I could do, such were my emotions. Jos himself was truly spent from his efforts and so we simply stood there in a loving embrace, staring down upon the waters that brought us together.

Preparations for our nuptials began immediately. Kezia, who greeted our news with great enthusiasm, threw herself into the planning with gusto, helping me with every little detail. Each evening at the close of business, I would again take up my needle and thread, setting to work on a wedding dress that I hoped would be the most beautiful ever seen by Jos and Hobarton. Bearing in mind Jos's reduced circumstances, I didn't want to spend excessively, so I contented myself with a pretty, pale blue cotton, which I hoped, through clever workmanship, to bring alive. The blue would match my beloved ribbon that I intended wearing in my hair, and afterward, the dress would serve as very suitable day wear.

My lovely bridal creation quickly took shape and was hanging proudly in my workroom when I discovered I was carrying my intended's child. I could not be surprised, for by that time I had been lying alongside Jos for several months, and a warm glow filled me when

I thought of the bairn, our child. There was little time to ponder how to tell my beloved, before he came to me, excited by a proposition he wished to lay before me.

'I was thinking, my darling, that for our wedding tour, I should like to take you home.'

'To England?' I all but sobbed.

Jos looked at me with surprise.

'Yes,' he confirmed. 'You could visit your family, meet my mother, and the children would be overjoyed to see you again.'

My heart sank, and lowering my eyes, I quietly shook my head.

'Don't you want to go?' he queried.

'It's been my dream for so many years,' I admitted. 'But at the moment it is impossible for me to make such a long journey.'

Jos looked at me, confused for a moment before I gently took his hand and placed it upon my small belly. I will never forget his face when he realized that I carried his child.

'Oh, Hannah. My sweetheart,' he sighed lovingly. 'A baby.'

Falling to his knees, he rested his cheek upon my belly and began to sob. I had never witnessed such violent sobbing. I gently caressed his dear head. He clung to me so tightly, so desperately, that I feared he might never be consoled. Eventually, he was soothed.

'You have given me everything, my dearest girl. There are no words to tell you how much I adore you.'

'This bairn will be the first of many wonderful things for us,' I assured him.

As there was a child on the way, Jos declared that our wedding should be brought forward and we decided to marry as soon as possible. Before we did so, however, the celebrations to mark the Cessation of Transportation would take place. Having been a staunch supporter of the Anti-Transportation League, Jos was kept busy attending meetings, organizing protests, and enlisting support for the cause. Now having succeeded in his quest, he was occupied throughout much of June and July, organizing the celebrations.

On the 10th of August, all of the planning came to fruition, with a day of festivities held across the colony. Bells started peeling at six o'clock in the morning and continued at intervals throughout the day. There was very little business done in either the town or port, and the idle boats in the harbour were decorated, their brightly coloured flags gleaming in the brilliant sunshine. Salutes were fired from the port throughout the day, the mariners doing themselves proud.

At eleven o'clock, we attended a service of thanksgiving at St. David's Cathedral, after which we proceeded to the wharf where the entertainment was underway. Mr. Hoggins, whose pastries often tempted our tastebuds, produced a magnificent cake decorated with a kangaroo in icing. The cake was displayed on a stand draped in the Union Jack. This gentleman also supplied the numerous sandwiches and tarts on offer alongside ginger beer and lemon syrup.

As part of the celebrations, Kezia and other children were issued with a ticket entitling them to a medallion commemorating the event. Kezia would end up saving that ticket for two years until the silver medallions arrived in the colony. By the time of their issue, further attempts had been made to throw off our convict past, one of the most crucial being the change of name for our tiny island from Van Diemen's Land to Tasmania.

Our day of celebration was completed in spectacular style with a huge fireworks display, the nearby hills of Richmond also set alight with beacons. That I made merrier than many others present is beyond a doubt. I suffered greatly under the cruel system of transportation and its wickedly harsh punishments. In five months' time, our bairn would be born into a world where this brutal practice was now at an end. It was truly gratifying.

Whilst our initial plans were to marry directly following these celebrations, our nuptials were further delayed by a serious health crisis in the colony. The scarlet fever epidemic of which Kezia and the Johns's children were all victims was still prevalent across town and there was a desperate search for its source. Some blamed the rivulet, others the state of the streets. The fact that the disease was on the rise in Hobarton whilst Launceston remained virtually disease free proved it was a localized problem. Jos did what he could to alleviate pain whilst helping to discover the origin of the disease.

One benefit of the delay was the granting of extra time in which to establish our new home. Whilst my business would remain in Hampden Road, Kezia and I would be moving to the house at the back of Jos's surgery. With our reduced means, it was gratifying to discover the previous occupants had left a small assortment of furniture that, once properly cleaned and restored, proved perfect for our little family. Mirroring my work once so lovingly completed at *Brynmawr*, I again set about creating soft furnishings for my new home. Jos's financial situation meant that the quality of fabrics I worked with were far inferior to those of the past, but I soon found that I could make a pretty design look equally as good.

For Kezia, the move would cause great upheaval. She would be leaving the place she had called home all her life, and whilst she would continue seeing the Johns children each day, and be schooled alongside them, I knew that parting from them each evening would break her little heart. I understood how difficult it would be for her to live separately from the four lively children whom she thought of as much-loved sisters and brothers. It would take a great deal of adjustment learning to sleep by herself for the first time and in a strange, lonely room.

It was a blessing, therefore, that the sweet and generous nature she inherited from her father meant she did not remonstrate but accepted the change without question. I was thankful that her temperament did not mirror my own for I would never have been so compliant. The great affection that Jos and she shared, as well as the eagerly anticipated arrival of her younger sibling, also softened the blow. As a farewell gift, Angharad gave Kezia her own kitten, a tiny bundle of grey fluff who was joined by another within weeks. Soon a puppy was added and our growing menagerie managed to offer Kezia a little extra comfort whilst she became accustomed to her new life.

During this time, my daughter was not the only one who needed comforting, for I had serious concerns for my own wellbeing. From the beginning, my pregnancy was unlike my first and I was crippled by severe morning sickness, which saw me take to my bed far more than I would have wished. Both Jos and Doctor Bell counselled me well and, whilst I initially feared I might lose the bairn, I was much relieved when I felt my child move for the first time.

Throughout this time Bronwyn continued to prove herself the truest and best friend anyone could wish for. Whilst I could thankfully continue producing garments for my clients, oftentimes I was unable to meet with them in person. Bronwyn happily attended to them in my place, helping them with fabric choice and selection of trimmings. Angharad, who was by now a very mature and sensible thirteen-year-old, was also an excellent help being able to cut patterns with precision and whose fine and delicate needlework was faultless. In the quiet hours, Bronwyn would sit by my side, her company and lively chatter ever so much loved and appreciated.

It was during this time that Jos and I were gratified to receive a letter from Jos's ex-wife Sophia, announcing that she too would soon be wed. Lord Charles Grey, the man for whom Sophia left Jos, finally proposed and she would be Lady Grey at last. Lord Charles was from the Grey family who had inhabited various residences in Groby, Leicestershire since the 1400s, and could count among their number Lady Jane Grey, Britain's Nine Day Queen. Handing me a thick envelope, Jos informed me that Sophia included it for me.

'Dear one,

Josiah writes that the two of you are to be wed. May I offer my congratulations and wish you every happiness. Be assured I bear you no ill will, you will be much better suited to life as Mrs. Markham than I ever was. You will be content with the love and care Josiah will give you, I was not. I fell in love with a handsome, young doctor with great prospects. When he lacked the drive and ambition to bring these to fruition, it was a bitter disappointment to me. I am not so black-hearted, however, that I do not realize that I was lucky to have such a kind and gentle husband and I know that Josiah will make you the best husband that anyone could wish for. That he has loved you for a great many years I am certain and I am pleased he will finally have a wife to love him as he so deserves. My children are extraordinarily excited that their father is to marry you, far more so than when they heard of my own upcoming nuptials. I suppose it is only natural, for they have loved you oftentimes better than they have loved me, and understand their father's infatuation.

Now, I must speak of something I should have done many years ago. When my brother fell in love with you, he asked for a ring in my possession that had been passed down through several generations of Gresley women. He wanted to give it to you but I refused him. That my brother and I had become estranged by the time of his death has always saddened me. I wish to make a gesture of friendship towards you, something that would have pleased Samuel. I am therefore sending you the ring, a little late, but better than never. I hope that when you wear it, you will think of me with kindness and remember how much my brother loved you. In time, I hope that you will pass it on to your daughter, Kezia, I believe. Josiah's mother, whom I see when she avails herself of the privilege of visiting her grandchildren, informed me that her son wrote of how Kezia resembles my family, and of how she walks in Samuel's image. Is she very much like him? It gives me so much joy to know that a person dwells upon this earth within whom my brother lives on.

Though I may not always have shown it, I was very fond of you Hannah, and I want to wish you great joy.

Sophia Gresley.'

The ring finger of my right hand was quickly adorned with Sam's beautiful ring. My eyes often lingered upon the pretty piece and as Sophia hoped, I thought of Sam and the great love we shared. Jos was pleased for his former wife and wrote to wish her joy. It was only right, he mused, that she should be as happy as he was now. Jos knew his first marriage had been a mistake, and celebrated that both parties were marrying again and prayed all would finally be content and happy. We enclosed a portrait of Kezia taken at Mr. Bock's 'Crystal Palace' photographic studio so that Sophia and her family might see the beauty of Sam's child. Sophia did likewise, enclosing a recent portrait of the children captured in London.

It was seven long years since I last saw their gorgeous faces. Now here they were more lovely than ever. Georgina, at fifteen, was every bit the confident young lady, her fine features shown off to perfection. She sat in her mother's image, and everything from the setting of her golden curls to the quality of her gown and the unmistakable worth of her earrings and brooch had been planned meticulously. Whilst Georgina seemed very much at peace with her world, Lavinia's face was far less tranquil.

As a young child, Lavinia had been incorrigible and was often corrected for her outspoken and wild ways. Now though, whilst just as pretty as her sister, Lavinia appeared broken. Jos told me that it was Lavinia who had taken her parents' separation to heart and her melancholy was all too evident. She did not meet the camera straight on, allowed her own golden hair to fall freely over her shoulders and there was the slightest hint of a scowl upon her brow. I prayed that Jos did not recognize the disaffection in his daughter's face and that similarly, he would miss the sorrowful eyes of his youngest daughter.

Seated on the floor at Lavinia's feet, my sweet Ava rested her head upon her sister's knee, Lavinia's comforting hand caressing her shoulder. I could tell they were companions in their grief and was pleased that they had each other. The handsome 'man' of the family, William, stood proudly behind Georgina and Lavinia, a hand on each of their shoulders. Grown to be so very much like his dear father, I wondered how his mother felt about it. He was ten years old now. It seemed like only yesterday that I helped to bring him into the world. Jos stared at his children with such adoring eyes. I reached out and placed my hand on his own. As tears welled in his eyes, he turned to me.

'My darling,' he said, gently stroking my belly. 'You will never know what it means to me that this little one will not be torn from my arms and that in you I have found my true soulmate. I hope you know just how grateful I am for all that you have given me.'

Having endured seven long months of waiting, the day finally arrived for me to don my pretty new bonnet and marry darling Jos. My dress which would have been so beautiful if worn when first made, was altered to fit my expanded figure. Though not as lovely as I could have hoped, the material was still pretty, and I had the satisfying and joyful knowledge that it was the carrying of my beloved's child which forced the alterations. I was more than content. In my hair, I wore my blue ribbon, something which until that moment, Jos was unaware I had kept. He looked at me, his face full of emotion at the discovery of my true devotion. I described how I sewed it into the lining of my petticoat, and told of the time I hid it under my tongue to avoid detection. I would have done anything to keep that ribbon and the memories of Jos that accompanied it.

My dearest friends, Bronwyn and Huw attended and stood as witnesses. When it came time, I took up the pen and signed my name. It was a momentous thing. That I could write at all was incredible, that I signed a marriage certificate to become the wife of a well-born and highly respected doctor proved just how far I had come since I was herded onto the *Garland Grove* as a convicted criminal eleven years earlier. I prayed Jos and I would live a long and prosperous life together.

And so, I was finally Jos's wife. Our union signalled a new start for both of us. Married to the most admirable and lovable of all men, I had my daughter and another bairn on the way, and I would finally have a family of my own. Together we spent our wedding night as tenderly as we could, accompanied by my seven-month bloom. Early the following morning our blissful slumbers were interrupted when Jos was called upon to minister to a dying patient. Over the coming months, I would learn to reconcile myself to the fact that as a doctor, Jos would often be summoned at inopportune moments. He was constantly on the move and, being highly respected, was in great demand.

At times, I felt totally ill-prepared for life as a doctor's wife. Whilst I soon became accustomed to the strange offerings of livestock, fruit, vegetables, and other produce that appeared on the doorstep, it was far harder to adapt to the anxiety and loneliness. I remembered how I used to fret over Jos's absences during my early days at *Knypersley*. Now, as his wife, my fears increased tenfold. I battled endlessly to accept his late-night call outs, the long hours I was forced to be without him, and the terror I felt every time he was called to an accident or case of contagion. I learnt what it was like to miss someone so terribly that it was almost impossible to continue on until that person was safely by your side once more. Sadly though, these fears for my husband's welfare were soon eclipsed by concerns for my own.

During preparations for the wedding, I suffered from a growing number of headaches, something which I put down to the increased busyness of the period. As time progressed, however, they increased in severity and were accompanied by blurred vision and the occasional loss of balance. Jos was anxious about my health and that of my unborn bairn. Complete bed rest was ordered and I was established in my room with everything Jos could think of to keep me amused. Each evening, he would escort me outside and, whilst I sat breathing in the soft scents of spring, he would join me to read aloud and tell the day's news.

As Christmas approached, any expectations I had of attending Christmas fairs and dinners were vetoed, but I was content to sit with Jos as we reminisced about our first Christmas together. He had shown me kindness and bestowed the gift of my cherished blue ribbon, gestures which meant so much, particularly when I was still mourning the loss of family and friends. Jos told of how his heart ached for me, being so young and brought so low, and without anyone at Christmas.

And so it was, that as I woke from my slumbers on Christmas Eve, a sharp pang seized me, and I realized this was the day my bairn had chosen to make its appearance in the world. With Jos having departed earlier that morning to attend upon another, and although my hours of trial were still in their infancy, without him by my side, panic began to take hold. My bairn was coming around four weeks earlier than expected but would wait no longer. Bronwyn was soon beside me and I was pacified. In preparation for this event, Kezia packed a small overnight bag in order to stay with Bronwyn and Huw. When it came time, however, she refused to leave my side. Perhaps a little more like me than was good for her, she stubbornly resisted being moved, demanding to know why the bairn was hurting her mother. Bronwyn did her utmost to soothe and coax her away, though I know she remained, listening intently at the door whilst I laboured inside.

When Huw's attempts to locate Jos failed, Doctor Bell came to my aid and eight hours after my ordeal began, I was delivered of a daughter. I named her Annis in honour of darling Granny Ravens. I quickly discovered, however, that I was not yet done. Now it was clear why everything had been so very different this time, for another bairn was on its way. Doctor Bell and I were to labour on for a further half an hour, a time when a son was born and named Gethin after Jos's highly esteemed father. Doctor Bell was much gratified that we came through the ordeal safely and that his friend and colleague was now the father of twins. I had been truly blessed.

As luck would have it, Jos returned home just thirty minutes after the twins' arrival. I will never forget how the colour drained from his face, and the sight of his distraught eyes peering gravely over Bronwyn's shoulder as he enquired how I survived the birth.

'Hannah. Is Hannah alright? Please tell me she's well.'

I was awake just enough to whisper my husband's name and to hold out a hand to him. Tentatively coming forward, he stood beside the bed and I could see tears upon his cheeks. He took my hand in his own and kissed it. I smiled. With this, he sat upon the bed and burying his head into the covers, sobbed pitifully.

'I should have been here. I should have been here,' he kept repeating.

I soothed him, stroking his hair, assuring him I was perfectly well.

'We have twins, Jos,' I said attempting to cheer him. 'A beautiful girl and boy.'

Jos lifted his face from the covers and looked at me. He was completely exhausted. Bronwyn brought Gethin forward and placed him into his father's arms, before gathering Annis into her own. Once he was assured I was well and did not suffered excessively, Jos was very proud of his new bairns and felt fortunate I had carried and delivered them safely. As a doctor, he knew the extra risks associated with a twins' pregnancy, and how hard it was to carry one baby, let alone both, to full term. Twins were notorious for causing perilous journeys for expectant mothers, and Jos had seen women lose both babies well before full term, whilst others had delivered one living and one stillborn child. In the saddest cases, two stillborn children were delivered to unsuspecting mothers who received no indication that something was wrong.

With the freshness of a cool breeze caressing my face, I opened my eyes the following morning as the curtain billowed gently out across the room. Taking little Annis into my arms, I felt such joy and contentment. I clutched her close to my heart and kissed her tenderly. My beloved sat close beside me, gazing at his new son in wonderment, his little finger gently fondling the bairn's cheek. He was simply mesmerized. Marvelling at the tiny lives we created together; I loved like never before. Eager to become acquainted with her new siblings, Kezia rose early begging to hold one of the bairns. Transferring Annis into her arms, I watched as she gently rocked her sister. I could not help but think back to Kezia's birth, and of all the precious moments like this one that were stolen from us. I reached out and stroked her hair.

'I love you, my darling.'

A smile beamed forth from her lovely face and she bent forward to kiss me.

Whilst I was now the mother of three, Jos was the father of six and as such was one of the many proud men who were fathering a new nation. All our children were born free in a land where opportunity was great. They would live in the warmth of the Australian sunshine, in a country of soft breezes, clean water, equality, and prosperity. I knew that my little ones had such prospects for a happy, healthy future.

10

WALDEN PARK

'**'M**id pleasures and palaces though we may roam, Be it ever so humble, there's no place like home.'

John Howard Payne, 1823.

In his meticulous care for our dear little family, Jos decided it was imperative that we move from central Hobarton to a lovely new home in Holbrook Place. He had seen how easily infection could take hold, especially in young bairns who lacked the proper resistance, and he wanted to save our own children from the insidious diseases he witnessed in town on a daily basis. Originally the home of a sea captain, the house was placed on the market following this gentleman's return to England, and Jos's diligence and self-sacrifice allowed us to purchase it.

With stunning views over Sandy Bay to the Derwent River and, most importantly, Mt. Wellington, it was built to capture views of the picturesque landscape. The rooms posed no obstacle to my placing furniture in order to soak in the delights of the area. Our bed was positioned so that I might see Mt. Wellington upon waking each morning. Outside, the property possessed some beautiful formal gardens that assured me many happy hours of wandering, and I knew how they would similarly entice our children as they grew older. At Jos's suggestion, we named our new home *Walden Park* in memory of my birth-place.

When our move was complete, it was time for rejuvenation. With my husband's fortunes on the improve, I was supplied with a house-keeper, and thus relieved of all household chores, I was able to indulge in one of my greatest delights, spending time with my children. Of the twins, Annis became the first to sit up and attempt to say 'mama' and 'dada', whilst poor little Gethin, although the first to crawl, also owned the dubious honour of being the first to cut a tooth. The operation of my salon also continued, my work managing to take a little of the sting out of the dreaded hours when Jos was absent from home. With Bronwyn's home a mere fifteen-minute walk away, I decided to continue working from Hampden Road whilst cherishing the extra time it allowed me to spend with my dearest friend. Kezia would accompany me each morning as she made her way to the schoolroom, whilst I proudly pushed the twins in their carriage, the Johns family always adoring and eager babysitters.

People must have seen me as an interesting second choice for the attractive Doctor Markham. The stunningly beautiful, statuesque blonde, Sophia Markham, possessed great wealth and privilege, her intelligence and talents making her highly attractive to all. I, Hannah Markham, now appeared amongst them by way of perfect contrast. True, I had regular features and more than one person noted my sweet face and supposed "pretty eyes", but I could never be called striking. Undoubtedly, comparisons *were* made in some of the better drawing rooms of Hobarton although I only ever heard words of appreciation for the joy that I brought their cherished doctor.

Thankfully I was never recognized as the young convict girl who had once been assigned to the Markhams. My past was a shame that must be hidden at all costs, a stigma with which my children must never be associated. This became all the more evident when seventy-five-year-old ex-convict Abraham Gavin came briefly into my life several months after the twins' arrival. Mr. Gavin was transported as a sixteen-year-old for stealing a beehive from his uncle. Having served his seven-year sentence, he now ran an extremely successful ferry business in Hobarton. Calling on Jos for a private consultation, Mr. Gavin noticed the twins and stopped to admire them.

'Never had no babes myself,' he informed me. 'Didn't want them to suffer because of what I done. I've brought two nephews out from England to inherit the little I own.'

I was astonished that this fear could be so profound that someone would deny themselves children. Oblivious to the fact that I, too, arrived in this colony under sentence, his words made a far greater impact than intended. As he passed through the room to Jos's surgery, my eyes fell upon my darling children; the twins on their woolly blanket, Kezia reading in the sunshine. Surely no stain tarnished them, they were as innocent and pure as any child. How could anyone believe such angels were tainted by vice? If there was any truth to the belief that the sins of the parent could be visited upon their children, I was positive it was not the case with my own sweet cherubs. I was comforted by the knowledge that none of my children would ever know the hardships that I had endured. The world was theirs to conquer. They could truly seize upon the advice that Granny Ravens once gave me and make the most of every opportunity.

Not all children, however, were as lucky as my own. As I moved about Hobarton, I was increasingly concerned by the number of vagrant and destitute children on the streets. Van Diemen's Land was now supporting an entire generation of young people who were, at best, the children of transported convicts, at worst, and most alarmingly, children who grew up in orphanages and asylums. Stolen from their mothers, the title of orphan had been loosely applied before they were apprenticed out as servants or labourers, many never seeing their mothers again. Having renewed his previous association with many of the benevolent institutions of Hobarton, Jos now worked with these young orphans tragically stuck in a life of disadvantage and abuse.

Witnessing firsthand the effects of the brutal convict system on the next generation, Jos treated young boys who, having grown up in the orphan schools, were undersized for their age, the consequence of a poor and inadequate diet. With bodies often too small and weak to do harder, back-breaking work like road building, they were considered the fortunate ones, gaining employment as herdsmen and labourers for settlers, some of whom were ex-convicts themselves. Luckier still were those who managed to acquire skills through these assignments that would allow them to be self-sufficient in later life. For many, life could be fairly good, their masters having a legal obligation to provide them with good meat, drink, lodging, clothes, and medical care. For numerous children, however, the damage was already done.

The girls too were undersized and shared the boys' pale complexions. Years of living in dimly lit, often completely darkened rooms, had taken their toll on this generation's sight and their eyes were often restless and painful. None, however, were supplied with glasses to correct their affliction. Others also suffered the effects of serious accidents and burns obtained at the orphan schools, many being poorly treated, or worse still, left untreated. Jos was truly devastated by the number of young women he treated who had been sent into service only to return to the institution carrying unwanted children, bairns forced upon them by rogues who then absconded. He was equally distressed by the young wives he met, girls who avoided going into service by being married off to men often much older than themselves. Many were ill-treated, some forced to carry bairn after bairn, their husbands' thirsts insatiable.

In the course of his benevolent work, my husband also became familiar with many stories of youngsters who absconded from their masters to search for missing parents and other family members. Many walked great distances during their search only to be arrested and returned to their master or reassigned. Some of these poor children were sentenced to gaol time, one young boy of thirteen spent a month in custody having been dragged from the arms of his newly-discovered mother. The luckier ones found their parents, others being handed over to the care of older siblings. Many of these children had been raised in the Queen's Orphan School, a dreaded institution that often caused me nightmares. Had I not been so fortunate as to rescue Kezia from Dynnyrne, this place would have been her destiny, her doom. She, however, was one of the lucky ones. Educated, loved, and housed comfortably, she was safe from suffering anything as dismal as the experiences of these other poor girls. Her future was secure.

When the twins were six months old, I was granted the opportunity to visit my beloved *Brynmawr* once more, something that until that time I failed to have the courage to do. The fate of my dear little mountain home had been constantly on my mind since the events of 'Black Thursday' wreaked havoc in the area just under four years prior. I will never forget that day of terror. News that the entire state of Victoria was on fire reached us by early afternoon, and smoke clouds from the fires had already travelled as far south as the north of our state. The children became fearful when they could smell smoke. Bronwyn and I did our best to calm them with the assurance that the smoke was from the Victorian fires.

Gazing from the window, however, my eyes noted that smoke was beginning to fill the streets of Hobarton and my gaze was instinctively drawn towards my mountain. Instantly, I saw plumes of black smoke billowing from its cherished slopes and hurrying down the passage, I threw open the front door and raced into the street. I looked up to be greeted by a terrible sight. Flames were threatening to engulf the entire mountain and I shielded my eyes from the horror. Staggering, I leant upon the wall to steady myself before sliding to my knees, consumed by sorrow. Bronwyn rushed to my side and, taking me into her arms, tried her best to ease my pain.

That afternoon and evening the sky turned deep orange, a dreadful, threatening hue, so unlike the brilliant oranges of a tranquil sunset. Whether my treasured *Brynmawr* survived the flames I knew not, and I now questioned my resolve to visit again. Was I simply causing myself more heartache by seeking something that had perhaps vanished or, at best, changed beyond recognition? As our carriage rounded the final bend, I closed my eyes to shield them from the harsh reality.

'Oh, it's beautiful!' cried Kezia.

With her astounding declaration, my eyes flew open and came to rest upon a *Brynmawr* unchanged from the day that I was torn from it. It was still the loveliest and most serene place on earth. Alighting from the carriage, I stood hesitantly upon the verandah.

'Would you like someone to go in with you?' Jos asked.

Shaking my head slowly, I tottered towards the door. Laying my hand upon the old, familiar handle, I turned it and cautiously entered. The darkened hallway reached out before me. The door to Sam's study lay open, and I mechanically walked towards it. Someone had covered the furniture to protect it from dust, but otherwise, everything was exactly as Sam left it. It was just my mind playing cruel tricks on me, but Sam suddenly stood before me in all his youthful enthusiasm, smiling with his usual tenderness. It was overwhelming, and I quickly retreated back to the verandah. I didn't tell my family of my apparition but merely asked whether someone might accompany me after all. Kezia took my hand, and together we entered what should have been her childhood home. Sam's study drew her interest as it had my own.

'This is where your father taught me to read and write,' I informed her.

She turned and smiled as she perused the numerous volumes upon the shelves. Sam's treasured specimens then caught her eye. Approaching his specimen cabinet, she delicately opened each drawer, carefully examining the contents with total fascination. There was no Sam now but in his place was his beautiful daughter, growing more like him every day. It seemed so right that she stood here in his study, similarly enchanted by the things he held so dear. I knew that Sam would be looking down upon us at that moment and would be exceptionally proud of this daughter of his.

Departing Sam's study, my eyes lighted upon the hat stand, positioned as it was near the front door. There was Sam's battered old hat, waiting faithfully to protect him from the harsh Australian sun. Beside it hung mine, the large brimmed offering Sam insisted I wear to protect my delicate skin. I sighed. Kezia squeezed my hand and we moved toward the bedroom. Entering the room where Sam and I once slept encased tenderly in each other's embrace, my eyes quickly rested upon his spectacular painting of Mt. Wellington which he so lovingly bestowed upon me. The painting, I determined, would be the only thing I would remove from the house that day. It would return with me to *Walden Park*, and again take pride of place over my bed. I saw too the little wooden crib sitting silently exactly where Sam had placed it. Of all the things I saw and the memories that consumed me that day, it was this crib and the recollection of the happy expectant father who made it, that affected me the most. With tears welling in my eyes, I told Kezia the story of how her father created it with so much love.

'Your father made it in secret as a surprise for me. He had never crafted anything before, but he was so excited about your expected arrival. He put all his efforts into making it and asked our overseer, a kind man named Charley, to help him.'

'How lovely,' sighed Kezia, taking me tightly in her arms.

Once composed, I opened the top of my chest of drawers, and showed Kezia my wedding attire, still laid out in readiness. Kezia gently reached out and ran her fingers over the delicate fabric.

'It's perfect,' she said. 'It's so sad you didn't get to wear it, but I shall. I will wear it when I get married.'

'It will be well out of fashion by then,' I smiled, touched by her declaration.

'Then you and I will put it to rights, together. Besides, wedding dresses are meant to be passed from mother to daughter.'

I agreed and Kezia gently closed the drawer once more.

Our visit to *Brynmawr* was still in its infancy when I noticed a man approaching on horseback, and as he came closer, I recognised the aging face of our former neighbour, Mr. Cuthbertson. Alighting, he knew me instantly.

'Mary and I saw your carriage pass. I rode over to see who was visiting.'

'Have you kept the house like this?' I queried.

Mr. Cuthbertson nodded.

'I owed it to Mr. Gresley. I've done very little really, just kept the weeds at bay and cut some bushes back. Mary has tended Mr. Gresley's grave, ensuring fresh flowers are placed upon it.'

I was speechless, so overcome was I with their compassion and generosity. Invited to take refreshments with them, we were warmly greeted by Mrs. Cuthbertson who was delighted to finally see the bairn I was expecting when we last met. Had Mr. Cuthbertson not already proven himself a trustworthy and honest man, he did so upon our arrival at his home, producing paperwork that detailed the sale of *Brynmawr's* stock and the subsequent banking of the acquired funds. Apart from a small amount retained to place an iron railing and headstone upon Sam's grave, Mr. Cuthbertson handed me the receipts required to reclaim the funds. Refusing to accept a penny, I insisted that our neighbours retain the money in payment for their kind deeds over the years.

'It's as I have always said,' Jos declared as we walked through the forest later that afternoon on the way to Sam's final resting place. 'I have met far more honest people amongst the ranks of ex-convicts and struggling settlers in this colony than I have amongst the gentry.'

When we reached the tranquil river and the peaceful tree under which Sam slept, I was fortunate that I had the love of my family to support me as emotion overcame me. Jos placed a comforting arm around my shoulders as I cried out all the day's emotions. I lay the bunch of roses I brought from *Walden Park* beside the lilies Kezia chose, and I fell to my knees, remaining beside the grave in silent contemplation for several minutes. When I could be drawn away, we returned to the house where I retrieved some of the treasures that I hid following Sam's death. I handed my engagement ring to Kezia, giving her permission to wear it henceforth, along with her father's pocket watch. Her face lit up in wonderment and she hugged me tightly as she clutched her father's watch to her heart. I then extracted the envelope that Sam received on the morning he died. I handed it to Jos and said,

'As Sam lay dying, he told me to take this from his top pocket and give it to you. He received it that morning. It seemed to make him very happy. He said that everything was going to be alright. I think it was from his mother.'

Jos read the offered letter. Laying it upon his knee once finished, he looked at me.

'Sam was taking you home,' Jos uttered with amazement. 'It's all here. His mother speaks of her excitement at his return and promises to speak to her husband on Sam's behalf.'

Jos held out the letter for me to peruse.

'But he was so happy here,' I assured him, refusing to take it. 'We had so many plans for the future of *Brynmawr*.'

Jos shrugged.

'His mother mentions a full pardon that Sam was seeking for you and acknowledges that once your child was old and strong enough, you would both be accompanying him to live on the *Knypersley* estate. She writes of her belief that he had made a wise decision to bring his wife and child home and to give them all the benefits that a move to *Knypersley* would ensure.'

Tears welled in my eyes. I thought back to the times when Sam would hold me in his arms and tell me of his dreams. He achieved so much at *Brynmawr* but somehow could never see himself as successful. He was always striving for more, to make good, and to give me everything he thought I deserved. It was now obvious that he made what must have been an excruciating decision to abandon all his dreams, all he worked so hard for, and to return home, a place where he felt confined and restricted by protocol and family expectations. He made this decision for me and our child, wishing for what he thought was best for his young family, putting himself, as always, last. Tears rolled freely down my cheeks especially knowing I could never thank him for his sacrifice, or tell him that just by being with him, I possessed everything I could ever have desired. Without him, life had gone on, but would never be the same again.

My struggle for survival following his death robbed me of my proper mourning period, but I grieved now. Jos was sensible of my need to be alone at that moment. He didn't try to console me, nor distract my mind from its dwelling. Instead, he encouraged Kezia to accompany him to Sam's study, where I had given her permission to choose her favourite specimen to take with her. When I was finally able, I took one final tour of the house before Jos aided me into our carriage.

As we slowly drove away from *Brynmawr*, I cradled Sam's beloved painting in my arms, whilst Kezia nursed her own treasures: her father's sketchbook from his voyage to Australia and a native devil he preserved through taxidermy.

Following our visit to *Brynmawr*, I became curious to know whether I could discover the fates of our three labourers, Charley, Arthur and Regan. I told Jos of the kindness that they showed me following Sam's death, of the reverence with which they buried my beloved, and of how they stayed by my side until the authorities came. It did not take long before Jos received some intelligence concerning my query. Of Charley, we received a favourable report that pleased me greatly. Not long after leaving *Brynmawr*, he applied for and was granted a full pardon. Lacking the funds to return home to England, he worked for several years on a property north of Hobarton until he saved enough money to buy a property of his own at Campbell Town. He apparently chose not to remarry, though records showed he was living with a woman by the name of Elizabeth. I truly wished him happiness. Arthur was sadly not as easy to find and Jos assured that the search would continue. And then there was news, or so we thought, of Regan. By the time the authorities returned to *Brynmawr* to retrieve the men, Regan had taken flight. Records could not tell us where he went but a man answering to his description was hung in Hobarton six years later for bushranging. Whilst I prayed that the Regan hung was not the one who had worked alongside Sam and me at *Brynmawr*, something inside me told me it was.

By this time, I had been in Hobarton for twelve years, and the town was remarkably different from the one I discovered upon first setting foot in the colony. A horse-drawn omnibus now ran along Elizabeth Street to New Town and the children and I took great delight in the novelty of this new mode of transport. Work had also begun on the new Government House, which, when finished, would have commanding views over the Derwent River and Botanic Gardens. Many citizens, myself included, hoped that the Governor and Lady Young would again host one of the grand balls for which former governors were famed.

Whilst I marvelled at all things progressive in the town, Jos took on new challenges to help its citizens achieve better conditions and equality. In June, he attended a meeting that focused on the poverty experienced by many of the lower classes around Hobarton. Subsequently, he became a member of a committee whose role it was to produce a report detailing the living standards of the poor. He discovered people existing in conditions unimaginable to most of us, hovels without the most basic of necessities. The committee's work attracted the attention of the Governor who promised his support to rectify the problem. It was atrocious to think that such wretched conditions could have gone unchallenged for so long.

The following month, Jos was there to welcome nearly three hundred German immigrants to the colony, after a treacherous voyage where measles claimed twenty-one lives. A crew member was also lost overboard, and five out of the six bairns born en route died before reaching port, the sixth shortly afterward. Jos visited them in quarantine and was there again to help Mr. Loch and other agents to find interpreters, housing, and employment for the new arrivals.

In the face of such suffering on our doorstep, I was never so thankful that my own little family were well cared for and loved. Come September, we had further cause for celebration when the *Champion of the Seas* delivered our beloved Ava safely back to us. Having grown disillusioned with life in England and yearning for the loving arms of her beloved father, she braved the long, solo trip back to Hobarton. She explained that Georgina was happy with life in England and the society it offered her, whilst in true Lavinia fashion, she had been too temperamental to make a decision by the time Ava's ship departed. Ava was certain that her sister would follow shortly. Young William had been desperate to return but both grandmothers united to keep him there to finish his schooling. The promise was made, however, that he could travel immediately after graduation and he grudgingly agreed.

The evening of her arrival, she came and sat beside me, resting her dear head upon my shoulder as in former times. Raising her adorable eyes lovingly to meet my own, she sighed.

'How I've missed you, Hannah.'

I assured her that no parting had been more painful than the day when I was forced to leave her behind. The silence that followed betrayed the depth of our emotions.

'I have a gift for you,' she proclaimed, before bestowing on me a parcel tied with pink ribbon.

'It's from Granny Ravens.'

'Granny,' I murmured with a quivering lip. 'Dear Granny.'

With trembling hands, I untied the ribbon to reveal the most beautiful shawl, hand knitted for me by Granny. It meant so very much, a gift from home. I held the shawl to my cheek, closed my eyes, and thought of Granny sitting by the fire. There followed a few magical moments when I again stood in St. Paul's Walden, its familiar sights, sounds, and smells came flooding into my mind. It was such a long time since I breathed the air of my homeland, walked its charming green meadows, and felt the softness of the English sun.

When I finally managed to return to the living, Ava told me how she called upon my family, their inquiries regarding my fate having been ongoing for several years, and that dear Granny cried and cried upon hearing news of me. I was gratified to hear news of my family and to know they were all well. It was also extremely satisfying to know that they met my dearest Ava and knew of my life since leaving England. I became determined to write to dearest Granny as soon as possible, and to reconnect the chain broken for so long.

As Ava settled into life at *Walden Park*, I quickly learned that she didn't crave the social life of her mother and sisters, but was content to remain at home in the heart of the family. She adored her new siblings, and was idolized by them in return. Seldom did I see her without one of the twins in her arms or Kezia by her side. In everything I did and planned for Ava, I was careful to pay reverence to what her mother would wish for her daughter. Now fifteen years old, it was time that Ava was introduced into Hobarton society.

My first opportunity came later that month when Mr. Watson hosted his highly anticipated fancy dress ball at New Wharf. Whilst some were saddened by the Governor's absence through illness, the rest of the evening certainly didn't disappoint. Despite her husband's ailment, Lady Young and her entourage attended, Her Ladyship greeting Ava kindly, wishing her every joy in her new home. The attentiveness of Lady Young didn't fail to attract the notice of others present, and many came forward to greet sweet Ava, several recounting fond memories of her 'dear mama.' Ava took all the attention in her stride, conversing with those who gathered with great poise and warmth. I marvelled at her stamina, especially when I knew she would have preferred to be at home with a book.

Christmas that year was celebrated as usual with Bronwyn, Huw, and the children, their joyous company and friendship always enhancing the festivities. Ava was a welcome addition to our little gathering, her newly discovered talent for relaying very amusing anecdotes keeping everyone well entertained. When it came time for Bronwyn to take up her harp, Ava joined her at the piano, the pair producing truly heavenly airs. As the new year dawned, we joined the celebrations held to herald in our colony's new name, Tasmania, which officially came into being on 1ˢᵗ of January, 1856. With the day declared a public holiday, everyone was free to join in the festivities which included a Regatta and Horticultural Show.

As the idyllic days of summer rolled on, we were blessed that our renewed ownership of *Brynmawr* allowed us to spend many a blissful day in our mountain retreat. Enchanted by the picturesque landscape, Ava aimed to replicate it onto canvas and with a pinafore protecting her dress, she would stand for hours at her easel with an assortment of watercolours close at hand.

Her father's study became Kezia's domain, a place where she studied his collections, made drawings and notes of her own, and set out in search of new additions. Savouring my renewed barefooted freedom, I sat contentedly upon the verandah. I thought of the animals that once made *Brynmawr* home; of little Markham the Wombat and of the mother devil and her bairns. What joy they brought to my world. There was no sign of them now, and I wondered what became of them following my departure.

Sometimes I would take a stroll to the river where I would reminisce whilst bathing my feet in the cooling waters. Some nights, darkness would surprise us, and we would choose to remain overnight. How we relished those nights on the mountain. I loved to see my much-loved house coming back to life, winning its way into the hearts of a whole new generation.

I began working on this little piece of reminiscence during my period of enforced bed rest prior to the twins' arrival, and completed it during our tranquil days at *Brynmawr*. I hesitated at first to write my story. I know that I have been truly blessed, and mine is a story that many who were transported to this country could sadly not tell. Yes,

I suffered and endured great hardship, but I also had the rare good fortune of being assigned to dear Jos, of receiving undying love and protection from Sam, and of being rescued by the sweet Bronwyn. My children have all been born healthy, and it gladdens my heart to watch them running wild and free. They are my precious treasures, and possess lives I could never have dreamed of at their young ages.

With Granny Ravens' shawl around my shoulders, I acknowledged that she was a woman of great foresight. She assured me that with diligence and tenacity, I could make something of myself in Van Diemen's Land. Her prophecy had been fulfilled. She would be proud of me, and I was content in the knowledge that I kept my promise to make the most of everything that came my way.

Against overwhelming odds, I had triumphed over adversity and a brutal regime that destroyed so many. In finding love, I discovered true freedom. Whilst the seas of my life may not always be calm, with Jos and my cherished children by my side, I will find strength and spirit enough to waste not a moment in self-pity. In granting me my life, that stony-hearted judge bestowed a great blessing. I owed it to the women who succumbed, and to those dear ones who saved me, to live with a heart full of gratitude, knowing that my destiny could have been so very different.

Missy Birch is a teacher, writer, and historian based in Victoria, Australia. She has contributed to several publications for the History Teachers' Association of Victoria, including an article on Ned Kelly, *A Widow's Son Outlawed*. Her fascination with the convict history of Australia led her to contribute to *Convict Motherhood*, published by the Female Convict Press in 2025. Her debut novel, *Vandemonian Spirit*, received an Honourable Mention in the 2024 Historical Novel Society's First Chapters Competition. Her short story *A Ferndale Sojourn* won the Knox Heritage Festival prize, and *The Emerald Lady* earned a Terror Australis Award at the Scarlet Stiletto Awards. Missy's poem Old Man of the Sea was published in *The Liquid Mirror* anthology. Missy wishes to thank Lucy, Bonnie, and Finty for their undying love and patience whilst she wrote this novel.